Harlequinned

New Writing

Published by the Centre for Creative and Performing Arts, the University of East Anglia.

Typeset in Centaur MT

Printed by Mackays of Chatham PLC, Chatham, Kent.

British Library Cataloguing in Publication Data. A catalogue record for this book is available from the British Library.

ISBN 0 9515009 6 1

Harlequinned

New Writing

An Anthology
from the MA in Creative Writing
at the University of East Anglia

Introduced by *Malcolm Bradbury*

Acknowledgements

The editors would like to acknowledge the assistance of Malcolm Bradbury, Jon Cook, Russell Celyn Jones, Ellen Moorcroft, Mike Oakes, Phoebe Phillips, Anastacia Tohill, Andy Vargo, and Vicki Winteringham.

Thanks also to the Norwich School of Art and Design, and the Esmee Fairbairn Trust, for their support of this project.

Editor-in-Chief *Katherine Brown*
Design *Ferne Arfin, Katherine Brown*
Production *Ferne Arfin*
Associate Editor *John de B. Pheby*
Editorial Assistant *Johnny Boyne*

Cover and illustrations *James Brown*
http://sunsite.unc.edu/otis/pers/Moose.html

Contents

Introduction
Malcolm Bradbury 7

The Pharos at Alexandria
Thomas Guest 13

from Perhaps a Woman
Katherine Brown 43

from X 20
Richard Beard 57

from The Only World I Know
Johnny Boyne 73

from The Awakening
Ferne Arfin 91

Simon Wrigley-Worm Boy
Tom Shankland 109

Moriarty
Toby Litt 127

A Sprig of Basil
Sue Hubbard 141

from The Nihilist Evangelist
Bo Fowler 155

from Music Practice
Claire Hamburger 177

On the Steps of Lalita Ghat
Jim Gleeson 195

from Oxford
John de B. Pheby 215

from Columbus Day
Janette Jenkins 241

Introduction

Malcolm Bradbury

Malcolm Bradbury

Introduction

For several years now the members of the MA course in Creative Writing at UEA have brought out an anthology of some of the fiction that has come out of the year's course. These anthologies have been created by the students themselves: usually by a group of them who have taken the publishing option at the Norwich School of Art and Design. Over the years, these UEA anthologies have spread through the bookstores and been quite widely read. And anyone who cares to hunt back through the pages of the previous ones will find a first sight of a considerable number of stories, or segments of novels, that would later appear in book form. In short, these collections have proved an important showcase for new writing, by new writers, and they've often marked the first publication of authors who have later made significant reputations

Over the years, I've introduced several of these volumes, as have Rose Tremain (who taught the course with me), Ian McEwan (who was its first student) and Adam Mars-Jones. But this one is just a little different – because, after 25 years of working in the programme (as long as it's existed, in fact), I'm about to leave it and hand over to an excellent successor, Andrew Motion, who will take over as Professor of Creative Writing next year. This great change of life tempts a certain amount of looking back. During the course of these 25 years, some 200 writers – most of them new, though not all of them; most of them young, though not all of them; most of them writing what the publishers generally like to call literary fiction, though by no means all of them – have been in the programme. About a third of these have since become published writers of fiction, or non-fiction, or screenwriters and TV playwrights.

It so happens that 1995 has been a year of good harvest, with more than ten novels or story collections coming out from former students in the course. They include Kazuo Ishiguro's *The Unconsoled* and Deirdre Madden's *Nothing Is Black*, Philip MacCann's *The Miracle Shed* and Louise Doughty's *Crazy Paving*, new novels by Ann Enright, Denise Neuhaus, Mark Illis, Suzannah Dunn and Glenn Patterson – a reminder, at least, that the writers in the programme have been, not just interesting, but also remarkably various. It's also been a year in which an anthology of short fiction from the 25 years of the course, *Class Work*, has been published by Hodder and Stoughton.

For all these reasons, the 1995 anthology, perhaps, has a special pressure on it. There's a history there now – and what's more the mid-nineties isn't perhaps the very best of times to be adventuring into serious writing. There's a degree of recession in publishing; there's pre-millennial anxiety about literary directions; there's a dip in the cultural mood; there's also a climate of expectation. Finding a voice, finding a subject, exploring a lifetime direction, discovering the authority of authorship: that's what the struggle of writing is all about. A creative writing programme can help with this only to a certain point. Many people will say that writing can't really be taught; and, to a considerable degree, I think they are right. Writing is a personal and an internal discovery, and it can't really be pushed too hard from outside. However, there's value in the community of energy, ideas and literary experimenting that can develop in an energetic, committed group of people who take writing seriously, and what goes with it – the shaping and making of forms and structures, the working through of the powers of language and the potentials of narrative.

25 years ago, when the course started, I had the idea – mostly drawn, I suppose, from my own solitary and untaught situation as a beginning writer – that writing prospered best when you found a community of people who shared their experiences

together. Writing has always clustered round movements and manifestoes, clubs and pubs, magazines and salons. In some ways I'm less sure about that than I was: there are a great many writers who prosper best on their own. It's possible to become too self-analytical: it's also possible to be too willing to adapt to the opinions, judgements and influence of others. But working alone is what most writers do most of the time, for most of their lives. And there's a lot to be said for taking advantage, at least for a year, of the fact that writing is indeed also a debate, a shared set of problems and difficulties, a transfer of lessons, a confusing medley of voices, who nonetheless share some things in common, including a commitment to the imagination, a fascination with form, an obsession with the powers of narrative. Writing takes each one of us off in his or her own direction, toward goals which probably never become totally clear (or you wouldn't go on chasing them forever) but which do become increasingly confident and purposeful. To keep, extend, develop an individual identity, while learning from the common difficulties and possibilities, is perhaps about the best that can be asked and offered.

Which is why the stories that follow may have, by comparison with previous anthologies, a character all their own, but they don't follow any single very distinctive trend, or resemble a school. They're a set of different and firm directions, taken by writers who have all shared common problems and who take their writing seriously. There's the short story as a reflective and reflexive commentary on writing; there's the short story as the distilled account of an experience. There's the novel as near-poetic experiment in prose, and there's the novel as an enterprise in the complexity and suspense of narrative. There's fiction that directly addresses some of the dramas and preoccupations of contemporary Nineties culture – from feminism to smoking, you could say – and there's fiction that uses the conventions of realism and constructs a significant relation between the present and the human past. There's fiction that comes out from the particular drama of these islands (conflict in Ulster, street life in London), fiction that comes out of the identities of

American life, fiction as fantasy. There's fiction as anecdote, fiction as myth. There's narrative interrupted, narrative that drives hard toward its end. There's play and experiment with genre, with stereotype, with image, with text. There's new fiction opened out by the play of the computer; there's formatted screenplay, screenwriting now forming an important part of the programme. and there's an overall complexity and originality of voice which is, in its way, the complexity of current life, with its many universes of discourse, which in turn are changing the nature of the story, the situation, the character, the novel.

There's a certain bittersweet pleasure in introducing the anthology from this 25th year. I'm delighted it's such a good one, and that it has its striking share of writers of real promise (some of them have had their work accepted for publication already). What else? Well, this was a year when Rose Tremain departed the course (alas) after teaching it with me for seven or so years, since her writing commitments had so multiplied. Her place was taken by Russell Celyn Jones, a writer I greatly admire, whose own new novel *An Interference of Light* came out this year. Rob Ritchie co-taught the screenwriting course, Andy Vargo, of the Norwich School of Art and Design, taught the publishing course and helped make this volume. The Centre of Creative and Performing Arts at UEA and its director, Jon Cook, helped with financial support for publication. But, of course, the true achievement here is that of those who wrote and also edited it. I hope, like me, you feel excited, delighted, refreshed by what they've done.

Malcolm Bradbury

The Pharos at Alexandria

Thomas Guest

Since graduating in Mathematics from Cambridge in 1985, Thomas Guest has worked as a computer programmer in England and Los Angeles; a bicycle courier in Sydney; and a banana picker in Israel. He has completed one novel and is currently finishing a second. The following short story is taken from his linked collection, *Seven Wonders.*

Thomas Guest

The Pharos at Alexandria

"Like music, do you?" The left hand corner of Deedee's mouth turned down as though the word music was sour. "Eh? D'you like music?"

The kid said nothing. Just stared. His eyelashes grew too long for a boy's, his irises shone in the sunlight. And the way the kid stared; people didn't look at Deedee like that, directly, dispassionately. They'd pretend not to be looking, but they'd look all right; sidelong glances.

"I expect you like music," Deedee pressed.

"What's music? How d'you mean music?"

"You're kidding me, right?"

"I don't know what you mean. What's music?"

"Noise like the gypsies make. Picking at strings and puffing through tubes. Singing, whistling, hooting, all sorts of nonsense. That's music." And he frowned. "Like it, do you?"

"It's all right."

"No it isn't all right. You hear me?"

The kid shrugged.

"I said Do You Hear Me? It isn't all right."

And the kid – at last – looked down and bit on his lip. Bloody kid, thought Deedee. That won't work on me.

"I'm telling you, You Do Not Like Music. It's all crap. Infects the whole body. Avoid it."

The kid's lips were trembling. Deedee pressed on: "What are you – a gypsy then are you?"

A shake of the head. The oiled coils of the boy's hair fanned out like the dark seaweed that floated up some mornings in Deedee's pool. The seaweed he'd skim and let dry in the sunlight. It would wrinkle, shrivel, grow brittle. The bladders would blacken and crisp in the heat. Grew everywhere, that seaweed did. If he didn't keep an eye out it'd choke up his pool.

"Not a gypsy are you?"

"I said."

"You didn't say anything."

"I'm not a gypsy."

The kid's eyes swelled liquid in the corners. Tears sparkled blue-green. Even when he cried he was pretty.

"Like to muse, do you kid?"

No reply.

"Like reading. Like – what's it called? – poetry? Poems? Words that sound sweet?" His mouth twisted further with each of the words, muse, reading, poetry and sweet.

The kid looked up. Speaking through tears, his voice remained steady.

"No I don't like poems. I'm not a gypsy. I don't like music. OK?"

Deedee smiled, a sidewards sneer forced on him by his disfigurement.

"Like music do you kid?"

The kid left in a hurry. Deedee felt his heart pause for an instant. Just for an instant he wanted to call: Come back, I'm sorry. But he didn't.

Up spiralled the sound of feet slapping the stone stairway. The footsteps receded, and then there was the bluster of the wind shredding itself on the square cut pillars supporting the cupola, the whirr of the burnished bronze mirrors tracking, the swish of the circling pendulum, the rustle of dried dung incinerating below, and further below, the waves shuffling pebbles and sand on the shore. Threading through all these noises, almost imperceptibly, the whine of a string instrument playing somewhere in the city.

Deedee spat. Spittle slipped over granite. He ground bubbled saliva into stone with his thumb.

The boy had discovered the man a week ago. He'd been drawn by the winking lure of the lighthouse and had spied the man tending his garden at the foot of it. He crept closer.

The man was bent over a line of radishes, easing the seedlings from their packed row, rubbing sandy soil from their roots, spreading them in his fingers and pressing them into a second, more extended row.

The boy watched the man's fingers shuffle aubergine leaves, uncoiling tendrils and letting them spring back again. Black vegetables, revealed, gleamed in the sunlight. The man snapped some yellowed leaves from the coriander; the boy sniffed at the air.

The man heard him, turned and glared. The boy tensed, ready to run, but saw bewilderment mixed in with the anger. He saw the man's deformed face, shiny on one side and matt on the other. He stayed rooted. And the man turned back, continued working, ignoring the boy. His movements became brusque.

Suddenly the man stood and shouted: "Out of here! Piss off! Bloody Gypsy!"

The boy trotted away, flustering a squad of seagulls into the air. But he wanted to see what the man would do next.

When he crept back he found the man at the shore, inspecting the contents of a lobster pot. The man pulled out a veteran lobster, barnacle encrusted, slowly waving its eight and a half legs. It arched and curled, twitching antennae as the man admired it. The man knelt, placing it back in the water.

Then the man turned and caught sight of the boy. The boy smiled and the man sneered back. He watched as the man slid a knife between the eyes of two crabs, tossing their bodies in a clatter on the pebbles. An octopus was lobbed beside them; the creature squirmed, oozing sepia. This time when the man shouted the boy did not run away.

Deedee found it unnerving, the kid watching him with that unnatural stare. He could normally scare people off, no bother, and be on his own, the way that he liked it. But while he went about business as usual, the kid tracked him, always at a distance, like one of the stray dogs which slunk between the boulders and would occasionally, piqued by hunger, approach him.

He responded as he would to a dog. He ignored the boy. He shouted; that worked the first time. Then he played it like he was mad. Tried all this muttering and twitching. What would happen when he had to go to his pool? He even thought of calling up the authorities but he'd always shunned dealings with them.

The time came. Deedee needed privacy.

"Come here, kid."

The kid walked forward; didn't even look scared.

"You can't follow me. I'm going somewhere alone now."

And, to his amazement, the kid had turned and sloped off, though when he returned the kid had been waiting.

Deedee was shadowed in this way for a week. He gave up trying to scare the kid off, assuming he'd get bored and eventually leave. The kid, though, gave no sign of leaving. He'd sometimes run off and play in the sand-dunes, but always showed up again. Deedee could feel those eyes on his back. One morning he left some food out. The kid was too skinny. The food was eaten.

And, every afternoon when he wanted time on his own, the kid would back off. Deedee liked that.

"You must never follow me when I go off on my own," he said, a week after the kid's first appearance. "Promise me."

"I promise."

Deedee believed him; he trusted those eyes, their irises the colour of sea shelving away from the shore. When he came back from his pool he questioned the kid.

The kid was articulate enough, though his accent gave nothing away. He answered no direct questions about his past or his future. He'd shake his head and look down. Deedee offered him a room of his own. He tried to make this seem casual, but it felt like an adoption.

The boy remembered the moment. The man had said, "Stay here if you like."

The boy hesitated. The man's pink eyes gave him away; a

sudden flinch, an appeal. The boy walked into the small, bare, space. Sunlight shafted through a vent cut high in one wall. The air was suffused with the scent and sound of the sea.

Later, the man had allowed him up to the cupola at the top of the lighthouse. The view had been breathtaking; the wave-flecked expanse of sea, the reed-bristled delta, the deep blue of the harbour, the receding grid of the city. He'd never realised the world was so big.

"It's beautiful," he said.

And that was when the man had turned on him with questions about music and poetry and gypsies.

Having put the kid in his place, Deedee stopped asking questions.

All the same, he did sometimes wonder.

For instance, how had the kid negotiated the heptastadia, the spur of land between island and city? How'd he climbed the clamber-proof wall?

What Deedee reckoned, the kid was a gypsy. His eyes suggested as much, the twist of his hair. Or he could be half-gypsy which might explain why he'd turned up like that. The gypsies had this thing about purity of blood. No screwing outsiders, that was their attitude. So if the boy was half-gypsy he was also an outcast.

Deedee had had one of them once, a young gypsy girl. All look alike in the darkness, he reckoned. Which wasn't true about him any more. He looked and felt different. And didn't do that sort of stuff any more. But he'd done enough in his time, no question of that.

And now he despised gypsies. They lived rough in the gardens, or behind the columns at the back of the library. Smoke from their fires charred the limestone. Their music polluted the air. Just as seaweed threatened to choke up his pool, those gypsies would choke up the city. One thing; he'd keep them away from his island. Let one of them try coming out here!

Then he remembered: maybe one of them had.

Stubborn, the kid was. Wouldn't even admit to a name.

Deedee liked that. He'd grow up perverse just like him.

Deedee wasn't Deedee's full name. It was a sweetening of Daedalus. Nor was he Daedalus, not really. He'd adopted the name back in his youth when he'd wanted to be an inventor. He'd moved out to the island, to join the scientific community and study alongside Eratosthenes, the astronomer, Archimedes, who still kept a hand in, Euclid, Apollonius, Aristarchus and the others. No one called Deedee by his real name, Alexander. He hated it. Everyone in Alexandria was called Alexander, and he wasn't just anyone.

As things turned out, he never graduated to being an inventor. He was smart all right. Good with his hands. Able at geometry, philosophy and arithmetic. Cunning even. But what he lacked was that extra spark of insight to see beyond what existed already.

And so when they suggested that he tend to the fire and regulate the mirrors, that he should man the great harbour lighthouse, the Pharos, he took on the job.

He served out his apprenticeship under a man called Julius, who'd turned out a right fool. Maintaining one's inner beacon, Julius had called it. "Are we shining this morning?" he'd say, and, "Remember, Daedalus, this is not a labour, it's an illumination. We've both heard the call."

Deedee hadn't heard any such call. A job's a job, he would say, though admittedly this one was better than most. He got solitude when he needed it. The chance to separate out his thoughts, to tease insights from nonsense like fibres from cotton and lay them out on the vast fabric of the water.

He'd done plenty of thinking. Back then.

Julius died suddenly. His apprentice took over. At last, Deedee could do things the way that he wanted. He ran the lighthouse efficiently. Evenings, he often found time to go into the city. He'd met up with women. All sorts of them. He hadn't been fussy.

"I operate the lighthouse," he'd tell them.

"You *never*," they'd say, eyes opening wide.

Then Deedee carelessly, stupidly, leant against one of the

burnished bronze mirrors in the cupola. Mid-day, and the metal had heated up to red-hot from reflecting and focusing the light of the sun. His flesh turned to wax in an instant. He felt his own molten skin slip over his cheekbones, his shoulder, his left arm, his left flank. He screamed. He screamed while his flesh seared on hot metal. A stench of hair and meat burning stained the air. The blustering wind tugged round the mirror. Seagulls rose shrieking.

Somehow he peeled himself away from the mirror and crawled down the stairs.

Like marinating meat, they poured lemon juice on him. Then olive oil. They salted him. Then he fainted.

He was swaddled up like a baby. Wrapped in lint. Immobilised for a period of months. In this enforced silence, his language changed, became coarser. Words and imagination became enemies. As did music; he hated the way it tormented his feelings. Filaments of cynicism within him spread and connected. His own mind turned inward; he needed things to hold, to work with, but touched nothing except soft cotton; he had nothing but thoughts, and used these for self-torture.

Members of the leadership council came to encourage him to recover. He knew why. The prophecy. Alexandrians were worried about the beacon. In his absence the lighthouse was operating a minimal service. They wanted him back there. The medics, however, insisted he rest.

Deedee defied them by discharging himself. Even by moonlight, when he peeled off his bandages, grinding his teeth to master the agony, he could see what had happened. No more pigmentation. Him a North African, now paler than the pasty faced Celts drawn to the city because of its library. His hair was white, white and frizzed, as though it had absorbed texture and tone from the lint he pulled from it. Specks of dead scalp fell away. His skin also; white; the scorched areas smooth, the rest of it flaky. Heaving his limbs was painful; he succeeded by willpower – with his freedom to strive for, he had plenty of that.

Even in the darkness his deprived senses were overloaded. He hallucinated wildly: that he was burning under the sun in the desert; that he was his own ghost, pale, ectoplasmic. These tricks of his imagination were worse than the physical pain. He zigzagged the road grid, crossing avenues and canals. Roosting flamingos, lock-legged, knee deep in water, fixed him from beady eyes shaded by fringes of pin feathers. He crawled along the vacated colonnade of the heptastadia, heading back to the luminous tower of the lighthouse, its watery beam wafting the sea. He'd have that beam scouring the sea again, like it used to.

Julius would have been proud. Julius had been single-minded, and had seen everything in relation to the lighthouse. Now Deedee cloaked himself in that same obsession. What had been a job became a compulsion.

He subsumed himself in doing things properly; meticulously. Each evening he'd use offcuts of papyrus to get the fire started. "Too good for books, this stuff, burn it all," he'd mutter. Orange-red flames would strip shadows from the hollow which bored the heart of the lighthouse. He'd spiral upstairs and reset the mirrors' aspect, so that now they reflected the flames below instead of the sun. Up in the cupola, Deedee would, for a moment, be surrounded by beauty; fading sunlight weaving the waves into a magical tapestry, gilding the delta, smoothing and shading the city buildings. Quickly he'd turn and dive back down the stairs.

Through the nights he attended the fire, snatching fragments of sleep. Sometimes his suppressed imagination escaped into nightmares and he'd wake, clammy with sweat, to the echo of his own tormented voice.

Mirrors swivelled; stars etched out their slow passages. Occasionally, astronomers would visit. Deedee would help them focus the auxiliary mirrors. Silence would fall over the chattering group, for there, reflected in the burnished surface would be Saturn's slim rings or the red eye of Jupiter.

By day he monitored the conical pendulum's swing; checked it scribed long plumbed circuits of the lighthouse's hollow centre. He hadn't quite figured the mechanism – one of Archimedes' inventions – but it worked. A ring at the peak slid along a spiral of wire. As the spiral spun open, the ring would glide downwards, and the pendulum wire would swing in opposition, half a cycle behind. The bit Deedee couldn't understand was the escapement which converted the pendulum's circling into the back and forth of the mirrors. But all he had to do was lubricate and align the mechanism each month, and, each morning, raise the ring to the peak of the spiral and set the pendulum in motion once more.

By the shore, the oxen were tethered, Taurus and Minos. Deedee brought them fodder. He smoothed down the close packed hair on their flanks. He polished their horns with olive oil. Deep inside they'd resonate contentment.

"A job's a job," he would say.

The boy saw the messenger first. Coming out to the island, carrying a papyrus scroll. He'd been living alongside the man for a couple of months now. He was afraid. Had he been tracked down? Would he have to leave?

He watched the messenger walk across to the lighthouse; saw Deedee scowl as he took the papyrus, opened it.

The boy's instinct was to hide, but curiosity drew him forward. He approached Deedee cautiously.

"Guess what," Deedee sneered. "Guess what the matrix leadership says?"

The boy backed away.

"You've been appointed my successor."

The boy did not understand.

"My apprentice."

The boy gasped, smiling widely, and saw Deedee control his response to a scowl before pivoting to walk briskly away.

"Are we starting?" asked the boy, catching up.

"No. I'm going off on my own now."

Deedee picked down a rocky descent to the North West of the island, where the limestone collapsed in shuddering boulders into the sea. He checked no one could see him. Soon he'd be covered, hidden from view by the rugged surroundings. The only sign of human life on the island would be the peak of the lighthouse, with its twinkling mirror, and, atop the cupola, the gleaming gold statue of Poseidon. Rock primroses shivered in crannies. Sea parsley. Glaucous sea holly. Fat bumble bees yawed and rocked through the air; flowers leant under them.

He arrived at his secret place, his pool. Rocks cradled the water from the disturbed surface of the sea. Deep underneath, light filtered in through a submerged hole connecting to the sea, illuminating his garden. This liquid light imparted on the sea plants a golden patina. They shone like filigree. Gilt crabs picked clockwork courses across immersed contours. Anemones fluttered shining tentacles. Fish flickered like light in a crystal.

As a gardener, Deedee was not green fingered, he had the Midas touch. His hands, in the water, became coated with gold and studded with quicksilver bubbles. He'd made his own tools: a long handled grab, a knife bound to the end of a pole. But really he did very little. He lifted out refuse that floated up to the surface. He'd weed out plants that suddenly dominated, or unknowingly blocked out the light.

That day he undressed and swam. His body, with its one withered side, gleamed like Mercury's. He transcended reality, becoming immortally beautiful.

His secret.

"Come here kid," said Deedee.

The kid emerged from the sand dunes dishevelled.

"You want to look after yourself, you know that," said Deedee. "Easy to get lost in those dunes. I've told you."

"I won't get lost. I can always see the top of the lighthouse and head back towards that."

"I know that. Just be careful, that's all I'm saying."

But Deedee hadn't known, though once he'd been told it seemed obvious. Archimedes had the habit of seeing through problems like that. Would his son – already he thought of the kid as his son – become an inventor? Would lighthouse keeping be too simple for him?

"Listen kid, I've got a name for you."

"What is it?"

"Guess."

"Can't." And the boy turned, started to trot back to the sand dunes.

"Icarus, back here at once!"

The boy turned again. Dragging his toes in the sand he walked back. "Icarus?"

"Like it?"

"It's all right I s'pose. Icarus."

"Icarus," repeated Deedee firmly. "Don't wear it out."

He smiled softly, not realising he did so, as the boy ran back through the sand.

Icarus, after being named, was taken on as apprentice. He found the man pedantic, imparting knowledge slowly, resentfully. Icarus soon realised that Deedee was not quite as clever as he thought; he knew how things worked, but not why; he'd try to cover up what he did not understand.

First came reading and writing. Time after time Icarus would have to scrape letters on slate. One error, and the whole sequence would have to be started again. And then there was Euclidean geometry, necessary, Deedee claimed, for aligning the mirrors.

"When can I try aligning the mirrors?"

"When you've done with your learning."

"I'd learn faster if you let me do something real."

"No!"

Icarus bored of the routine. Lemma, proof, lemma, theorem. A tedious catalogue of straight edges, scribed circles, arcs and parabolas. He'd drum his legs in frustration, hardly able to wait for his escape from the classroom. Then he'd rush from confinement and over the sand-dunes. Sometimes he'd look across the harbour to the city and wonder what it was like there. He contemplated running across the heptastadia. But it was late and the old man had this thing about being on time for dinner.

Icarus was not allowed to touch anything. Not until he knew the names of all the equipment. His teacher seemed obsessed with detail. "This is the oil," he would say, "to lubricate the escapement. Whereas the oil in the large amphora is used for starting the fire. And this – are you listening? – is the frankincense we drizzle in the oil on special occasions. Such as?"

"Don't know," said Icarus.

"And what is it called?"

Icarus shrugged.

And so they'd start all over again.

Detail became important to Icarus too, for the simple reason that he wanted to get on to the next stage. He realised that Deedee intended him familiar with all the terminology first. From this realisation he learned quickly.

Deedee attributed Icarus' sudden interest to the thoroughness of his teaching. He went into yet greater detail. Sometimes it was difficult to believe the kid had ever seen Alexandria.

"Have you been to the museum?" he asked. "The library?"

"No."

"The Sema? The hippodrome? The agora?"

"I don't think so."

Perhaps now was the time to explain. They were sitting up at the top of the tower in its cupola where Deedee had finished demonstrating, patiently, step by step, how to align the great mirrors. The two of them sat against the cool stone wall, allowing the breeze to ruffle their hair.

"See Icarus, this place was built to be great. Built by the greatest leader of all. Know who that was?"

The kid shook his head.

"Alexander. None other than. He had this thing about Oracles. He asked the Oracle if this was the place for his city."

"So what did the Oracle say?"

"Said a city built here would shine like a beacon."

"The lighthouse."

"Right. Of course, the muses would say the *library* is a beacon of learning. But this is the real beacon – right here – one of the Seven Wonders, it is."

And then of course the kid had to know what the other six

were. Deedee saw that this explanation business might take some time.

Icarus listened attentively at first. Geometry came to life as the man told him how the city had been laid out.

"Designed by architects," said Deedee. "Got that? Architects, engineers, geometers, surveyors, builders. Practical people."

Straight lines and right angles formed the basis of the design, a grid. Perpendicular roads intersected; between these flowed alternately deep and shallow canals. The grid had sixty four squares, like a chess board.

Whereas spirals, arcs, conic sections – forms of the sea, the man called them – provided the basis for the lighthouse's structure.

"A Wonder," the man emphasised.

It *was* a wonder. Icarus would often look at it. The tower spiralling upwards, gleaming white from its ivory coating like a huge sea-shell. On the exterior of the first stage a frieze was carved. From a distance this seemed no more than the pattern of waves in a storm, each curling into the next. But as you got closer, in the form of the waves could be seen the torsos of tritons. The tritons chased mermaids.

Sometimes Icarus believed he saw mermaids. He saw them out to sea when the sun reached its peak. Their hair seemed to flick, pure white, like the crests of the waves. On stormy nights he heard their singing cut through the noise of the wind.

"Shit! Get down, kid!"

As Deedee swung his open hand round the kid jumped clear.

"How many times have I told you? Keep clear of the mirror!"

Deedee spat on the mirror and saliva sizzled on bronze. He'd pulled his slap so it became – almost became – a caress. Even the caress didn't land. Perhaps he should hit the kid. That'd teach him. Now where was he?

"Mermaids."

Deedee continued: "Alongside the tritons and mermaids are dolphins. Where can you find a sculpture like that in the city?"

"Deedee?"

"What?"

"Did you burn yourself on the mirror?"

"What!"

"Is this where it happened?"

"No."

Deedee was furious. He should have hit the kid.

He finished his speech quickly.

Told Icarus about the library, how it had grown bloated on scrolls of leather and papyrus, had grown over-crowded with muses and poets who wasted all day – God help them – thinking ideas. The building even smelled rotten. It smelled of poorly cured leather and poorly washed thinkers. And its backside was infested by gypsies.

"So I'm warning you, keep clear of poetry."

What else? The kid could find out for himself.

Only when he'd got halfway down the stairs did Deedee realise he'd forgotten the point of his speech. He'd meant to warn the kid about gypsies.

What was the buzz-phrase? An integrated multi-cultural city? All sorts of people, it meant. Which was OK by Deedee, though being African he reckoned he had more claim than some. Each group had been allocated their own grid square at the start: the Libyans, Egyptians, Nubians, Hindus, Jews, Ionians, Macedonians, Thracians, Rhodians, Cypriots, Cretans, Dorians, Carians, Ethiopians, Celts, Saxons all had their own space.

The city had no single leader; Alexander had died while mapping out the extremes of his empire and returned in a coffin. Now there was what the muses called a matrix system of leadership. Said it was appropriate for a city designed on a grid. The idea being each citizen had their own voice. Except for the gypsies.

Like chess pieces, the citizens moved from square to square, mixing and matching. Some nudged forwards like pawns, others swept like bishops or rooks. Deedee had made the most of it. Back in the old days. He'd hopped all over the board like a knight.

Only the gypsies refused to join in. They lived rough. They burned smoky fires. Their kids ran wild and were not to be trusted. And they played music. All the time they played music. Wild, dirty, music.

Bookwork complete, a period of initiation followed for Icarus. He'd learned how to handle the man now; you had to let him feel in control. Not to ask questions, rather to wait for the answers. Similarly, he'd learned that privileges unrequested would be granted.

So he watched and helped unbidden when he could, quietly fetching fuel blocks for the man to position, or being in the right place with the oil. He instinctively knew what Deedee regarded as his, and didn't trespass.

Icarus found his guardian fascinating. Why did his skin drip like wax on one side? Why did he do things so thoroughly? Why was he so touchy? Icarus applied his patient approach to their relationship. He never pressed questions.

Most of all, Icarus wanted to know where the man went in secret each afternoon; but he accepted he must never ask about that. After all, the man let him keep his secrets.

Sometimes the man would reveal the aesthetic side he tried hard to deny. "The colour those clouds are, it's like the inside of a conch, all pink and shiny," he'd say, when they sat in the cupola after lighting the fire. This statement quickly followed by, "Talking crap, aren't I?"

Icarus said nothing. The man had caught it exactly. That evening, for the first time, he was allowed to align the great mirrors, aiming their beam at the sea. Icarus' steady fingers hid the fervour inside him. Slowly, reverently, he adjusted the aspect, double checking for the benefit of his instructor. He suppressed an urge to whoop when he finished.

When Icarus turned he saw the old man gripping tight to the cupola with both hands, one withered, one sound, and staring out at the sunset.

"Can't call you a kid no more, can I?" he said gruffly.

Deedee trusted the youth more and more. He appreciated Icarus allowing him time to himself. He had never been followed to his grotto, nor even been asked where he went.

Sometimes Icarus called him Daddy. A mistake – a corruption of Deedee – but he liked it. It could have been so, after all; that gypsy girl. He shook his head. She'd been all right, she had. He checked the colour of his eyes in the mirror. Apricot, but the bronze dishes stained everything yellow. Probably pink, without pigment. Even his eyes had been drained of their colour. He tried to remember what he'd tried to forget – how he'd looked. He thought they'd been turquoise, he thought they'd been the same shade as the lad's.

He snorted. Imagine him, Daedalus, looking in a mirror!

He often looked at Icarus. Puppy fat had turned into muscle, toughened by fetching and carrying. Well defined calves, what with all of the stairs. Sometimes the lad scrubbed his skin down with sand mixed with olive oil. And then it would gleam and smell wonderful.

Each had their own room, but sometimes, in the early days, the boy had been frightened by nightmares. He'd come to Deedee's room chest heaving, eyes dampened with tears. Deedee would comfort him. There were no sea monsters. There was no fire burning out of control. There was no terrible fall. The child's breathing would slow and his budded fists would fall open. He'd sprawl into sleep.

Deedee imagined having the young man sleeping next to him now, being next to that taut, animal body. He never touched the lad – he didn't touch anyone – but he'd like to. There was nothing sexual in it. Something in the lad's casual beauty reminded him of his own unblemished youth.

Since the accident Deedee had been sexually functional, but out of action. Living out at the lighthouse kept women away. Now, though, the youth brought the whole problem up again. What if Icarus took an interest in women?

"Shit, kid, there ain't enough fuel for the fire."

Deedee kicked at the embers so sparks flew upwards.

Icarus hitched the oxen and hauled up some more fuel. In fact there'd been plenty.

Having proved himself capable, Icarus had been allocated duties. He aligned the mirrors each morning and evening. "Young legs are better at stairs," Deedee would say, though he overhauled them, always.

Icarus also reset the conical pendulum. And he looked after one of the oxen, the smaller one, Minos.

"When I'm gone you'll have to look after them both," said Deedee.

"Don't talk nonsense."

Recently the old man had taken to saying things like that: When I'm gone! He still had many years in him yet.

Icarus' curiosity was piqued by the things the man sneered at. The city, particularly its music and gypsies, fascinated him. Why should he be warned so strongly against them?

Each afternoon, when Deedee went off on his own, Icarus would race into town. His bare feet pummelled the marble flags, the blows echoing back from the columns, as he ran across the heptastadia.

Sometimes he'd walk the streets, searching for ones he had not found before. Sometimes coy – and yet not so very shy – girls approached him. "What's your name?" they asked, and their eyes added, Cutie. They'd giggle. "Where do you work?"

He'd point up and across to the domed tip of the lighthouse, where it seemed as though the golden Poseidon pointed back with his trident.

And they'd giggle again. "You *never!*"

He'd kick up his heels and run off. Sometimes one would catch his eye and walk meaningfully, swinging hips that she didn't yet have, towards one of the densely palmed parks. He wondered if he was meant to follow. He'd find his face glowing without knowing why. Instinctively he knew that he shouldn't ask Deedee.

He spent his allowance, the drachmae the old man gave him, on felafel, honey cakes and grilled ribs of lamb. He'd seen one radish too many. He sat up on a bridge above a canal guzzling rich food, grease and honey besmearing his cheeks.

Powerful swans sculled purposefully underneath him, curling their necks and clapping their beaks. He let fragments of food drop and watched their heads snaking towards shards of pastry, scraps of bread and of meat. Deeper down, fat carp rolled like gold plated barrels, reflecting light through the murk.

On one such foray Icarus discovered the Sema, the park which doubled as Alexander the Great's final resting place. The dead leader rested in a casket of alabaster. The wafer thin stone allowed Icarus to see through to the shrunken corpse. A fountain played in front of the coffin, permanently weeping.

Tucked in the park's corner, it was the ring of tents, the fire, the music, which attracted Icarus. He pulled back ribbed leaves of banana palms, he ducked beneath curling fingers of fruit, and found himself facing a small, grubby, child.

The child stared at Icarus. Icarus stared back. Both stood rooted. The child's face crumpled up silently. A lean dog trotted forwards. The clearing was shrouded with wood smoke. From a tent came the slithering sound of a fiddle, underpinned by the melody of the bubbling fountain.

Suddenly a shriek. A girl – possibly the child's sister – rushed from the dark mouth of a tent and snatched the child away. For an instant she glared at the stranger. Her expression made Icarus's hair erect. A delicious prickling sensation. Air drying sweat to his scalp. His knees flexed. And then he was running. The hound yapped at his heels. The child was bawling.

"You all right?" Deedee asked.

"Sure I am."

"You look worried, that's all."

"Yeah?"

"What's the matter?"

The kid said nothing, just shrugged.

"Icarus, is something the matter?"

"I said."

"You didn't say anything."

"Well nothing's the matter, since you're so concerned for me."

"Where have you been?" The taboo question, at last, had been asked.

"Where have *you* been?"

Deedee fought to regain his composure. "Suit yourself," he said. "I don't bloody care where you've been."

And the kid left, leaving his dinner untouched.

Icarus changed.

The girl's defiance eclipsed his own so surely that he turned inside out like a jellyfish. She had hated him so perfectly that all he wanted was for her to love him with the same passion.

Taking his lead from the man he grew insular. Rather than walk into the city, he used the auxiliary mirrors, high up in the cupola, for spying. He kept his habit a secret, again using the time when Deedee would go off on his own.

He angled the mirrors into a telescope as Deedee had shown him. He viewed the gypsy encampment. He spied on the girl.

Sometimes she seemed like a child; she'd play with the children – who scuttled shy between the ferns and flowers; they'd hurl bananas at one another, soft yellow missiles; she'd hopscotch between lines she'd marked in the dust; she'd twirl her skipping rope and recite soundless doggerel.

And sometimes she seemed like a mother; she'd scrub the children clean and untangle their hair; she'd discipline them – slap them, tell them off, tell them stories; she'd sit with the adults, talking.

And sometimes, the times Icarus treasured, she'd be herself.

She'd find a quiet spot to sit with her fiddle and she'd play. Her brow would frown with concentration. Her lips would purse. Slim fingers scuttled along the neck of the instrument. The bow slipped back and forth as she coaxed notes from the strings. Notes that Icarus could only imagine.

Or she'd walk the far side of the gardens away from the encampment. Her hair coiled dark and sleek like Icarus'. She would pluck some bloom and thread its shaft through her hair.

She would sing to herself as she walked.

And occasionally she stripped in front of the fountain in the garden's centre, before the translucent coffin. Her body poured from its husking of clothes. Her limbs, dark at their extremities, grew more pale where they connected her body. She bent over the sprinkling water and soaked her hair. Excess water spilled from the stacked system of bowls. She squeezed her glistening hair, soaped up a lather, rinsed clean. Each limb in turn she submerged and in turn she washed them, her hands stroking inwards. She dampened the neat curls between her legs. Her nipples coned at the touch of the liquid. The water beneath her shivered and rippled.

She dried herself briskly, shaking off drips. Dressed efficiently. Olive green leaves enclosed her again.

In his tower, Icarus found that his breathing had frayed. He could feel the throb of his body.

He realigned the auxiliary mirrors and crept back down the stairs.

Icarus grew thin, addicted to hunger. Hunger offset the passion within him; it went with the way that he felt. No longer did he visit the city and supplement the island's meagre offerings with the rich food his body craved.

Deedee was concerned.

"Icarus, have some more radishes."

The youth looked down at his plate.

"Some goat's cheese?"

"I'm not hungry."

"Some bread then?"

The youth shook his head.

"Icarus, will you have some bread and cheese now?"

"I said, I'm not hungry."

"Suit yourself then." And Deedee pushed his own food away. The kid had spoiled his appetite.

Deedee traded the sea food he trapped for all sorts of nonsense to tempt Icarus. Cheese cakes sprinkled with sesame and aniseed. Shredded wheat soaked in syrup. Olives. Barley cakes.

Dried meats. The kid turned his nose up at them.

Deedee also grew thinner. He took up cooking, applying the same fastidious principles he applied to all tasks. He'd spend all day making a pilaff. The smell of simmering tomatoes, rice and sea-food haunted the lighthouse. Then in the evening the two of them would sit there, resentfully keeping their appointment, picking out the prawns and the olives. Next morning, the oxen feasted on leftovers. Delicious pide, spanacoppita, baklava; all met with indifference.

"Why won't you eat, kid?"

"Don't call me kid."

"Why won't you eat, Icarus?"

"I'm not hungry."

Icarus had fewer opportunities for his spying. The old man was spending more time cooking, working the garden, setting out his netting and lobster pots. He got tetchy when the weather was too hot and furious when black-fly invaded his beans.

"What's up?" said Icarus.

"Bloody insects."

The man ripped away the infected tangle of plants, stamping, kicking, flailing, wrenching, getting caught up in them. Swearing and cursing. He hurled them on to the bonfire he'd made.

Icarus walked away disgusted. He'd lost it, the old guy. Why couldn't he go off like he used to and let them each have some time to themselves? All Icarus wanted was to sit in the cupola and admire his girl. Instead, he spent time in his room inspecting its ceiling and savouring his hollowness.

"I'd like a flute," said Icarus.

"What!"

"Or a fiddle."

"What – did – you – say?" Deedee spoke slowly, grinding the words.

"I said, I'd like a flute or a fiddle."

"All right. All right. I heard you."

"And?"

"What have I told you?"

"Don't know."

"Of course you know. Don't give me that shit son."

"Don't call me son."

Deedee's pink eyes blazed. His lips thinned until both disappeared. "You Will Not Have a Fiddle. That's Final."

"A flute then?"

"NO!"

So Icarus stole one.

He slunk into town when the moon hid behind a silver-fringed blanket of cloud. He foot-padded across to the library. Every muscle taut, aware, inside him. At the back of the building, at the base of the pillars, lay a group of sleeping gypsies, their rags all entangled, their fire now extinguished, their dogs, even, asleep.

Icarus crept forwards. He'd done his reconnaissance using the mirror; while the girl took a siesta he'd spied on the back of the library. He knew where to find what he wanted.

Holding his breath he lifted dark rags releasing a smell of sweat that had dried then been moistened by more sweat. And of alcohol. He looked at the sleeping face of the man he was about to rob. So easy. He strode away, the fiddle tucked into his tunic. Not running, not guilty, but quickly.

When he reached the heptastadia he broke into a run. He whooped, slalomed the columns. His spidery legs flashed under him.

Deedee rose to find no sign of the youth.

"Where's the kid?" he asked Taurus. "D'you see him this morning?"

He stroked the bull's massive neck; massaged its ears. Moist breath steamed from its nostrils.

Minos chewed on the worzels that Icarus had left him, unwittingly answering Deedee's second question.

"What's got into him, eh? What's he up to?"

And again, when he went to the lighthouse he found the youth had the pendulum in order and the mirrors aligned.

Deedee refused to trust his apprentice's work any more. He doubled checked everything. Each day he double checked everything. The work was all perfect. The small tent of fire, ready for him to light in the evening. The arrayed blocks of fuel. Everything.

"Don't like it," muttered Deedee.

Icarus judged it perfectly, the old man's hardness of hearing. He took a similar route to the one which lead to Deedee's secret pool, across the boulders which stumbled to the west of the island, down wind. He reached the small cove where he kept the stolen fiddle hidden in a cranny. Tenderly he lifted it from the recess. He sat cross-legged. Around him, the rocks formed his audience.

Slowly, he learned. At first he wept frustrated tears at the clumsiness of his fingers. The jagged notes that blew out to sea.

He persisted. In the afternoons he watched the girl when he could. When she played he noted the set of her chin. The poise of her breasts. The steps of her fingers. Their delicate pressures. His secret tribute inspired him; one day, he knew, he'd play the music she seemingly mimed.

As Deedee hoed the soil, pulling weeds from his garden, sometimes he thought that he heard strains of music. Particularly days when the wind changed. Motes of music floating like ticks from dandelion clocks on the breeze. He frowned. Ragged music. Must be gypsies.

He walked into Icarus' room. Nothing there. It smelled musty; close. Quickly he went through the small heap of possessions. Nowhere a musical instrument could be hidden. He breathed deeply.

Then he lifted the mattress. Pressed under it lay sheets of papyrus, written on. His breath caught. He replaced the mattress. He went back to the door. He scanned the rocks and the sand dunes. No sign of Icarus. Just a thin strand of a note teased out by the breeze. He went back inside.

A diary, maybe?

Not a diary. Poetry! Love poems.

Bad ones.

The kid had defied him. He felt angry, betrayed and sad all at once. He didn't know what he felt. He thrust the papyrus back under the mattress. He walked to the lighthouse. The month wasn't up but he'd overhaul the escapement. He'd dismantle the cogs, ratchets, lever arms, springs, array them, clean and grease them, fit them all back in place again. That would calm his trembling fingers.

"Will you stop looking at me like that?" said Icarus.

Dinner time, and the man stared at him hollow-faced. Said nothing. Just stared.

"What's this about? Will you stop that looking at me!"

Still nothing.

Then Icarus guessed. He shoved aside his kalamare and ran back to his room. His poems had been crumpled. He tore the papyrus to shreds.

Deedee is worried, confused, out of his depth. Almost surprised, he finds the next morning that the oxen have been fed, the fire laid and so on. Perhaps life can continue as normal. With some relief, he bends to his own tasks.

When he finishes, he walks to his pool. To wash away the grime of deception.

Icarus watches.

Up in the cupola he swivels the auxiliary mirror to track the man's footsteps. He uses the view in the mirror like a knife, cutting into the scene.

He watches the old man undress. He sees that the man's skin, one side slack, wrinkled, on the other seems to drip like wax on a candle. The malformed whiteness, opposing his girl's perfect darkness, almost shocks him into stopping. Almost. Instead he tightens his fingers on the knurled controls, enlarges, focuses, prises the scene even more open. Deedee steps into the water, becoming Mercury, quick, coated with silver. The whole scene, the cove and its shimmering water, unhinges like a nacreous oyster.

Next, Icarus turns his mirror to the Sema, where his girl strips in front of the fountain. Her shift, her shirt, her sandals, her girdle. She wears nothing else.

He grunts as he tugs his erection. She bends over to douse her hair and he imagines he takes her, roughly. She likes it; she urges him. At last he has her.

Semen smears the granite under the cupola. Icarus releases his breath.

A piercing brightness lances the grotto. Sun reflects from the dish of the mirror. Deedee learns of his spectator only when he ceases spectating and turns his gaze on another.

Little shit! I'll fix him.

He doesn't bother dressing. Belying his years he scrambles like a monkey over the boulders. His scrotum swings under him. He sprints through sunlight that shines on the ivory tower. Up the stairs now, lungs heaving. Icarus' breath is in step as he reaches his climax.

Daedalus faces Icarus under the dome of the cupola.

The main mirror's beam reaches its limit and both men suddenly blaze in its spotlight. Reflected sunlight fans out like wings from both pairs of shoulders.

The moment is over, the main mirror tracks back again. Deedee is faced with his son. He feels like screaming. He feels like lashing out. He feels like crying.

Icarus continues to stare coldly, emptied of passion.

Deedee steps across to the auxiliary mirror. He sees the boy's naked gypsy still washing herself.

"Out! Get out! I told you. You'll never come here again. D'you hear me? Never!"

Banished, Icarus practices on his fiddle. His pupils narrow in the sunlight and his skin becomes darker. Each night he sleeps on the beach. During his dreams, the waves teach him rhythm. Using a shard of sea-shell and charcoal he scrapes tattoos on each arm, like a gypsy's. He etches a pattern of flames on his calves. Or the flames could be waves or the waves could be feathers. His hands become skillful, developing a life of their own. They scamper across the sway and curve of the fiddle. Their music takes shape.

He plans a duet with his girl that she won't even know about. From the cupola he'll watch and mimic her movements. Thus he will hear the girl's music.

He understands where music fits in with geometry and poetry. And he understands why the man hates music so much.

Deedee didn't know his crazed heart could actually break. He thought he was tough, thought he'd got over all that. Too late he realises he's had it all wrong; he's been too strict, too strait-laced in bringing up the boy. In bringing up – say it! – his son. If only he could find some way to see the boy, talk to him, explain. Somehow patch things up again. He can't face going down to his pool. All he wants is his son back.

He works. The beacon continues to beam, by day reflecting the sun, and by night the fires. Life functions.

Another six months. Icarus is ready. Shaggy-haired, wild-eyed, agile-fingered: he looks and he plays like a gypsy. The door that leads to the spiralling staircase is locked. As expected. No matter. He hugs the chest of a mermaid. He clutches the horns of a triton. He grapples a dolphin. His fiddle swings from his shoulders. He heaves himself upwards over the lighthouse exterior. Hands and then feet.

Too late to stop him, Deedee sees him, climbing the spiral horn of the tower.

From his garden, he watches the young man crawl upwards, corkscrewing higher. Deedee does not run. Nor shout. He just watches, mouth open, fingers shifting, gripping the hoe.

Icarus reaches the cupola and has to lean backwards to grip on the coping; the overhang. His legs dangle and flail in thin air. His wiry arms haul himself upwards. Then the fiddle slips from his shoulders. He turns to grab it.

And the turning continues.

Daedalus steps through his duties coldly like an automaton.

He says nothing. Words hold no meaning. His final official

task is to pass on his actions.

With undignified haste, the matrix leadership have sorted out an understudy, a new kid. Daedalus knows why. He knows they're saying his days are numbered. That he's become the shell of himself. That the art of attending the beacon needs passing on, and fast.

He actually heard one of them say to the new kid: Watch out for the old man, you might find he acts *funny*.

The understudy trots by his side as he goes through his rituals. Daedalus looks at the new kid; his face flickers; his eyes hold the question: Understand?

The kid nods.

As sunlight stings the sky into life Daedalus carries the amphora of oil to his pool. He has to go slowly to keep it from spilling. The sky is pale blue when he reaches what has become once more his secret.

He tips oil on to the water. It slicks the swell into stillness and smothers the surface with a deadly but beautiful rainbow.

Slowly he walks back to the lighthouse. This time he pours the oil on himself.

Daedalus smells his flesh and hair burning again. This time he planned it. He breathes deep, stilling the screaming instincts inside him. Oh yes, he'll act funny. Black smoke swirls up the hollow centre of the lighthouse and Daedalus sees Icarus falling again, spiralling slowly to earth like a sycamore seed. The fire has become a funeral pyre. The bob of the conical pendulum whips around his body; its wire twirling his spiral of flames, shortening, tautening.

Through a flickering veil he sees the new kid in front of him.

And now he's floating upwards.

And now his spirit sees everything.

Under the cupola, the mirrors jolt at the unexpected force from the pendulum and escape their escapement. Amplified sunlight is redirected to focus on the library roof. The rush covered rafters develop a melanoma, a dark spot. The spot grows, smoulders, smokes, burrows deeper. Flames ring it.

In the city, the beam from the lighthouse cannot be diverted.

The prophecy inverts and the library turns into a furnace, a beacon. Smoke can be seen throughout what was Alexander's empire.

Pausing at canals, gathering strength and then leaping, the fire edges eastwards, one square at a time.

Flames crackle. Webbed feet slap upon water as squadrons of swans stampede their take-offs. Massive birds race the canals, wings flared, shoulders heaving. Pinions scrape bridges. Pink clouds of flamingos rise gawkily, legs swinging under them.

Before the flames reach it, Alexander's coffin shivers then shatters in response to the blistering heat. Shards of alabaster twinkle and fall round the fountain. The corpse sighs and sublimes, falling inwards.

A gypsy girl steps from the Sema and into the street. Her skin gleams with sweat. The heat of flames is solid. She seems not to notice. Charred words fall around her. Coral and ivory feathers.

She tucks her fiddle into her. Her music is wild as the flames.

Perhaps a Woman

Katherine Brown

Katherine Brown was born in Geneva in 1968. She studied at King's College, Cambridge, and the University of Pavia, Italy. The following is an extract from a work in progress, *Perhaps a Woman*. It is dedicated to Claire.

Katherine Brown

Perhaps a Woman

She wove violence into tapestry, and had it put before her sister; the voiceless caught up in thread; the unknown unknowing, told.

Here, we are twone: two in one; as I speculate throughout those silences of word and gesture and look. You do not speak of it, perhaps cannot remember, but now I know that grainy space and time which first inhabit consciousness and crumble the self distractedly amongst the staring and the clamouring of those around. Now I know that speckled helplessness of thought, then the fear and suffocation which made you shrink from those who bore upon you. I know it is this, and much greater than this, which came to yank your body from my half-touch and pulled your hands to shake in front of face.

I know a terror shreds your heart. And I know that if I tender hand towards and near, you scream.

Still, we used to talk to you, waiting for some flicker, though none ever came. Still, we used to talk at you talk at you. And when you did not pull away, I would put my arm around your bony back and hold you, head hanging beneath the straggled hair. Let me be the memory for that time.

Twone; two from one. Later, and in this moment, as you are reading what I write: this book, your toes curl over and your feet tighten, to flick, one against the other, dryly. Your face again hidden beneath a swing of hair. But you do not shriek suddenly, and wrench the pages. That was the postcard torn and twisted and flung to the back of a hospital shelf, but not this, not now. Here I write, not to you, not at you, but search for words for both of us, and others.

No words no longer, no speech, no thought; she, shelled:
thrummed through with monolithic images of food; and in
dawn-encroached exhaustions her mouth opens and closes a
little, opens and closes, a baby's suckling;
not dumpling flesh, downy globe of head,
but papered brittleness pulling back to skull.

And I, I, while a car hurtles around a corner and a hag skids by in mortar with pestle, I journey frantically. I curl up tightly, then unfold, travel suddenly the aeons between saliva-forced swallow and pit of stomach. I am amongst the oceanic bellowing of the trees, the moon torn and spinning in wisps of cloud. Where the skull dances in the spaces beyond the window and between the walls, turning this way and that, laughing like a face, translucent like a shadow. I am where the girl-woman sits subdued by the fireplace and others, conspiratorial, cluster in the far reaches of a room that pulls and stretches into vast distances. I am in the city, in the forest; watching as a woman pushes past, skull tilted in a frozen grin purpled by the gloom. And another, hands raised and head moving through an easy arc, purses her lips in mimicry around a word half exhaled, whilst the night cloys around her mockeries and sinks the soundless syllable, invisible. Stumbling amongst tree roots wracked from their soil, I am all these places. And nowhere. Frantic and apart.

Oh but one, now, transvestised, leered with kohl-rimmed lids, pushes gaunted scalp in amongst my worlds, persists with stare and jut of jaw, whilst I clutch at my completions, and try to stay elsewhere;

like – no: not like domed snowscaped scenes, shaken by an

outside hand and throwing swirls of whiteness into slowing watered movements,

not like, no: rather birds that tear in windows, beaked with bloodied puppy fat, to shred the body of its last hangings of air.

She is flying towards me towards her, in pestle and mortar, with broom to sweep away her traces; bearing down towards meher in a car that shudders over the cobblestones steep between grimed walls, bearing

father it was father who gave me to the husband gave me to this woman gave me to her birds

or mother was it mother who promised me unborn in return for gluttoned gratification

travesty guilt is mine

I am falling through sleep. Know later that I must have been walking through that Venetian Square towards a passage between bar and church; know later that it was then that I began to tread amongst a squall of pigeons and an old lady's crumbs, throwing up confusion shaped like birds' wings and a madwoman's cries; recall later that I did not know until going, gone, was in the alleyway, that it was I who was being cursed.

But I am falling through sleep and watch what I must; feet seen from above amongst strutting plumped bulks. Not here the bed's familiar and unexpected lurch towards a sudden abyss. Not that, but a memory, commonplace, yanked and swollen. A greyness rushed upwards in a violence of wings; and my eyes flung open against the terror of my heart.

She, now: old woman, with crumbled spine and crumpled fingers, with sunken face, and eyes yet sudden, bright, she has eased herself against the slope of wet mud, and hand against tree trunk, has begun to inch her way down.

"Cussèd weather. Too old to be doing this. Oh botheration. Oh, this mud." And she lifts her free hand to rub it against her skirt.

Is she now the one, the chaperone, the widowed sister of the imprisoner, the one who watches over Tereus? She the one, who as a bird, looks in through the window while leaves darken to a falling day and the metallic hum of distant cars is drawn across the sky? The one who, like a mother, could once catch all her accidental thoughts, but now sees nothing, and brings a glass of water:

"Child, your appearance will kill us both,"

and the mirrors echo: Lady did I not say that your appearance would kill us: this the reproach of the bird-prince to his imprisoned lover, she having regained beauty in the fulfilment of love and desire

but here, hair slices the face in two, flings out one eye of brutal nakedness, hands yanked in front of mouth;

and then a glass shatters in the pit of the woman's heart.

and laugh laugh purpled mouths like cigarette-burned skin you're not going to touch me you cannot touch me do not touch me

This the real, the concrete, amongst all my imaginings. This, both the here and the there. And in the seams of the woodland there is a font, not visible at first, as dark glosses of leaves pull downwards over a discarded dustbin and knotted plastic bags, on towards a flattened emptied carton, lying in its fall across a slope of earth. Not visible as the eye first recedes to other childhood enclosures beneath branches and behind haphazard barriers; but then returns to founder in a startling of stone and gravel and sudden sunlit lawn. For here, at the borders: the basin, supported by prepubescent girls, coy in upheld arms and downcast eyes, hair frozen in its flow. And from where I am, I can make out a sideways slice of rain water, opaque as its pitted surrounds, and stagnant.

It was here that she had come to fetch the water flung back at her. There that she will go the day she washes her hands of the unspeaking child. But for the moment she continues to pulp left-over words, to scoop them into moulds, until, congealed like platitudes, she tips them neatly onto plates and puts them before her charge.

The crockery she uses is innocuous enough; cheap pastel china of squared forms, thickened edges and wide rims, with provenance unmarked, generic. Not unpleasant; the insides of the cups slightly stained perhaps, the inner circles of the plates a little drawn with scratches, the occasional chip which has taken off a triangle of pale green or yellow or pink and left behind whiteness; but, no, not threatening. And the phrases that had set and were being dished up were normal, appropriate, what you would expect.

"Swallow, don't chew. Take them in as they are," she would say as she pushed them at her.

But inevitably, invariably, the woman would find words mashed beneath the edge of the table, crumbled and pulped in the toe of a shoe, caked into pockets and encrusted around the necks of t-shirts, even caught in the girl's matted hair.

Inevitably, invariably; hypnotic and broken from the forms which once held them; I, wondering and wandering through dazed banalities. Then a dimpled stone elbow, rounded cherubic belly, and a bird that plummets with the rapid simplicity of a premonition.

"Talk to me. You're leaving me talk to me. Talk to me."
Broken ends which bob back into my silences. "Talk to me."

But no, that is not quite right. Why do I think it is she, trying now to reach me, when all along it was I, straining my body towards her, and then tightening so I would not touch too much. The words were mine, but not in those shapes, nor so direct nor short. I did not say 'talk to me', held no expectation, yet the suppressed plea which tugged all through my soliloquies was that. "Talk to me."

She never did, of course; not to me, not to anyone. She had no thought or feeling or perception with which to talk. She had left, and left a long time ago; her going not noticed until she was gone.

"But you were such a happy child." Or a thin smiling child; thinning more and smiling less. Until one day I went to put my arms around her; she who was doubled over, her smiling face upturned and drenched in tears. And when I encircled her waist, I felt her body tiny, loose:

but was that a dream that there were no ribs? Was that a dream?

Lady, did I not say your appearance would kill us, that sunken face and shirt fallen in a lurid cry of bone. But no, no, let thoughts skid and skate then settle in allotted safety, not this. Not her, but rather from a train's cradling hum, from a distance, the unseen lives of evening lit windows. The blackened rows of terraced houses and jolt after jolt of back extension pushed into L-shaped yards, then lean-to wooden fencing and a confusion of washing. Now closer, an empty milk bottle, an almost-memory of some ancient anticipation recalled no gone again; and here the wider streets with rusting railings, the fall beneath the pavement to windows buried and brutally exposed, their gouged existences with an overview of kitchen table and the shudder of panes at a passing car. And have these others known the childhood dream, the teddy bear in joyful replications secreted throughout the room? Have they too woken and searched above the wardrobe and in the bottom drawer, to be met with dust and empty clothes, and a disappointment that never leaves? To live now in the quotidian clatter of cutlery and the chaotic litter of endless looks?

But I had thought to leave her behind, and have returned only to the jack-knived violence of her body as she yanks from the woman's gaze.

The silent bowing leaves pull at me as the day quickens to darkness and dampness spreads through every brick and stone. Not the reddened warmth of a remembered tapestry; but why that now? The lady, and beneath besides above: beasts, handmaidens, and flowers; moments in a red muteness. But there are too many images and gestures discordancing amongst my containments. Need to throw them out, let them sink into leaves and sods of earth thrown black by last night's rain.

I return to it, my thoughts return to it, for our past has patterned our wrists and minds, and how could I forget?

Let them sink there, those relentless repetitions of voice and gaze. Rather this than a tightening, then snapping, in minutiae of fraying,

No, not a lady in an ornamental garden, but woman pushing head to hand, head to hand, elbow on the table at the borders of my consciousness. Head to hand, hand to head, and table not etched by mountains or charred by streams: oh girl, little girl, what are you doing to yourself, why are you doing this to yourself

And shall those voices resume their clamouring now that I am sitting still? I run to keep them in their voiceless moment, refuse them this, their harbouring of threat.

But inbetween moments you cut yourself. In that momentlessness we can never know,

Not mine a burying of the inappropriate, but a letting of the excesses into different forms which tip and sink in consciousness,

Pushing head to hand, hand to head, then watching from her crooked tilt of fingered face:

I don't know why you're being so funny about it.

But she does not say, and cannot say: you are breaking my heart, it is breaking my heart. Does not say. Instead; and running away with all the sentences she has scattered through the years and which keep on coming back:

come on now, stop being so silly

And yellow leaves begin to turn;

I don't know why you're like this, it's because you've got everything. We used to have what we were given, not like now and all the waste

Grittened bark of ancient trees catches in amongst my hearts;

here just a little bit. I remember one morning I went to feed the rabbits, but mother had cooked them the night before and there was no use getting all upset about it because that's all there was. Then they took away my cat

Skidding now, the earth is black;

and shot it, said it must've run off; it was for my own good, I was allergic to it; didn't find out the truth till years later. That's how it was then what've you got to be sad about we've always given you what you wanted everything

Sitting against a tree and crying;

you'd be better with something to keep you busy instead of brooding all the time. Here sort out these beads for me; there's a nice little job for you

And crying crying crying amongst the unheards. The leaves in their stillness and the muted settling of twigs in sodden earth.

When they came, they came in through the window. But I was not there. *I stir, touch against, buckle backwards: a clammed and fleshy thickness beside my head, on my pillow.* Not there as the tower room darkened in a wing-beaten silence beyond frosted glass. *I freeze in that lurch between dream and waking, for it is huge beside my face, a pored pulpiness.* And the tower room darkened and the windowed wall shuddered. Another thud and the pane, already uncertain at an edge, began to fall, fall inwards, was falling. *A hand: I realize it is a hand.* It fell in a hurtling of blackness; the glass splintering and shooting shards of blood across the floor, into the mirrors. *My own. On the pillow beside my head a hand and wrist and part of arm; myself.*

And she, hurled back against the mirrors, a terror of two backs, mouth straining as though to scream: no oh god no no no no. She, tendons knived from wrists, fingers splayed across peeled-back mouth, again bolted. And with beaks and claws they seized her, rent that taut and tightened air tensed around her thinnesses; seized her. She, hitting bone to floor, arms flung like wing bones over face and head; no oh god no no no. Feathers falling, and a broken blood-stained talon turning into an old woman's hand.

Now in the mirror, her expression; eyes whitened hard and wild as a hare's. Then a light switch flicked in another room and I start.

Oh, she thinks I do not know, when the voice on the phone is pale from loss of blood; when, unusual, it has lost its sheen, and worn away from glittered chatter; when, though not late, she is tired, already abed. And I did not know at once: only later, when thought turned back and tried to make its way across moments disjointed now and partial; came upon the white-chalked words.

Yet by then I could no longer see their edges, the points at which what she said and what she meant remained distinct. Instead their texture, their thickened dullness, swelled against the cut and shut me out.

"No, not now. Can't talk to you now. Go go away. Please go away. Let me be."

These, then, not the words, but they their weight, and held in my voice. For I, to the one who calls out: Hey beautiful lady xcuse me beautiful lady hey I said xcuse me I'm talking to you Well thank you my darling and may you have prosperity and long life Thank you; I too plead,

"Go, go away, just go away, please go away. Why can't you leave me alone, why can't you all just leave me alone."

And, she: tired, no not really. Later I saw the chalky face and bandaged wrist as she lent out of an upper window, forgetting -

shot the arm back in and retreated behind the wall.

I am watching you, watching as you sit alone, and do not know, do not feel the dislocations between each moment. Alone, are sitting on your bed: are sitting looking nowhere: are sitting on your bed, playing penknife into wrist: are sitting on your bed with blood. Do not know from one moment to the next.

And was not that body of beak and claw and wing? To wrench in detached deliberation each filament from its feather and laugh as sharp intakes fall against the spine? So only later then, and afterwards, do you draw breath within the purpled spines rucked from skin. Only later does what you do become yours, can be seen,

pulling bracelets into the nightmares of my sleep.

Of beads blue-black like the sheen of crows, strung and bound around your scars, still dripping with the clay that moulded them; of a rust coloured band worked large with holes and like a napkin ring too small; then the king's bracelet with glints giddying between thought and broken promises: what he said and what he did and did not do.

And you, were you not only ever as this, perhaps had been, perhaps had only ever been that smile-affixiated photograph behind the glass, flitting in their reflected partialities? Though now not glistened surfaces, but wool. Mattened in a tapestry's configurations, gestures separated, side by side: you spoke, fell silent, put out a twist of a smile, held the mocking blanks of beer mats to your eyes, pulled your hands into sleeves, were gone.

Even now uncomfortable to hold my wrist exposed like that; what was it? Not mine, but yours: roped thickly purple down its length so you would wince when you saw it, and girls on the bus would look and turn to whisper, breaking sentences into stares. And the one who was once your friend, that ginger haired porcelainity, gaze averted, stubborn equanimity, (do you think her heart at least rustles?), why she never knew you. And so you curl up close as I put my arm around you, but what else can I do?

Now, caught between the cracks of stone: the crow-black beads of clay; whilst out of sight and without its shape, the filigreed rusting band. Yet the king's bracelet, spinning still, snatches glints of colour and broken forms from the overturned room, then clatters against a mirror and shudders: turning turning, encounters other images; and falls away from metal and into dances.

Not the king's bracelet, but the courtly dance, that ritualistic circling. And in the orange rain of street lights, tossed and blown like gnats over a dirt track, glinting shapes like snow, she paces around each lamp post. Five then seven, thirteen, seventeen times. Five then seven, thirteen, seventeen, as people come to windows, move their mouths and stare. Hair matted over muddied eyes and gritted skin, she quickens each circling, rushing through numbers, desperate to get home. Still another lamp post, still five, then seven, thirteen, seventeen; five then seven, thirteen, seventeen. Numbers to hold back destiny against an impossible tumbling of worlds.

> The old woman: twisting wrist in hand and hand in wrist, pulling back to massage the soft and tendoned underside with edge of thumb, then buckling again the parched skin in that incessant circling,

With words like shiny taffeta threaded through her clothes, stiff and crinkling as hats pushed to the back of wardrobes and used for dressing up; glimmers caught in feathers; she is flicked from woman to bird and bird to woman, one to the other, simultaneously.

Pretended through with certainties, she moves from the fire which scorches her legs from too long sitting, to the red flagstoned pantry and plates greased with damp. And Tereus, in the time before that name, would shiver into tall beds with taut sheets and blanket upon blanket up to green coverlet, sheets so cold they felt wet, and slowly slowly would push toes down from scrunched-up body, crumpling and softening their austerity; whilst in another room playing cards would be set against the night and taffeta words drawn about more closely.

It was a time when sleep was sutured by the jolts of trains, drawn away by the liquid calls of crows and green curtained light, and dissolving in dark wood and mirrors tarnished like liver-spotted hands. Then when the dust hung idle in the mid-morning light she would pick through the old clothes still stitched through with words, hold them up against her body, play with adult conversation.

So I pull these spaces around me and lie against the afternoon.

Not waiting to be let in but on the other side, she stands at the mirror, her back through frosted glass grey grained as rain. And because she does not know, because she cannot know, does not, cannot, is not: mirrored flesh rippled out of reach and hurtled back to leer. In taunts of flip-flopped words as fat is thin is thin is fat is ugly is lovely is I don't know I don't know I don't know don't know which of the words is meant to fit.

Evening and a child begins to turn, beginning to turn, turning, spinning now round and round, spinning through outstretched arms pulling weight in circles pushing mud between toes cold clung with grass, reeling through duskiness glowing orange into street lights and drawing curtains tight, spinning beyond the cried-out name and calls to come inside, turning turning on and on upon herself.

X 20

Richard Beard

Richard Beard was born in 1967. He read English at Cambridge, and has since worked on Iona, in Kowloon, at the Dragon School, in Lunga Tower near Oban, and at the National Library in Paris. His work is often featured on Radio France under the pseudonym Marcel Barbon. The novel, *X 20,* will be published by Flamingo in early 1997.

Richard Beard

X 20

Day 1

Dr William Barclay, born 7 March 1936, died 3 March 1994, aged 57. Mysterium Magnum. The principle of all generation is separation, he used to say.

Distract your mind. Take up a new hobby. Occupy your hands.

He said that the mosaic virus could sweep through a field of sweet tobacco leaves or potatoes or tomatoes in a single day, causing devastation to entire agricultural eco-systems.

Try not to think about it. Spend time in public places. Keep very very busy all day long.

{365 x 20 x 10} + {2 x 20} (leap years). Equals exactly 73, 040. Plus 6 irregulars. Not give or take, not approximately, but exactly seventy three thousand and forty six. All the same, it's difficult to prove.

Walter once told me that the old steam-trains in the old days, all steamed up and stretching homewards, used to say Cigarettes tch tch, Cigarettes tch tch. The sound of a train then, an old train on an old track, steaming homewards, smoking.

I knew about this, the concentration. That concentration would be part of the problem. That a restless, dissatisfied mind would rip from one dissatisfaction to the next, like a child stuck in a hawthorn tree in a high wind, on a high hill, in winter. At night.

Lucy Hinton, big-bellied and surrounded by children. The back of her head turns into a chimney, the blackened smoke-stack of a steam train, steaming smoke-signals saying, at the very least, goodbye bye bye.

Stear clear of friends who smoke. Repress your desire.

Feeding the dog would distract the mind. Scientists experiment with animals to save people like me unnecessary discomfort.

Julian Carr, Dr Julian Carr, went to work in his sister's bra.

Breathe deeply. Indulge yourself in every other way.

Always boxes of Carmen No 6, and never soft-packs, although at one time soft-packs were very fashionable, especially in Paris, where I once was.

I hate and despise more things than I can name. My lungs ache. Avoid tense situations. Use public transport.

In the flat where we used to live above Lilly's Pasty Shop, he would hop once and jump once and Lilly would bring up a Large Pasty No Chips. He had a range of jigs for different orders, and I swear the cat could recognise the step which meant cod.

I wonder if Dr Julian Carr would have made my parents happy if he had been their only child instead of me. The Hamburg episode notwithstanding.

Carmen No 6 in endless white boxes, on the beds and tables and chairs, in all the pockets of my life. The logo of black castanettes, in silhouette, looks like a split scallop shell. Nowadays, the sign of the double castanette is most often seen beside the air-intake of Formula 3 racing-cars, or discreetly positioned in posters for the English National Opera.

He once said you can change the world and I said no you can't.

There is also hypnosis, aversion therapy, psychoanalysis,

acupuncture, electric shock treatment, and possible conversion to the 7th Day Adventist Church, who maintain that cigarettes are an invention of hell itself.

My name is Gregory Simpson. I am thirty years old. I am trying to keep my hands occupied.

Day 2

Some time ago, when I was still a teenager, my parents were proud of the fact that I didn't smoke. Each time I promised never to start they would congratulate me on my good sense, then stare silently for several seconds at the memory of my Uncle Gregory. My Uncle Gregory died of cancer at the age of 48, in the winter of 1973.

Every Christmas, before my uncle died, my father used to light a King Edward cigar at the beginning of the Queen's speech. He used to lean back in his chair, four fingers along the top of the cigar, smoking as happily as King Edward. Now, whenever I see the Queen, she smells of Christmas cigar smoke.

Thirteen years ago, in what turned out to be my only year at University, I was allocated a room in the William Cabot Hall of Residence For Men. My next door neighbour was Julian Carr, who smoked Buchanans No 1.

The wall between our two rooms was predictably, institutionally thin, and whenever he had visitors, which was often, it was easy to follow the gradients of his impressive voice. The smoke from his cigarettes and the cigarettes of his friends would gradually seep under the adjoining wall, over it, between the molecules of it, through the very centre of it. My mother would have called it attempted murder.

Julian Carr was studying medicine. His degree was being sponsored by the Buchanan Imperial Cigarette Company. All his Buchanan cigarettes were therefore free, and he chose to smoke their No 1 brand, blended and manufactured exclusively in Hamburg.

Ten years and one day ago, recently returned from Paris, I

met Dr William Barclay in the grounds of the Long Ashton Tobacco Research Unit, just outside the city.

"Call me Theo," he said, "everyone else does."

It was February and it was cold and we were both smoking cigarettes: the Research Unit corridors and labs were strict No Smoking zones. My cigarette, obviously, was a Carmen No 6. His was a Celtique from a pack he'd bought in French Guyana. It was cold enough to confuse breathing with smoking.

Theo had a tan which made him look unseasonably healthy, and which contrasted nicely with the starched white of his lab coat. But his hair was always the most striking thing about him. Already greying, it stood up from his head in a visual imitation of surprise. Different sections of his hair gave up growing at different lengths, and some bits just kept on going so that his head looked completely out of control, the hair escaping the skull in every possible direction. He also had a small vertical scar on his upper lip.

We wandered aimlessly through the landscaped grounds, past the cinder running track and the asphalted tennis court, timing the walk by the burn-speed of a cigarette, an instinct I still admired in others. Eventually, we reached the narrow pond which marked the boundary of the Unit, just inside the security fence. Theo asked me if I was new and I said I was.

"Got somewhere to live?"

I said I had.

He said he'd won the trip to French Guyana in a Spot the Ball competition.

Seven minutes and forty-five seconds ago, roughly, Walter arrived. Walter is one hundred and four years old, but he doesn't look much over eighty. He uses a stick and always wears a hat or a cap to cover his bald bare-headedness. What started as vanity is now habit, and today it is a green canvas rain-hat. There is an enamel badge pinned to the front showing the ruins at Tintagel with a red TINTAGEL printed in a crescent underneath.

Walter is sitting in his favourite chair beneath the framed publicity poster of Paul Heinreid and Bette Davis in the film *Now, Voyager*. He is smoking a pipe, peaceful as an Indian chief, staring into the middle distance of his memory.

He has already asked me what I'm doing.

"Writing," I said.

"Writing what?"

"This, that, anything."

"Why?"

"Distracts the mind. Keeps the hands busy. You know."

"Thought I'd just pop in. See how you're bearing up."

"I'm fine."

My lungs are shrinking and my heart aches: I am about to suffocate from unrequited desire. "It's really a lot easier than I thought it would be."

But Walter wasn't listening anyway. He was looking round the room.

"When was the last time you went out?"

"The funeral."

"Yes. Well the less said then."

My parents waved me off to University as though I was embarking on a single-handed sail around the world, when between the two of them they knew full well that the world was flat. It had always been flat: in their own lives they had found it nothing but flat. They stood cardiganed together in the frame of the doorway, in primary colours, waving imaginary handkerchieves.

Unexpectedly, unwillingly, I found I missed them.

My mother used to write a weekly letter in which she hardly ever used full-stops. Mostly, she wrote exclamation marks! She discovered how to make the events of her life tremendously exciting, not through exaggeration or alcohol or drugs, but simply through punctuation.

She was scared I would choose cigarettes to perform the same function in my new life at University, so often, fastened to the letter with a coloured plastic paper-clip, there would be articles cut from the The Daily Express or The Daily Telegraph, and sometimes from Cosmopolitan.

Half of all smokers expected to die from smoking-related illnesses.

Fifteen to twenty percent of all British deaths caused by smoking.

Smokers' chance of lung cancer increased by 980%.

I read endless columns of percentages of danger, and learned from them the equal and equivalent measure of parental fear, always fearing the worst. In my occasional written replies, and always on the telephone, I promised I still wasn't smoking and didn't plan to start. The repetition of the promise became a kind of ritual, a habit it was hard to break. More importantly, it became my easy and English way of saying I loved her.

Even though I didn't smoke myself, I soon discovered that I enjoyed the company of smokers. It was a kind of rebellion by proxy, each smoky room a moment of passive rebellion. I was particularly impressed by Julian Carr who could smoke before breakfast and in the middle of meals, and who could light matches into his cupped palms like Humphrey Bogart in Paris in *Casablanca*. I lent him sugar and gave him my last rasher of bacon. When he ran out of matches, I let him light his cigarettes from the glowing tube of my electric bar fire.

I learnt how many brothers (one older) and how many sisters (one older) he had. He openly admitted to a happy childhood, which made it seem true. Later, at school, he'd lost his virginity at fourteen and been captain of the rugby team. He'd sold marijuana to the fifth-form girls. He was reading James Joyce. I gave him my last egg.

In return, he invited me to the parties he was invited to, which were always the best parties. They had the biggest barrels of beer and the blondest girls, most of whom, at some time, came back to his room and smoked quiet cigarettes far into the morning.

That's how I met Lucy Hinton. Who had black hair.

Starting in his sleep, jumping and spluttering to attention in the trenches of the First World War, Walter wakes up suddenly, spilling the triangular ashtray perched on the arm of his chair.

I tell him it's alright. I calm him down. I pick up the ashtray and give it back to him.

"I was dreaming," he says.

"I should hope so. I'd hate to think you were getting senile."

"Did I ever tell you," he says, "about this monkey-skin pouch I once had, dyed the colour green, which I lost in the course of a boar-hunt in the forest of Compiegne in the Easter Vacation of 1903?"

But his heart isn't really in it, not like it used to be, and he remembers the Compiegne forests without telling them, stepping off alone into the vast protected reservation of his past.

Among other distinctions, Walter has the largest cigarette card collection in the county. Sometimes I ask to look at a particular set (Kings and Queens of England, for example, or Great Imperial Battles or The Way We Were) as a quick and always reliable source of historical reference.

"You're pregnant," I said.

"Well bugger me, so I am."

Lucy Hinton lay on the floor beneath the curtained window of Julian Carr's room in The William Cabot Hall of Residence for Men. Her shoulders and her head were cradled in a bean-bag, and she was wearing a denim maternity dress fastened up the front with big black and white ying-yang buttons. Her hands, fingers splayed, rested on her swollen belly. She had a single feather stuck into a thin beaded headband.

"It's difficult to make an effort," she said, "considering."

Her voice was languid, throaty, like a code which when deciphered always read a breathy *Hello Baby*, a message her pregnant body did its best to confuse. It was as if she was speaking two languages at once, making no sense at all.

I was sitting on the bed, watching her, ignoring Carr who was passed out on his collection of Suzanne Vega CDs. He was using the head from his gorilla suit as a pillow, and had unzipped and pulled down the top half of the gorilla to show a T-shirt with ***Buchanan's Silverstone Spectacular*** printed on the back. He was breathing deeply, evenly.

I was dressed as a doctor, with a white coat and a head-torch and a stethoscope round my neck.

"Bung me his cigarettes," she said. "I'm dying for a fag."

Carr's cigarettes were on the floor by my feet.

"Is it due soon?" I asked, "How long is it before it's due?" I didn't reach for the cigarettes. "I mean, how long is there to go?"

"Well, let's put it this way," she said, "I only go to parties with a full complement of medical students. The cigarettes?"

"You're not really going to smoke, are you?"

"Why not?"

"Pregnant women who smoke have a much much greater chance of giving birth to an underweight baby."

At the last minute, I managed to erase my mother's exclamation mark.

Theo finished his Celtique. He looked at the filter, then looked over his shoulder, then flicked the filter into the grass at the side of the pond, disturbing a duck which splashed into clear water. He offered me a cigarette, which of course I had to refuse. I noticed one of the cigarettes in his pack was turned upside down.

He smoked, then swore, then clamped his new cigarette between his teeth and waded down towards the water, found the previous filter, which he wiped against the grass and then dropped into the pocket of his lab coat. As he clambered back up the bank, he said,

"The tiresomeness of conscience. They told me at the desk you didn't have anywhere to live,"

"I'm in a hotel."

"Company paying?"

"Yes."

"I've a room free at my place."

I retreated instinctively and immediately, like a snail, a tortoise, any small scared soft thing with defence an option. I explained how I had to have my own room with its own lock. How I absolutely had to be left alone. How I needed to use the kitchen and the bathroom when no-one else was there. How what I wanted most of all was just a simple uninterrupted life, with no intrusions and no involvements and with the minimum possible peripheral activity.

I wouldn't even want to talk to anyone very much, to be honest.

Lucy Hinton gasped and slipped down the bean bag, her fingers splayed wide across her belly. "Oh!"

"What?"

"I think it's . . ."

"No!"

"No," she said, breathing heavily but managing to push herself back up the beanbag, "False alarm."

"Spontaneous abortion," I said, "is another well-documented risk."

"Medical student."

"History."

"Give me the pack of cigarettes," she said. "I won't smoke one, I'll just hold it, for old times' sake."

"Promise?"

"Promise."

I passed her the cigarettes. Our fingers touched, briefly, and I was even more disturbed by the difference between the *Hello Baby* and the baby baby. I glanced at the denim straining at the ying-yang buttons. I thought of the translucent surface of a snare drum and had the idea that if her skin were tight enough it might just achieve translucence in the last days before birth. All the workings of the baby and the belly would be visible like television.

"Did you want to get pregnant?"

"I wanted to have sex."

She took a cigarette out of the packet. She held it up to the light, then ran it along under her nose, her eyes closed.

She asked me if I smoked and I said no.

"It's only I was thinking," she said, "you could smoke the cigarette and I could just kind of *smell* it."

Uncle Gregory died when I was nine years old.

It is breakfast time. Uncle Gregory has come to stay. I'm about to leave for school and he is going to take me in his van. Mum is washing up at the sink under the window facing the garden. Uncle Gregory is in the garden, lighting a cigarette.

Mum shouts at him that it's almost time to leave for school. He can't hear her so she taps on the window. Still smoking his cigarette he steps around the whirligig washing line, spinning it like in a musical, and says "What?" with his mouth moving very clearly. He cups his hand to his ear. Mum shouts at him that it's almost time to leave for school. Uncle Gregory mouths "What?"

He eventually understands what she's saying at the exact moment he finishes his cigarette. I can't remember if we were late for school or not.

I did nothing about finding a place to live. I could hardly see the point. Then the Company said they'd stopped paying for the Bed and Breakfast.

In those days I still had to go up to the Unit twice a week, and on the Thursday I took my break when I saw Theo kicking the dew off the grass as he sauntered down to the pond, smoke sometimes enveloping his head like an extension of his hair. I caught him up and took a light for my Carmen. I asked him if we were the only two smokers in the place.

"Looks like it," he said.

"Don't they give them free cigarettes or anything?"

"Sure. But most of them have seen what it does to the animals."

"You'd think they'd need a fag after that."

"Yes, you would." Theo smiled. "In fact, I said almost exactly the same thing once. To somebody I have successfully forgotten. They told me they thought it was in bad taste."

"Do you? I mean you yourself, are you, experimental? I mean do you personally work with the animals?"

"It's not a wildlife park."

He lit another Celtique and I opened my mouth to say I'd been thinking about the room in his place when

"Shhhh!" he said, "Did you hear that?"

"What?"

"Shhh!"

There was a rustling in the reeds by the pond. It was like the sound a blackbird makes in forest undergrowth, pretending to be

a rat or a badger, fooling passers-by, exciting them unecessarily.
"It's just a bird," I said, but Theo was already half way down the bank.

"You *have* smoked at least *one* cigarette before, haven't you?"
She held the unlit cigarette between her lips. She pulled off the beaded head-band, and caught the feather as it fell beside her. She placed it on her belly, where it quivered as she breathed.
She took the cigarette out of her mouth, looked at it, and then put the cigarette back in her mouth.
"Would you smoke *this* cigarette, if I asked you nicely?"
"Really, I don't smoke."
"Have you ever heard what a womb sounds like?"
I looked at her belly, rising and falling, the feather trembling, the denim warping to the ying-yang buttons.
"Would you like to? You can put your ear against it."
I had stopped breathing through my nose some time ago and the air in my mouth seemed unusually coarse, clogged with seductive impurities. I slipped off the bed and onto my knees so that I could shuffle towards her, not really trusting language any-more, certain that I was about to experience . . . about to HAVE AN EXPERIENCE. This was life. And living. As advertised.
She held out the cigarette to me, filter first. In her other hand she had a disposable lighter which she scratched into life, the flame lighting up her face, religiously.
"Smoke this cigarette for me," she said. "I just want to smell it. Then you can listen to my baby."

For twenty three years, my Uncle Gregory worked as foreman in a factory which made industry-standard fire-proof doors. He supervised the delicate process of sandwiching a layer of asbestos between two layers of wood. This type of door is believed to have saved thousands of lives, both in civil and military specification.
My Uncle Gregory smoked filterless Capstan full-strength. When his leg was playing up, he often used to cut down to forty a day. His hobby was motorcycle racing.

Theo's death makes me angry. Or, I don't know, I'm angry all the time and I'm thinking about Theo being dead and therefore I think it makes me angry.

Visualising him is easy. He comes through the door in his white coat stained with the residues of strange experiments. His hair is utterly mad, as usual, and he creeps up behind Walter's chair, motioning All Quiet with a finger to his lips. He nudges Walter slightly and then whispers in his ear: "Prussians!".

His bad teeth, his terrible teeth and, his teeth excepted, his obvious and robust good health from the toes on up. His body looked like it had miles of life left in it. It was only his head that made him look like a crazed professor, wryly smiling, eyes full of old mischief.

Theo's dog also makes me angry, lying on my feet and whimpering occasionally, purely from habit. I could never understand why Theo liked the dog. The dog is disgusting. In fact, the dog is like a particularly pure idea of idle disgusting dog, and it has never been anything else but useless and disgusting. It has no feelings, this dog, only appetite: it whines constantly at the length of familiar time between now and dinner, not even knowing what's familiar about it.

If I fed him now, I could both distract my mind from cigarettes and fool the foolish dog. Unfortunately, this wouldn't distract my mind from the dog.

Every day since Theo died I have received at least five letters of condolence. Today there were seven, six of them pushed through the letter-box by hand. One woman carried her baby all the way from the Estates to hook a wreath of braided dandelions on the brass knocker, next to the polished sign which says The Suicide Club.

"I don't smoke." I said.

"Please, just this one, for me."

"I'm sorry, I don't smoke."

"Don't you want to hear the baby? Don't you want to touch it?"

She flicked at one of the buttons and it popped open and there was her belly tight against a kind of ribbed undershirt.

"Don't you want to?"

"I don't smoke."

"Oh for God's sake," she said.

She put the cigarette between her lips and lit it and drew in deeply, threw the lighter aside and stared at me. She drew in again and exhaled smoke through her nose.

Then she started to cough.

Her body bucked forward and now she was coughing and choking and staring at me, her eyes surrounded entirely by white, her tongue curling into a cylinder every time she coughed.

I tried to take the cigarette out of her hand and she screamed

"OH MY GOD!"

And I was on my feet and I was fussing over her and I was leaning over her and my hands were alternately grabbing for the cigarette and for her hand to comfort her and for her shoulders to keep her still and pinned back against the bean-bag and to try and get that damn cigarette off of her and out of her hands.

The coughing died down and she grabbed at me, the filter of the cigarette crushing between her fingers. She was breathing very heavily, her body trembling.

"What?" I said, "WHAT?"

"SPONTANEOUS ABORTION!"

She ripped open her dress and one of the buttons flew off and whacked hard into the CD player. She clawed at her stomach, tearing at her dress, her undershirt, her guts, at her baby, her very own baby, throwing out towards me an endless ream of red intestines, screaming at me to save her aborted baby.

There was something moving under the long grass on the bank that led down to the pond. It was trying to free itself, or trying to hide. Theo pulled back a handful of grass: something brown, alive, like the brown feathers of a female duck. It was trying to escape.

Theo cleared away more grass, and the half-blind thing blinked in the daylight. It was a kitten, it's fur matted with damp, it's small red-rimmed eyes too weak to open properly.

Theo picked it up. It didn't have the energy to struggle, and instead it hid its small face in the lapels of his white lab coat.

"No," he said, "I don't do animal experiments. I'm strictly a plant and natural history man."

She was laughing so hard, she wouldn't have seen me pick the still-lit cigarette from where it was burning a hole in one of Julian Carr's plastic-covered medical text-books. I crushed it out on the inside rim of the metal wastepaper bin. She was laughing so hard, and rolling around the floor, that the vest she was wearing under the dress had rucked up slightly, letting me see the top of her knickers through the hole she'd made between the buttons of the dress. She laughed so hard I saw her navel prettily indented on her mildly concaved, unpregnant, newly articulate stomach, reaching in and out with laughter.

One by one, I picked up the red nylon rugby socks which had been stuffed inside a pair of woollen tights. I held them in my hands, stupidly.

Walter says:

"It's not the same, is it?"

But I don't want to talk about Theo. I ask Walter how his daughter is.

"Same as ever," he says. "Nearly enough."

He asks me what I'm doing, and I wonder if he's forgotten that he asked me the same question earlier, or whether he just says it for something to say. He whacks out the remains of a pipe.

I tell him again I'm just keeping my hands busy, but this isn't entirely true.

When I was seven years old and in Primary 3, I had Miss Chisholm for English Composition. Miss Chisholm smoked a single Embassy Regal in the Top Field every day after Period 5. She used to go through the gate and hide behind the high wall where she thought no-one could see. I have a vague but insistent memory of Miss Chisholm in English Composition teaching us that the narrator can never die. That if the narrator died at the end of the story, how could he possibly tell it?

So this is the second reason I'm writing, the reason I don't share with Walter. I'm hoping that Miss Chisholm was right, and the narrator can never die.

The Only World I Know

Johnny Boyne

Johnny Boyne was born in Ireland and has lived variously in Dublin, London and New York. The joint recipient of this year's Curtis Brown scholarship, he has been published in several magazines and newspapers throughout Britain and Ireland. In 1993, he was shortlisted for a Hennessy Literary Award for Best Short Story. What follows are two excerpts from a novel in progress.

Johnny Boyne

The Only World I Know

How I Tried to Rid the World of Womankind (Allegedly)

Believe it or not, I've always wanted to be an actor. It's just one of those major dreams that I've always had. Something I just can't seem to shake.

I'm not totally sure why I want it. I don't know if it's really so much for a love of the craft as just a simple desire to be famous. A star. A teen sensation. I've always wanted to have lots of fans. Groupies even. Gangs of teenage girls following me down the street screaming as they run –

Spit on me, Johnny! Spit on me!

I'm probably quite deluded. I've been told that I live in a fantasy world.

One thing which I think would just be the coolest thing that could possibly happen would be to have little models made of me and sold in shops. Like those characters from *Star Wars* or *Star Trek: The Next Generation*. And if I was a famous actor then that could really happen. That would be excellent. I've got a little Deanna Troi on my bookcase at home, you know, and she watches over me as I go to sleep. She's like my guardian angel.

You can just imagine the look on some little kid's face on a Christmas morning when he opens up his presents to find a little six inch replica of ME on the inside. The delight! The sheer joy! It's probably a long shot but there's no harm in dreaming.

And I have to admit that I have had my moments when it comes to acting. When I was in school they used to stage whatever play was being done for the Leaving Cert course each year and I was in every one.

I started off in first year when I was only about twelve or thirteen when I played some airy spirit in *A Midsummer Night's Dream.* I just had to run across the stage every so often, flapping my arms in the air and looking like a member of the lunatic fringe. I got to wear a green body suit and I loved every minute of it.

After that I got better and better roles every year because the way it worked was that the sixth years played the leads, the fifth years got the next best roles and so on and so on.

By the time I got to sixth year I thought I was ready to take the plunge and play one of the big roles so when the auditions came around for *King Lear* I decided there was only one role I wanted and that I'd do anything to get it. I wanted to be Edmund. The bastard.

So I tried out.

I got up on the stage and marched around for ten minutes doing the *Now Gods, Stand up for bastards* speech and I was rolling my eyes and trying to look very dramatic, God love me, and by the time I was finished I was sure I had the thing in the bag. I was convinced I'd be the biggest and the best bastard in the school.

But I still didn't get the part.

The cast list went up the following Monday in the middle of the drama class and as it turned out Jimmy Peterson had got the role. He was a big rugby player type and he had dark hair and the weirdest eyes you've ever seen – they were blue but the pupils spread right out and there was hardly any white there; scary – and the drama coach, Mr Hargreaves, had picked him over me. I was very disappointed.

Now there had been an outside chance – very outside – that after all my years in the DramSoc that I'd get the chance to play Lear. I mean I hadn't tried out for the role but they knew what I was like and they knew I was pretty good and after all, it would have been their chance to say sorry for not giving me Edmund and to reward me for all my years of hard work and dedication.

But Simon Harris ended up getting the part of Lear. Again, I was not a happy laddy.

Mr Hargreaves was hanging around and so I asked him what had been wrong with my Edmund, why he hadn't given me the role, and he said that I was far too angelic looking to play the villain of the piece. He said that whoever played Edmund had to look like a real bastard.

When he said that, Father Higgins, who was passing by at the time nearly had heart failure and asked Mr Hargreaves what he thought he was doing using such language to a sixteen year-old boy in a good Christian school. Mr Hargreaves explained the context of the remark and asked Father Higgins whether he had ever read *King Lear*. He hadn't. Father Higgins then said that he thought it was disgraceful that we were putting on a play with such language in it and that he'd be going to the head about it.

Then Mr Hargreaves suggested that he leave us alone to get on with our work and stop acting like such an oul' eejit and Father Higgins took the hint and left.

But I didn't. I was still there waiting for an explanation.

"Look Johnny," he said, trying to appear consoling but failing badly. "There was no way I could make you Edmund. The audience would never believe that you're an evil bastard. You look too nice. It's your hair that's the problem really. If you were darker it would be one thing, but as it is..."

I protested my bastardy but there was no swaying him. And you know, after Edmund I wouldn't have minded being either Kent or Gloucester – whichever one of them gets his eyes gouged out; I forget – but I didn't get that either. Still, I hadn't been left out altogether. I was given a major role, even if it wasn't the one I wanted.

"You have one of the best roles in the play," said Mr Hargreaves. "One of the best roles in the whole of Shakespeare. You'll be wonderful."

So I swallowed my pride and accepted it. And I have to admit that for the fortnight we staged the play Jimmy Peterson made a damn good Edmund, the bastard. And Simon Harris was pretty impressive as Lear too.

Actually, I got to know Simon pretty well while all that was going on. The Fool hangs out with Lear a lot.

...The first thing I did when I started college was to try to join the Players. The morning I first went into Trinity as a student it was Societies Day and the whole of the walkway from the Front Arch, past the chapel, and round to the Arts Block was strewn with stalls looking for members. I checked a few of them out but I knew what I was looking for and anyway, there wasn't any chance of me joining the Windsurfing Society, or the Chess Club, or Young Fianna Fail.

Not in a million years.

So I got a leaflet from the Players stall and the next day I went over to the theatre to sign up for a try-out. When I went in the only person around was this guy sitting up on the stage writing an essay. He didn't look around for a minute but eventually he cried out *another one bitten by Thespus' Bug!* and spun around to look at me.

He was a weird looking guy. He had blonde streaked hair – obviously dyed – and it came down past his shoulders but real straggly. His clothes were way over the top and on the ground beside him was a fedora hat. He thought he looked the business but really, he just looked a bit stupid.

He asked me my name and I told him it was Sean but that most of my friends called me Johnny.

"Stick with Sean," he said. "Go for the ethnic look. There's never been a decent or even a successful actor called Johnny. Stick with Sean."

I asked him *what about Johnny Depp?*

He said *he's no Sean Connery.*

But I let it pass. He told me his real name was Seamus but that everybody called him Corbin because he looked like that Corbin Bernsen from *LA Law*. I couldn't see it myself but I didn't bother to tell him. He looked more like one of those guys from Duran Duran. The one that left and went to America to join the Power Station and be an American rocker and who no one ever heard of again. Weird hair those guys had.

Anyway, SeamusCorbin told me that I could come back the next day and try out and he asked me what I was going to do. I told him that I'd had some experience in Shakespeare so I'd probably do something from him.

You would have thought I'd just insulted his granny.

He let this huge roar out of him and said *the bard? THE BARD? Are you demented, child ? You can't do him!* I asked him why not and he said there was a ban on Shakespeare in Players because he was too old hat.

"When we want to go Elizabethan," he said in a very snooty voice, "we do Marlowe. We hate Shakespeare here. You should too."

I told him that I didn't want to hate Shakespeare. That I sort of liked him but he brushed me away.

"Who *do* you hate then?" he asked me in a real patronising voice and I shrugged a bit. There wasn't really anyone I hated. "All artists have to hate *someone*," he told me then, "and if you want to be an actor you're going to have to decide. The whole basis of any art form is to hate everyone else who's doing it. That's why people who have any sort of talent generally waste it by just going around fighting with each other, bitching about each other, and backbiting behind each others' backs. That's what the whole world of art is based on. Nastiness. Take it from someone who knows."

I wasn't too sure what he meant at the time but I think I'm learning.

I went home and looked through my books and figured out what it was I wanted to do if I couldn't do Shakespeare. I thought I'd try and really impress them and play both Maggie and Brick from *Cat On A Hot Tin Roof*. One of those early scenes where they're just lashing out at each other all the time. I always thought that was really sexy because, you know, all she wants is a good shag and he won't give her one. Excuse my crudity.

And I could kind of relate to that so I thought it was the play for me.

So the next day I got a pair of crutches for Brick and a glass of drink for Maggie and got up on the stage and started to play both roles for all I was worth.

I put on a Southern accent – probably pretty bad – and told myself that if I thought I was never going to make love to myself again then I'd, why I'd just kill myself. I'd do that. Then I told myself that I was waiting for that click to go off in my head, that click that makes me know I'm heading off into that oblivion I need so much. I talked about Big Daddy's illness, tried to get myself to sign the card for his present, mocked Sister Woman and her little no-neck children. When I brought up Skipper – a sore topic – the judges told me to stop.

There was three of them there; SeamusCorbin, a girl with plaits who, retrospectively, looked like Angel from *Home & Away* and some other guy who said nothing at all but just smoked a pipe throughout. SeamusCorbin asked me why I had played both roles and I said it was because I liked the scene and I thought it would be something to see whether I could do them both.

Then SeamusCorbin and Angel from *Home & Away* shook their heads and, almost as one, informed me that the reason I had played both roles was because of my inherent hatred of women. Angel from *Home & Away* said that I wanted to desex women, and take them away from the stage altogether. She said I wanted to destroy their entire sexuality and probably outlaw them. She said I should start to confront my own relationships with women before I started to systematically slaughter them. She said I should confront my fears.

I said no, that I just thought it would be fun to play both roles.

SeamusCorbin said there was no place for sexist little grunts like me in his Drama Group and that he'd eat his fedora before he saw me begin my holocaust on the female sex. He'd not have it, he said. Not while he had a breath in his body.

So that was that. I was out. And I haven't really acted since except in a Christmas production of *Grease* with my department. I didn't get to play Danny Zuko – and, despite what SeamusCorbin and Angel from *Home & Away* thought, I didn't even try out for Sandy – but I did get to play one of Danny's friends and I got to sing *Greased Lightning* on stage and do the *wella wella wella huh!*s in *Summer Nights.*

And the only time I ever went to see a Players production was when they put on *My Fair Lady* (*My Fair Lady!*) and Angel from *Home & Away* played the part of Eliza Doolittle to great applause. Her accent was a little off at times but other than that she was pretty good.

But I still want to be an actor. And one of these days I'll do it too and I'll be rich and famous and they'll make little models of me for the Christmas market. And then, as God is my witness, I'll never be hungry again.

The Popular Steadies

When I was in school there were two characters above all others who stood out as heroes for me. Everybody loved Colin and Jane. It was the rule. Somebody somewhere had written it down in stone. If you had sat down with any boy or girl in my year and asked them who they most admired, they would have said their names. We couldn't help it; we adored them.

Colin was the head of the rugby team, the captain of the school, and he had a fine head of hair on him. He was pretty smart – I mean he always did okay in exams – but he acted dumb enough sometimes to make him one of us too. I mean it wasn't like he wouldn't talk to us or something. He didn't think he was better than us or anything like that.

He was one of the boys. He'd go out with a bunch of us on a Friday evening to some underage bar and get really drunk and stuff and start making stupid jokes but by closing time he'd always be the one organising the taxis, offering beds on his floor, checking that no one was cycling under the influence.

He was our leader.

And what Colin was to the boys, Jane was to the girls. And then some. She was beautiful. *Extremely.* Always had the right clothes, the right hair. But she was really friendly and she always made you feel like she really liked you. I mean none of the girls were even jealous of her she was so nice and that's no mean feat, especially considering the fact that practically every boy in the school was lusting after her.

And of course, needless to say, Colin and Jane were a couple. Life seems to be designed that way.

They were kind of a sickening couple though, I have to admit. I mean they took all the same classes so they wouldn't be apart. They held hands everywhere they went. They sat together all the time. Yuk. But still, it was kind of sweet too. Their closeness made us all love them even more. They were just perfect.

Which is why it took me so much by surprise when I met them again one time during college, about two or three years after we'd left school in the first place. I have to admit that, despite how much I'd liked them, I hadn't really kept in touch so to see them again was pretty strange.

Now if I had been asked a couple of years back what would have happened to Colin and Jane after school, I wouldn't have been slow with the answer. Colin was going to go to a business school, get a great job, make lots of money and live happily ever after with his beautiful wife Jane, who by then would be making more money than him, a fact which wouldn't threaten him because hey! he'd be such a modern guy.

A future to die for. And nobody would have disagreed with me either.

But then I ended up at this party one night – I didn't even know anyone there; I'd just gone because a friend of mine had dragged me along – and everything that I'd thought about them before seemed to fade away. And some weird stuff happened.

My friend had disappeared off into a scrum of guys he was clearly very intimate with. I had a drink in my hand and another few in my stomach so I was quite happy to just linger in a corner on my own, letting my thoughts drift, my eyes wander over the bodies of the Beautiful People, my whole body relax.

Then out of the blue I was kissed.

Now don't get me wrong. I'm not averse to someone coming up to me and kissing me while I'm staring off into the sunset. I have no problem with some besotted young thing deciding that words have no place in our relationship and getting down to the nitty gritty immediately. I mean I can be as cheap as the next guy. Ask anyone.

But when you don't expect it, and you're already half drunk, a pair of lips suddenly pressing in on you is enough to give you a bit of a start, to put it mildly.

And that's exactly what was happening.

One of my two ideals from way back in school life, one half of the couple that I envied and loved more than any other, one of the only people who had really stayed in my mind after about three years away from school, was standing before me, pulling back after planting one enormous smacker on me.

And it took me by surprise.

"Colin," I said, stunned and thrilled to see him, amazingly thrilled, the kind of thrilled you only get when you see old friends when you're drunk. The kind of thrilled that makes you want to just throw your arms around each other and talk forever about the supposed glory days. "I don't believe it."

He grinned at me and threw his hand through his still perfect head of hair and punched me in the arm.

"Alright Johnny?" he said and I just shook my head in disbelief, as if I was trying to snap myself out of a daze.

"I don't believe it," I repeated. "This is brilliant. Where did you...? How come you're here?"

Colin was gatecrashing. He knew a man who knew a man who knew a man and he'd had nothing better to do so he'd just walked through the door. So he said.

"But what *happened* to you?" I asked him, instantly regretting the way that sounded as I took in his dishevelled figure.

"You think I've changed?" he asked, grinning so much that I thought his face might crack. Yeah. I thought he'd changed.

It wasn't his face or his size that had altered. It wasn't the fact that he was dressed like the student from hell in a grimy black tee-shirt covered in bizarre stains, some recognisable, some not. It was more the general picture of himself that he was presenting.

He was no longer the hero of my youth, but some dirty, smelly student, clearly broke, drunk and stoned on something, whose hair was unwashed, whose fingers bore early nicotine stains, whose slouching figure displayed his boredom.

This wasn't the guy I used to look up to anymore. This was something better; this was someone I could *relate* to.

We stumbled off to the top of the stairs away from the party and sat near the top, a row of beers in front of us that we'd stolen from the fridge – I say stolen, but it was a party after all – and with a lot to catch up on.

"Colin," I said, almost unable to find my voice through my excitement. "Don't take this the wrong way or anything, but what the hell happened to you? You look so..." I struggled to find the right word. "*Sordid*. What *happened*?"

"Sordid," he said quietly, biting his lip and nodding his head up and down in time with some interior rhythm. "I like that. Sordid." He stopped talking then and just started to laugh to himself. I watched him, smiling, waiting for him to say something more but after a few minutes I realised that it wasn't going to happen. It was like he'd forgotten I was even there.

"Colin?" I said and he jumped. "Jesus!" he said, putting a hand to his forehead as if he was checking his temperature. "I just drifted off. I hate it when that happens."

I nodded and smiled dubiously and wanted to laugh. It's marvellous when the mighty fall down to your level.

"So?" I said, shrugging my shoulders to urge him to tell me about his life from leaving school to that day. "I guess you never became an accountant, right?"

"Why do you say that?" he asked and I looked him up and down to suggest that he didn't really look like accountant material. "No, I never did," he said, smiling. He looked shy, like a little boy who's been discovered doing something he shouldn't.

"Things haven't really come together for me yet. I left school and went to college but I dropped out after -" He paused and checked himself. It was like he was trying to remember his story. "Well what with one thing and another, I left. It was kind of a mutual decision between me and the college."

"Really?" I said, but didn't inquire further. It didn't seem like he was ready to share yet.

"But I've got a job alright," he said, nodding furiously and grinning manically as if this meant he could still be Mister Perfect. "And I haven't, like, been arrested or anything so I suppose I'm doing okay."

"I always pictured you heading the Past Pupils Union or something," I said. "I always thought you'd be held up as an Inspiration To Us All."

He looked at me as if I was mad.

"Jesus, Johnny," he said. "Is that what people thought about me?" He looked almost worried about it. "So tell me about you," he said after a while, opening another can and taking a long drag on a cigarette. "What happened to you? You look much the same. Little more of this though."

He indicated the place under my mouth where I had, after much soul-searching, grown a thin half-Goatee. He pulled at it a little and then did something that felt like he was smoothing it back down. I was just waiting for him to say *cool*. If there was ever a time for it, I thought, it was then.

"I like it though," he said defensively, looking at me for all the world as if he'd just insulted my mother. "I mean I'm not trying to be rude or anything."

"That's okay," I said, laughing, delighted by his seeming innocence and desire not to wound me. "You can say it. I'm thinking of shaving it off again anyway. It kinda comes and goes."

"No, no don't," he said suddenly, leaping to the defense of my Goatee. "Don't do that. It looks good on you. Don't do it."
"Okay, okay," I said, trying to relax him. He seemed so highly strung that I was almost nervous of him. "I won't."

And I knew that I wouldn't either.

... "I used to really look up to you, you know," I said after a while as we both polished off a couple more drinks. "You were like my hero. You and Jane. Everyone wanted to be you."

Which reminded me...

"Jane!" I said, grabbing his arm as if I'd get the information quicker out of him that way. "Whatever happened to her?"

He shrugged and grinned and looked a little sheepish.

"She's okay," he said. "Same as ever I suppose."

"You two aren't still *together* surely," I asked. "After all these years?" He shrugged his shoulders and avoided my eyes. "I guess," he said. "Kind of. She's right downstairs, you know. She's here too."

My mouth fell open and I stared at him in disbelief. "No way!" I said and I felt like crying. I really thought I was going to just burst into tears. I had to keep swallowing to stop myself.

"Yeah, she is," he said quietly as if this wasn't really such a big deal. "Mark," he called down the stairs to some guy that was passing by at the bottom. "Tell Jane to come up here, will you?"

"I thought you said you didn't know anyone here," I said and he didn't answer me. Just took a long drink, another smoke and nodded towards the bottom of the stairs by jutting his chin out and pointing.

There she was. Jane. The woman of my dreams. She had walked out of a room downstairs and started to climb them before looking up. She was almost on top of us before she looked at me and realised who I was. I stood up, a little awkwardly, and shuffled slightly in the confined area.

"Hello," I said and grinned at her. Her eyes blinked and her face brightened up into a smile. She shook her head and I thought she looked like she might cry too. Finally we had something in common.

"Johnny," she said and shook her head some more. I grinned and nodded and tried my best to look bashful and sexy and wished that I'd worn that black waistcoat I like rather than this old Levis tee-shirt. But it didn't matter. Before I knew it, she threw her arms around my neck and grabbed me to her. She gave me a kiss that started out for old time's sake but seemed to develop from there. I was just getting into it when I remembered Colin and pulled away.

"It's great to see you," I said, sneaking a look down at Colin to see had he noticed. If he had, it didn't look like he gave a damn. Then I looked back at Jane as if I was in a dream and she looked like she wanted to kiss me again and I sat down in wonderment.

That was two in one night. I was on a roll.

She held my hand as we sat and the other she draped over Colin's knee and in towards him. She didn't look at him once.

"Just tell me everything," she said. "Everything that's happened to you over the last few years. From the start."

And I did. I told her everything. I started to talk and I just couldn't stop. Unlike Colin, she hadn't changed that much. She was as gorgeous as I remembered her. Even better.

"You look terrific," I said. "Really great." "Thank you," she said. "So do you. You look a lot more..." I edged forward, waiting for the word, praying it would thrill me.

" Swarthy."

I felt a tingle in the base of my spine and shivered suddenly.

"Better than when you were a kid."

God, I thought, if you exist, take me now. Just take me now.

"I told him the Goatee suits him. Don't you think so?" This was Colin, back to join us after a few minutes' silence. "I do," said Jane. She still hadn't looked at him but now her head spun around and she looked directly into his face. "It suits him. You should consider one."

Colin laughed. A little too long and loud to make him sound fully sane, but it was a laugh nonetheless. Jane laughed too and I looked from one to the other. I'd made Colin and Jane laugh. I could be a hero too. I grinned soppily and looked from one to the other like a little puppy dog.

"Sweet," said Jane eventually, pulling me closer to her and touching my blushing cheek while Colin reached out and ran his hand through my hair. I pulled my head back – out of reflex more than anything else – as if I thought he was going to hit me or something. "Okay," I said, somewhat at a loss for words. I nodded and stared.

...Colin was lying draped over a couple of stairs now, looking tired and happy. He had a wide smile on his face and his eyes looked watery.

"Were we awful back then?" asked Jane eventually, indicating her lethargic boyfriend and herself. "I mean were we rotten people?"

I looked at her as if she were mad.

"Are you kidding?" I said, astounded that she could even think such a thing. "Look, every class, every school, has their ring of heroes that everybody wants to be friends with but only a few can. It's like the way every class has their fair share of meanies too. You and Colin -" He sat right up and looked at me when I said his name and he looked suddenly miserable. "You and Colin were the best we had. And you were nice to everyone. There were so many people in that group back then who got their kicks out of just being nasty to each other. I mean none of them ever realised that we could have all been great friends if we hadn't all just gone out of our way to hurt each other. The meanies were everywhere in that class, you know? Everywhere. Why would you think that you were terrible to the rest of us?"

"What do you mean the rest of you?" she asked. I shrugged and looked at her as if to ask whether she really needed me to explain it.

"The rest of us," I said. "All us lesser beings. The ones that weren't as perfect as you two. The ones you ruled over."

Jane looked like she might cry. Or hit me.

"Is that what we were doing?" she asked me quietly and I felt depressed suddenly, as if I had spoilt something. As if she had made me see what a mistake I had been making all these years. "God, Johnny," she said and looked down at the floor.

...We sat talking for a little while more. Our initial heartiness returned and I began to hope the evening would never end. Colin was sitting up now and talking again and he seemed as excited as he had a couple of hours earlier. I thought I'd get risky. After all, we were all so drunk. I looked down at my can and smiled self-consciously.

"I, eh," I said without looking up and I knew that I had their attention and that they were staring at me with so much love in their eyes. I figured I could say it.

"I used to have a real crush on you, you know. I used to, like, have these crazy dreams."

I blushed a little and liked that I was. It made me feel that they'd know how honest I was being. I didn't want to look up until one of them spoke.

"Really?" they both said together. *I never knew,* said Jane and at the same moment Colin said *you should have told me.* I looked up at them, from one to the other, and must have looked confused. They both thought that I'd been speaking to them. They reached out a hand each and pressed my arms; Jane touched my right arm, Colin tapped my left. I opened my mouth to speak again, as if to clear that one up somehow, but found that I didn't actually have anything to say.

"You know what I always think?" said Colin and his voice came through strong and clear like the way he used to talk. "I think it's really weird that you can sort of be obsessed with someone and never tell them and they'd never know and all the time, someone else, someone you wouldn't expect, could be really obsessed with you. And you'd never know. Or they could feel the same way you do and just never tell you. That's what I think."

I looked at him and tried to piece all that together in my mind.

"I think that too," said Jane and she smiled at me. "Just nobody ever says it."

They were beginning to fall back into each others' arms and I asked them, laughing, whether I should leave them alone. It was only a joke because I knew that all three of us were enjoying each others' company, but they took me seriously and sprung back to life immediately.

"No," they said together. "Not at all," said Colin. So I stayed where I was and we all three moved off into one of the bedrooms and lay down with the intention of going to sleep and we didn't talk much more that night.

•

It was nearly half past eleven in the morning when I woke up and I jumped like you do when you wake up in a strange place. I opened my eyes but didn't sit up and squinted so that I was staring at the ceiling. I didn't feel like I wanted to look around me.

I knew that I was in a bedroom, lying on a bed, and that I wasn't alone. I could feel someone's head on my lap, moving in sleep every so often but I could also tell that there was someone beside me, warm against me. I swallowed and felt nervous and my mouth felt dry. I couldn't remember too much about the night before.

My legs must have jerked slightly because they both woke up, first Jane, lying across us both, using our bodies as pillows, and then Colin. We all three sat up slowly and groaned.

"If this was the old days," I said to Colin to break the silence, "you would have seen to it that I got home in a taxi last night. Remember you used to do that?"

He turned and looked at me and said nothing and I had to look away, his stare was so intense. But as I turned, Jane caught my eye and smiled.

"You really have both changed," I said nervously. "A lot."

Then Jane started to laugh. And once she started it felt like she wasn't going to stop. She just laughed and laughed and laughed. And then Colin joined in until they were both practically on the floor. And I ran a hand through my hair and stared at them and tried to laugh just because they were but I found I couldn't do it. I just looked at them and couldn't help but wonder. I wanted to stand up and leave but I couldn't find my feet. I lay back down, aware that the other two were looking at me and draped the back of my hand over my eyes, blocking out the sunlight, blocking out what I was remembering.

Colin and Jane quietened down and edged towards me.

"You think too much of us, you know," said Colin and I could tell that he was smiling at me. "If you really thought all that of us back then, you must have hated us more than you realised. Can't you see that?"

But I couldn't. I sat up and looked at him and shook my head and wanted to cry. I looked at him and wanted him to know how wrong he was.

"How could I?" I asked. "How could I have hated you when you were both my idols? How could I?"

Colin and Jane, they looked at each other as if they knew something I didn't and pulled me to my feet.

"Breakfast," they said.

The Awakening

Ferne Arfin

Ferne Arfin was born in New York and is a graduate of Syracuse University. She has worked as an actress and journalist. Now freelance in London, her stories have been accepted for *Bête Noire, Writing Women,* and *Iron.* She is also the author of two non-fiction books. *The Awakening* is extracted from an untitled novel in progress.

Ferne Arfin

The Awakening

A Crossing

Boundaries, limits, ends, beginnings. Doors are for opening, streets for crossing, walls for climbing over. *Push out, push on, push beyond. Come, imagine, see.* The spirits have no limits. *We have danced in the sky.* They have no conscience.

One day, you will go too far.

A pebble plunged towards the East River, unimaginably distant. Rachel, pressing her face against the cast iron railing, waited to see it splash and sink. The pebble, the last one in her apron pocket, disappeared, swallowed by the lively air beneath the Williamsburg Bridge. Her decision was made.

Duvi, who went everywhere and knew most everything now that he was a runner for Tammany, said the bridge was so high and the currents beneath so fierce that if you dropped a rock the size of your fist, you'd never see it hit the water. Rachel had decided to use this amazing information as a test. If she saw just one of the pebbles she had gathered at the foot of the bridge hit the brown water, it would be a sign and she would go home. But two pockets full of the biggest she could find had now vanished.

Breathing deep, she turned towards Brooklyn, committed to serious adventure and her first deliberate act of disobedience. It was the Spring of course. It could not be helped.

Spring astonishes the city. All at once the crabbed sycamores of pocket parks are feathered yellow green. Overnight, tamaracks push up tenement air shafts and tangle in clothes lines. Where the sidewalk is cracked, new sumacs and locusts force out the iron coloured winter weeds.

And the smell, so insistent and pleased, riding in across the East River on the backs of gulls.

Over the pushcarts and underneath the El, conversations lengthen with the days. Coatless children play *potsie* and *skellie* in the streets, scattering like startled sparrows and gathering again around the passing trolley cars.

Life moves out of doors. Sticky windows are forced, open sending cheap muslin curtains fluttering like checkered flags. On the fire escapes, women flushed with kitchen heat refresh themselves with glasses of lemon tea, their stockings rolled down to their ankles.

The inner life of the tenements, seething all winter behind windows steamed with human breath, boils over into the streets. The Lower East Side turns inside out, like a peeled orange.

For weeks, Rachel, seven years old in the late spring of 1914, had been tormented with the scent of restlessness.

"What smells, Mama? Can you smell it?"

"Can I smell it? Who can *not* smell it when Rosa stuffs cabbage?"

"No Mama, not that one, the other one..."

Sophie straightened, letting Jacob's shirt slide off the scrubbing board into the tepid suds. Dramatically, she sniffed the air.

"Child, I can smell washing soda and oil cloth...and your Tanta Rosa's terrible cooking. *That* is what I can smell."

Rachel looked for Spring in vain among the frail trees of Jackson and Seward parks. She followed her nose, eyes closed, to the far end of Delancey Street where the roadway swept upward onto the Williamsburg Bridge.

May called, unmistakably, from the other side, a wilderness of almost remembered fields and woods. The bridge was the gateway. But the Williamsburg Bridge, with its trolley cars and subway tracks, its pedestrian ramp crowded with colourful, hurrying people, was forbidden by Papa. The bridge end of Delancey

Street was the end of the world.

Fancy women from Allen Street took the air on the Williamsburg Bridge. Irish gangsters, Italians and atheists. Rowdy gentiles of every sort.

"What are fancy women, Papa? Atheists?"

"May God forgive you for asking."

Rachel, with the rest of Miss Keogh's second grade class, cut paper flowers for Mothers' Day. Miss Keogh said they should think about all the things their mothers did for them so they could thank them on this new special day that Mrs. Jarvis had begun in Philadelphia. Rachel drew Roses of Sharon and listened to the names of faraway places. *Philadelphia. Alasehir. Rabbah.* Bubbie Ruchel watched with some interest. From the top of the coat cupboard, she scowled. On the way home, Rachel tore up the paper flowers and threw them in the gutter.

She knew what Papa would say if she asked for a penny to buy real ones.

"What holy day? In school they teach you to celebrate gentile holy days?"

"But Papa, it's not a gentile holiday. It's an American holiday."

"American shamerican. There are Jewish holy days and there are goyesha holy days. I have no pennies for pagan stories."

Which is why, on the Sabbath, when she should have been playing quietly or thinking about serious things, Rachel, all by herself, was crossing the Williamsburg Bridge to Brooklyn.

This was the most wicked thing she had ever done. Before this Saturday in May, misbehaviour had almost always been an accident. The grown up world was full of rules you never knew about until you had broken one. This was a real plan. And if Papa found out, there would be real punishment, maybe even the strap.

It was going to be worth it. She was sure she could see Brooklyn already. It had open, rolling hills covered with nodding blooms. How glad Mama would be to have real, alive flowers for Mothers' Day. In Brooklyn people sat on the backs of horses that didn't pull carts; horses that bent low and tore the long soft grass with their yellow teeth. When the Levitzes from upstairs moved to Brooklyn, Sonia Levitz told Mama that she would have a big back yard, with room for chickens to scratch.

"But Sonia, so far from the schul," Mama had said.

"Herschel says there is a *minyan* already for schul in the Rabbi's house. So, we will build a new schul. My Herschel says we came to America to be pioneers. So, *schon,* I will be *eine richtige* pioneer!"

Pioneers. Open spaces. Cowboys and Indians. Like the pictures in the soft covered books that Duvi hid under his mattress. So, it was with more than a little disappointment that Rachel skipped off the bridge into rows of tenements just like her own. Perhaps they were newer, perhaps a little bigger, but they were much the same. The only chickens scratching were in wire crates outside a poultry store.

Crushed, she sank onto a curbstone and stared at her scuffed shoes. How could this be? She had been so certain. If she hurried back across the bridge, no one would ever know she had been gone. But what kind of adventure was that? She was thus deep in thought, considering what to do next, when a thickening presence made her look up.

A man was standing over her. He wore a long black coat although it was summery warm. His flat black hat had fur around the edge of its wide brim and his beard was much longer than Papa's trim whiskers. Rachel thought he looked like the men who were arriving every day now from places in Poland and Russia, where Bubbie Ruchel was born. She had heard Mr. Kandel tell Mama that these new people were running ahead of a war. When she asked about that, no one but Duvi would tell her anything and all he wanted to talk about was soldiers and blood. There had already been too many soldiers and too much blood.

"Maydeleh, are you lost?" The man's voice was gruff but friendly.

Rachel shook her head. "I wanted to pick flowers. For Mothers' Day. But there are none."

"Ah, but of course there are. There are always flowers somewhere. That way," he said, and he pointed just beside the sun.

Rachel followed the direction of his arm with her eyes. As far as she could see, flat, paved streets, lined with sidewalks and tenements, ran to neat, square corners. She wanted to ask him how far but when she turned he was gone, vanished among the push carts and storefronts near the base of the bridge.

Come. Walk now until your shadow races ahead into the darkening day. Come. The city thins but never ends.

Rachel had no idea how long she had been walking. After the paving ended, she had followed a line of telegraph poles, crunching down streets of crushed rock. Now the wooden poles and power lines marched along empty dirt roads, the advanced creepers of a strong, delicate vine that would soon drag the city behind. If she squinted she could see it shimmer on the alien landscape of tilled fields and sandy hills. Here the houses were only big enough for one or two families. They clustered in little groups, surrounded by pale yellow waste ground and tough, coarse grass. Stands of *sukki* weed waved their seedy heads above her and sang wind songs that drew her on.

It was so quiet. Rachel had never been alone in her whole short life. She was not alone now. A peddler with a stout black stick tramped along way up ahead of her. He bent forward under the weight of his sack and sometimes she could hear the familiar clattering of his pots and pans. If she stopped to lace her shoe, the peddler stopped too. Sometimes he seemed to be waving her onward, yet, as she ran, she knew she would not catch up with him. In the few settlements they passed, small knots of people went about their own business paying them no attention. The peddler never stopped to sell anything. Once a farmer trundled by on a flat-backed wagon loaded with sacks. Like Uncle Shoe, he wore overalls and big, dirty boots. He waved at her.

"Hey kiddo, you lost or something?"

Rachel shook her head. Behind her, the road pointed straight to the sun and home. She waved at the farmer who shrugged and drove on.

Only the big sky was crowded, populated with greedy mobs of sea gulls who tilted and screamed. Now and then, they settled on a field, scaring up clouds of iridescent starlings.

By now, Rachel had forgotten her reason for setting off. So filled was she with sounds and scents and sunlight, that the journey was its own reward. She spread her arms wide and danced slow circles, listening, with the tips of her fingers. She would have passed the little pond, behind a screen of scrub pines, had not the call of fine sweet water surprised her with an urgent thirst. Suddenly, nothing was more important. Heedless of her Sabbath clothes, she pushed through the stunted trees and bramble, scrambled and slid down steep, soft banks and, plunging her face into the dark surface of the water, drank like an animal. Only when she sat back, dripping, muddy and dazed, did she notice the riot of Spring wildflowers at the water's edge.

Daisies, dandelions, clover, water iris, buttercups, lady slippers, purple loosestrife. Queen Anne's Lace, smelling of sweet carrots. Sturdy black eyed susans. The names would come later. Now there were only colours and a swelling hubbub of strutting, preening, wheedling.

Unable to choose, Rachel grabbed for anything that would give up its hold of the black slime. The cattails refused to let go, but a bunch of sweet flags came up in a slick suck of roots and mud. She yanked and tore and snapped until, her arms full and her chin yellow with buttercup pollen, she sat back, panting.

If Rachel had started for home, she might have arrived with the last of the daylight. Instead, she took off her squishy shoes and waded into the pond. Her tired feet sank into cool mud. She wiggled her toes and watched the play of sky on water, smiled and thought of nothing at all.

A solitary gull swooped and tore at the pond. It rose and hovered low, barely as high as the twisted scrub pines. It sat on the air so close to Rachel that she could see the drops of water on its sharp smiling beak, shiver at the wisdom in its dense, unblinking eye. It invited as before it had welcomed, *balanced in our windy wake while we crossed the pitching night under a million stars.*

When I would not part for you again, you cleft me with your sharp keels. If I let you, you can ride me like a lover. If I want you, I will keep you for my own. I am in you. You are scattered as the stars in the firmament. Everywhere. And where you are, so also am I, rocking in the rhythm of your blood. Always.

We are a drawing apart. We are a coming together. Forever.

Rachel was running, her wet shoes and a few woody stemmed black eyed susans crammed in her apron pocket. The packed dirt road disappeared and she ran across a shifting pan of white sand, gritty, glowing and warm. Ahead of her, dunes, held together by a silver tracery of *dusty miller*, hid the source of the now thunderous chaos of voices. Laughing, sighing, shouting. *Come. Hurry. See.* Or was it the reply of her own rushing blood as she struggled upward, the soft sand sliding away underfoot?

She crested the dune and stopped, stunned before the living water. More water than she had ever seen. More than she, or anyone, could understand. It rose in swells of glassy green that broke with a roar then teased and nibbled the shore. It stroked the gentle slope of beach with sinuous, vanishing fingers.

And where it ended, there was only sky. Rachel had never before seen a horizon uninterrupted by the works of man. She held her breath . When she released it, her long sigh was taken and entwined in the throbbing song of the Atlantic. Something was growing; something enormous. It spread out in every direction, curving across the face of the water and beyond. Exhausted and nearly fainting with hunger, Rachel sat back into the sand and slept.

She dreams of swimming in a blood warm sea. Is this swimming, this weightless dancing on the thick green sky? She dreams of beautiful creatures with silky coats of dense brown fur, whiskery faces and warm, dark eyes. They breach then dive and roll, looking back up at her through swarms of phosphorescence. One of them swims beside her. His eyes are not dark like the others, but clear and light, as though they have trapped the sky. She wants to touch him, but he is always just beyond her reach. Again and again he darts away from her outstretched hand.

Perhaps it is a game, but it is tinged with the sadness of desire. And cold. Now she is shivering under the blinding stars. With each juddering gasp, her mouth fills with the bitter, salty taste of the cold. The creature with the sky in his eyes dives and rises beneath her. He is warm in the cold green sea. He is harnessed with water weeds. She rides on his back to the shore.

Rachel awoke, shivering, into a cloudshadowed moonrise. Two fishermen with long poles and strings of flat brown fish, knelt by her in the sand. One of them spoke.

"Piccolina, cosa fai qui da sola?"

She stared at him, searching her memory in vain for understanding.

The fisherman took off his sweater and wrapped it around her shoulders. "Little girl, what you do here all by you self?"

Still, she did not reply.

His companion raised his hands in a gesture of helplessness. "Maybe she doan speak no English, you think?"

But, though his accent was strange, Rachel did understand his question. She simply had no idea how to answer it.

In my cold wet arms, I will rock you warm. I am restless in your blood. Forever.

Advent

We are a drawing apart. We are a coming together. We have watched each other through so many eyes. When I was a wandering beggar, you gave me sweet wine. You have dreamt me awake in a northern sea. You are my peculiar treasure. Comfort me with apples.

It would have been so easy to lie. Who could believe a child of seven would walk nearly ten miles? For no reason at all. At the stationhouse, the policemen fed Rachel sandwiches and milk while in another room they questioned the two Italian waiters for more than an hour before they accepted their story. That they had gone fishing between shifts at the Sheepshead Bay Inn. That they had been on their way back to work, loaded down with a good catch of bluefish and flounder, when they found

Rachel sleeping in the sand on Brighton Beach.

A policeman questioned Rachel as well. Had she taken a ride from a stranger? Did someone, some man, offer her sweets? Where had she been when she was snatched from the street?

Rachel could have colluded. She could have constructed an elaborate scenario from these puzzling questions that continued during the long ride back to Rivington Street. If she had, she would not have been punished.

Instead, she might have been bundled off to bed, consoled by Mama's tears, sweet warm milk and *mandelbrot* for dunking. Tanta Rosa and Uncle Abie might have come down from upstairs with all her cousins, Uncle Abie bringing his flute to cheer her up and Cousin Chaia singing all her favourite songs. Of course Tanta Rosa would have told her a good story. Her sisters and brothers would have treated her with the awe and respect due an invalid. She might even have enjoyed a night alone in the bed she shared with Ruth and Bea. These comforts had a certain appeal.

But Rachel wanted to be at the centre of a different kind of fuss. She was the prodigal returned and she wanted a prodigality of admiration. She wanted Ruth to hang on her every word; even her older brothers and sisters to be impressed. She had crossed the Williamsburg Bridge and felt the subway trains shiver the world between water and sky. She had studied the faces of strangers, godless and pious, listened to their incomprehensible tongues and eaten their forbidden food. Hadn't she walked across Brooklyn all the way to the Atlantic Ocean? Hadn't she listened to its songs and dreamed sea dreams, seen the moon rise from the water? Best of all, hadn't she ridden all the way home in the front seat of a real gasoline buggy?

Naturally Papa would be very angry, but that prospect was thrilling too. At last, she would feel the strap he never used to punish the girls. How she had envied Duvi when he raised his shirt to show off the red welts on his back; when Mama soothed him with cool water and honey cake. Surely, now she had earned the strap. Her palms itched where they had clung for hours to Mama's flowers, the few damp, wilted black eyed susans that she had stuffed in her apron pocket. Mama said itchy palms meant riches to come. Rachel felt protected by an aura of special distinction. She insisted, in the face of disbelief all round, that she had walked all the way, without help.

Eventually, the evidence could not be denied. Yossel, Sarah's young man, pointed out the holes in the soles of Rachel's shoes and stockings, the matching blisters on her feet.

Papa, scowling and silent, stalked out of the bedroom. Mama, already swollen eyed from weeping, fell sobbing into the arms of Tanta Rosa and Uncle Abie, who led her away. It was left to Sarah, tight and prim, to paint a picture of the commotion Rachel had caused.

When Rachel missed lunch, Mama had sent them all over the neighbourhood looking for her. After she failed to appear for supper Ruth had to be put to bed in tears, worrying that Rachel might never return and alternately hoping that she would stay away to avoid Papa's wrath. Papa, Mendel and Uncle Abie had gone off with a policeman and a posse of neighbours to search for her. And Duvi's friend, Councilman Tierney, had sent firemen to scour the sewers and conduits near the docks. "Now everybody knows our business," Sarah said. "Even the *goyem.*" By nightfall, Mama was so hysterical, she nearly fainted. Twice. "And to be so wicked on Shabbas. God forgive you."

Rachel knew this last was for the benefit of Yossel, who wore his habitual deathwatch expression. She tried to mimic his mournful face to create a semblance of remorse. But the fiddler plays a wicked tune and Rachel was not sorry. There was a mysterious, peaceful pleasure, a calm in the eye of this hurricane. She had been the least and now she was the greatest. She sat back and waited for the inevitable. But the punishment, when at last it came, was not what she expected

The wooden chest, under the kitchen window, had come with Rachel's parents from the old country. Rachel didn't know much about what was in it other than the sabbath candlesticks and Papa's extra *tallis,* the prayer shawl he was saving to be buried in. The chest was locked with a big metal padlock. The authority of this lock was purely symbolic. Jacob kept the key hanging on a nail by the sink, in plain sight. But no one would dare touch it. Even Sophie had to ask Jacob to open the chest when she needed the brass candlesticks to make Shabbas.

Now, Jacob sent everyone but Rachel upstairs to Rosa and Abie's. He sat before the chest, fingering the key. Rachel stood before him, still, curious.

"Rachel," Jacob said. If you had not known him, you might have imagined he spoke gently. "Do you know you are not allowed to go on the bridge?"

She nodded.

"Why?"

Rachel thought about all the things she had been told. About the gangsters and hooligans and gentiles. About the crowds who could push a little girl off the platforms onto the subway tracks or into the path of a trolley. About the ladies who wore shiny dresses, the ladies Mama always crossed the street to avoid. She was about to list these dangers when Jacob, as was his habit, answered his own question.

"Because," he said quietly, "I have forbidden it."

"But..."

"This is not a discussion!"

Jacob looked down at his laced fingers. Slow seconds hauled the moon across the night. On the fire escape, a blue jay chuckled throatily. Rachel wondered why so many things were forbidden. But she did not ask. From across the street, another blue jay answered the first.

Jacob was still looking at his fingers when he said, "I want your solemn promise that you will not go on the bridge again."

Rachel said nothing. She listened to the birds and wondered about their particular, chattering voices. They were laughing. She stared at her father until he had to look up at her. His eyes were dull, a faded blue. Outside an evening breeze gossiped in someone's snapping laundry. Why had she never before noticed how watery and weak his eyes were?

"Do I have your word before God?"

Still she was silent. Spittle glistened in her father's whiskers and a piece of slimy whitefish, the remains of his breakfast, clung near the corner of his mouth. How small and stooped he looked. His *yarmulka* didn't fit. It rested at an odd angle, pointing peculiarly on his skull.

"I will have your word," he demanded, but he seemed to falter under Rachel's steady gaze. He had to look away to continue.

"Since you are so disobedient," he said, "and wander where I have forbidden you to go, you will not leave this house until I have your word...Take off your clothes."

Rachel heard him speak as though from a great distance. Because it did not seem to matter, she obeyed. She untied her muddy apron and handed it to Jacob. Then she undid the buttons and hooks of her cotton dress and pulled it over her head. Jacob waited. She wriggled out of her petticoat and gave him that as well.

"All of them," he said. But, although he watched the pile of her clothes grow on the floor, once again he looked away.

She pulled off her lisle stockings. Beach sand hissed to the floor when she slipped out of her cotton bloomers. How easy this was. How silly.

For the first time, Jacob seemed to notice that the kitchen windows were uncovered. He closed the flimsy curtains, then went into the bedroom and emerged carrying Rachel's other dress and her night clothes.

He put all the clothes into the wooden chest, locked it and hung the key on the nail by the sink, all this without once looking at Rachel's hairless, naked little body.

Was that it? Where was the strap? Rachel shivered, but it was only because of the cold.

Now Jacob stood up, his back to Rachel. Light from the bare kitchen bulb made his jacket shine. When he spoke, his voice was flat. She could hardly hear him over the gossip and laughter that had been growing until it bounced off the walls in all directions.

"There they will stay, until I have your solemn promise," he said. "Now, go to bed."

Rachel did not hurry to the bedroom. She took her time, listening, trying to understand the clarifying refrain of the murmuring voices. It was an old song. So old. It was about power. It was about fear. It was about the smallest seed at the heart of the world. *The least will become the greatest.*

And it was why her father was ashamed to look at the smooth ribs of her chest, her round belly, the warm little triangle between her legs. Ashamed. He was *ashamed.* Rachel wrapped this new knowledge around herself with the bedsheet. She hugged her shoulders, enjoying the cool, warm, firm softness of her flesh. *Restless, restless in your blood.* She smiled.

A week later, while Jacob, Rabbi Meyer and a delegation of men from the schul discussed charity for the refugees, she was still in the bedroom. Still hugging her secret. Still smiling.

•

Miss Keogh had been a young woman when she first visited the cold water flat at 75 Rivington Street. In the Spring of 1917, she was no longer young, but she still wore a shirtwaist dress and a hat with daisies on it. She had never succeeded in her mission to persuade Jacob Isaacson to allow his children the freedom of a complete education – as complete, at any rate, as the New York City Board of Education could provide – but she continued to try.

He was an odd one, she reflected, as she climbed the four flights of stairs. So rigid and old fashioned when so many others were taking up every opportunity with relish. Not only for their children but for themselves as well. Her heart swelled with the patriotism that only an immigrant can feel – for Miss Keogh was an immigrant too – when she thought of the enthusiasm of her night school classes at the Settlement House. People old enough to be her grandparents struggled with English and Citizenship and Geometry to earn High School Equivalency Diplomas. Didn't he realise that here his bright children could do almost anything, become almost anything they chose, if only he allowed them to be taught?

Miss Keogh believed she had good reason to equate education with freedom. As one of the youngest of twelve children, and sure to be lacking a dowry, she might have been locked up, like three of her sisters, with the Poor Clares or the Ursulines, had not a scholarship to the State Normal School at New Paltz given her the freedom to make her own way.

She had first visited Isaacson with the enthusiasm of a young teacher enchanted by an eager pupil. That had been little Bea, who at ten had been so hungry for history that it broke Miss Keogh's heart to see her dragged from school. She had come again for Davey, then Ruth and now Rachel, the youngest.

Miss Keogh's visits were unofficial. It was Isaacson's right to take his children out of school when they reached eleven. If he had complained, she might have even received a reprimand from the School Board. But Miss Keogh was a generous and childless woman who lived to help her students get on in the world. Although she knew she would be greeted with the same stiff necked scorn as before, she prepared herself to face Jacob Isaacson for the last time.

She took some comfort in the knowledge that without his cooperation, his children seemed to find their own paths anyway. All except slow, shy Ruth who would add little to the world but expect little from it in return. Perhaps, she reflected, it was the place that gave the freedom and not the schooling after all. Perhaps that was it. The right sort of spirit could flourish in this place.

Look at Bea, soaking up the history of European socialism wherever she could find it. At the Settlement House, at the Ethical Culture Society, at the East Side Socialist Club. Miss Keogh was proud of Bea, at 19 a leader of her union local. She had campaigned to get New York women the vote. Soon women would have the national vote, Miss Keogh was sure, and when that happened, who could guess how far Bea and her colleagues at the International Ladies Garment Workers Union might go?

Then there was Davey. Miss Keogh was less sanguine about his prospects, but certainly he had achieved freedom of a sort. The local political machine had been quick to spot the advantages of his agile mind and fast legs. She wondered whether Isaacson, when he sat across the Sabbath table from the son he called Duvi, knew what being a cadet for Miss Harriet Klien's Dance Academy and Social Club really meant. Two of Hattie's "ladies" were taking math classes at the Settlement House because Hattie couldn't find a bookkeeper who could keep his mind, and his hands, on the books.

And what would happen to Rachel? Miss Keogh stopped to catch her breath at the third floor landing. She was a puzzling child. Although Miss Keogh would not have called her bookish, she was sure that Rachel had gone through every book in the grade school library. Like Davey, she was quick with numbers as well. But there was something else about her. Something penetrating and still. From remarks overheard in the schoolyard, Miss Keogh concluded that some children thought Rachel had the evil eye and were a bit afraid of her.

Of course, Miss Keogh reassured herself, that was nonsense. But she could not deny that Rachel's independence was striking and unusual in one so young, especially, among these people, in a girl. She never wanted help with her school work, preferring to puzzle through on her own. And, unless she believed she deserved it, she rejected the praise and encouragement that other children seemed to demand.

Miss Keogh remembered, now, the first time she had seen Rachel's spirit manifest. It had happened three years before. Rachel, who was seven at the time, had been absent from school for a week. Miss Keogh visited to investigate, to see if, perhaps, a nurse from the Settlement House should call.

When she arrived, Isaacson and a group of men were holding some sort of meeting. Rabbi Meyer was there and several others. Rachel, it seemed, was being punished. Miss Keogh vaguely remembered that she, herself, might have been involved in the cause. Something about Mother's Day. She was explaining to Isaacson that keeping a child out of school for such a reason was against the laws of the State of New York, when the bedroom door opened and Rachel appeared, completely naked. She stood for a moment in the doorway, smiling at Miss Keogh while the men gasped and shielded their eyes with their hands. The rabbi actually put his hat in front of his face.

Isaacson jumped up, his body shaping itself into a shout that seemed to wither in the rays of the child's sweet smile. He sank back into his chair.

At the time, Miss Keogh had been dismayed. She found the men's modesty ridiculous and somewhat disturbing. What could be more harmless, more beautiful really, than the nakedness of a child?

While the men cowered, Rachel had crossed the room. She had taken a large key from a nail beside the sink and had used it to open a wooden chest that sat under the kitchen window. The chest seemed to contain a collection of garments. Miss Keogh watched Rachel pick through them, considering first one, than another, like a young woman choosing for a party. A striped, fringed shawl, one of those shawls the men wore in their synagogues, slipped from the edge of the chest to the floor. Absently, Rachel bunched it up and tossed it back in. At the time, Miss Keogh remembered thinking how peculiar it was to keep a child's clothing under lock and key. But she supposed there must be some reason for it.

Eventually, Rachel had selected a night dress. She started for the bedroom, then stopped in the middle of the kitchen near the men. She shook out the night dress, gathered it and lifted it over her head.

Once again, Isaacson had risen from his seat. But before he could collect himself for action, Rachel had shrugged into her night dress and disappeared into the bedroom.

It had all happened so quickly that thinking of it now, three years later, Miss Keogh was not sure she trusted her memory. But at the time, she believed she understood why the men covered their faces in fearful, shocked modesty, one of them muttering a prayer.

For as she turned to go, Rachel had glanced at Miss Keogh. Her round, brown eyes glowed with a look Miss Keogh would never forget. Now, her hand raised to knock, for the last time, on this door, Miss Keogh saw it once again, full of knowing satisfaction. For the merest fraction of a second, before her native common sense reasserted itself, she had been certain that she was looking into something more than the eyes of a child.

Simon Wrigley-Worm Boy

Tom Shankland

Tom Shankland was born in Durham in 1968. Since graduating from Sussex University in 1990, he has spent his time making films and videos. *Brotherly Love,* which he directed at film school won two awards in the 1994 Fuji Film Competition. Tom has just finished work on a short film for Channel 4. He is currently working on a feature film script.

Tom Shankland

Simon Wrigley-Worm Boy

1. EXT. A TRAIN TUNNEL. NIGHT.

The entrance of the tunnel. ***Titles*** *over the darkness that fills the screen. The sinister rumbling of a train getting closer. And closer. And closer.*

The train thunders on to the screen, the windows whipping past like the flashing scales of a serpent sweeping through the moon-light.

The train passes, revealing a housing estate which stretches into the distance. The bottom end of the estate runs along the railway track and stops near the tunnel where woodland begins.

SIMON's house is the very last house on the estate. Upstairs someone switches off a light.

2. INT. SIMON'S HOUSE. KITCHEN. NIGHT.

The kitchen, like the rest of the house, is spotlessly clean and plasticly modern. SIMON, a thirteen year-old hypochondriac, sits at the kitchen table, staring glumly at an untouched plate of pie, mash and boiled veg. He sighs when he hears the toilet flush and KAREN hurrying down the stairs.

KAREN is SIMON's mum, 30. She dresses very femininely but underneath is actually really tough. SIMON scowls, watching her through the kitchen door, as she makes quick adjustments to her make-up in the hallway mirror. Last minute doubts about the mini; she tries to wriggle it a bit further down her thighs then is annoyed to catch sight of SIMON staring at her.

KAREN

What are you looking at?

SIMON looks down, glum. KAREN softens.

KAREN

I'm only going out for a drink with him.

SIMON screws up his face as though he is in great pain. Concerned, KAREN goes over to him. She sees his untouched food.

KAREN

You haven't eaten your tea.

She strokes SIMON's head.

SIMON

I feel poorly.

KAREN gently pulls SIMON's hair back so he has to stare up into her eyes. She peers at him suspiciously. SIMON, feeling pressured to supply some evidence makes an unconvincing whimper. KAREN glares at him. She releases his head.

KAREN

I want you in bed by ten.

SOUND of a car pulling up and beeping outside. KAREN anxiously glances out of the kitchen window. The headlights beam into SIMON's face forcing him to look away squinting.

KAREN takes a last hurried look in the mirror.

SIMON squints at her, acting like he can't see her properly.

SIMON

My eyes have gone all funny.

KAREN is already out of the door.

KAREN *(OS)*

Ten o'clock!

The front door slams shut. SIMON pushes away his plate of food. He sighs deeply. He glances at the window. A breeze makes a twig tap eerily on the window. SIMON shudders at the sound and looks round the room nervously.

His gaze comes to rest on a very high cupboard. The beginnings of a smile flicker on SIMON's face.

3. INT. SIMON'S HOUSE. KITCHEN. NIGHT.

Standing on a stool, SIMON fetches down a cake tin.

4. INT. SIMON'S HOUSE. LIVING ROOM. NIGHT.

11.15 on the porcelain-dog clock. SIMON is enthroned in the settee surrounded by biscuit tins, crisps, chocolates etc...watching a football match on the TV. He flicks through the channels with the remote until he is suddenly hypnotised by a sex scene. Without taking his eyes off the screen he flicks off the lid of a biscuit tin.

Feasting on the biscuits are a number of small, thin, grey worms. SIMON's hand reaches in and clutches a couple of biscuits just as the sex scene is coming to a climax.

SIMON, entranced by the screen, takes a large bite of the biscuits. Chewing on his biscuit, he feels something moving on his hand and glances down. He sees a worm hanging off the half chewed biscuit in his hand and drops the biscuit instantly. Confused he turns slowly to the biscuit tin.

As soon as he has laid eyes on the writhing tin, he leaps out of his seat and sends a mouthful of half chewed biscuit across the living room.

He hears the SOUND of the front door opening. He rushes out of the living room.

5. INT. SIMON'S HOUSE. HALLWAY. NIGHT.

SIMON bursts through the living room door but stops dead in his tracks when he sees TREVOR follow KAREN into the house. TREVOR, 37, is a sales rep who thinks he's God's gift to women. Just inside the door he pins KAREN against the wall and tries to get his hand up her blouse. KAREN giggles.

KAREN

What're you doing man?

TREVOR

Just helping you find your keys. Heh heh.

KAREN cuts a laugh short when she sees SIMON. She pushes TREVOR's hand away.

KAREN

Simon man! What are you doing up?

SIMON glares at TREVOR. TREVOR stares back unsmiling.

TREVOR

All right.

SIMON looks at KAREN, tears welling in his eyes. He opens his mouth to speak but then catches sight of TREVOR's sneering smile. On the verge of tears SIMON turns and runs up the stairs. KAREN, concerned, looks up at him, but is distracted by the SOUND of TREVOR pulling down his fly.

TREVOR

I found your keys.

TREVOR grins. KAREN laughs in spite of herself.

6. INT. SIMON'S HOUSE. BEDROOM. NIGHT.

SIMON lies in bed staring tearfully up at the ceiling. A SOUND of a train getting closer. SIMON cautiously peers under the bedclothes. His small stomach rises and falls with his anxious breathing. SOUND of the train thundering past the house.

SIMON stares in terror at his stomach. When the SOUND of the train fades away he can hear the SOUND of KAREN and TREVOR having sex next door. SIMON scowls at the wall then turns angrily on his side.

PAN TO an envelope, carefully positioned near the door. On it SIMON has scrawled, 'To be opened in the event of my death.'

SIMON snores peacefully.

7. INT. SIMON'S HOUSE. BEDROOM. DAY.

A train passes outside. SIMON slowly opens his eyes. Surprised to see the sunlight streaming through the window he jerks back the bedclothes and prods his stomach. He grins, jumps out of bed and walks out of the door. A corner of his 'To be opened in the event of my death' *letter sticks out from beneath the bedclothes.*

8. INT. SIMON'S HOUSE. KITCHEN. DAY.

Toast on a plate. SIMON takes a bite. The Big Breakfast blares out of a small portable TV on the counter. Someone falls fully clothed into a pool. SIMON laughs, his mouth full of toast.

TREVOR's hairy, ringed hand switches off the TV.

SIMON nearly chokes on his toast. TREVOR glares down at him dishevelled and bleary-eyed wearing his boxers. SIMON furiously reaches out to turn the TV on again. TREVOR grabs his hand.

They both hear KAREN coming down the stairs. TREVOR lets go of SIMON's hand. SIMON switches on the TV with a triumphant glint in his eye. TREVOR picks up SIMON's remaining bit of toast and tears off a big spiteful bite on his way out of the kitchen. He gives SIMON a 'just you wait' smile just before closing the kitchen door. SIMON turns down the volume of the TV and listens to TREVOR and KAREN's exchange.

KAREN *(OS)*

I can't, I've got to run him up to school.

SIMON smiles but the smile soon fades when he hears the muffled SOUND of whispers and giggles then the SOUND of a door closing.

9. INT/EXT. BUS AT A BUS STOP. DAY.

Simon slouches in a seat near the back of the bus staring out of the window at the estate. KIDS in school uniform making their way to the bus stop.

The bus fills with noisy SCHOOL CHILDREN. These are the KIDS from the estate; lower middle class, clean cut. GARY, KEVIN and COLIN get on the bus. GARY is pleased to see SIMON. He breaks away from COLIN and KEVIN and sits down in the seat in front of SIMON. GARY is not too bright. He likes SIMON more than SIMON likes him.

GARY

What you doing here?

SIMON shrugs and looks back out the window. GARY fumbles for more words.

GARY

You feeling better then?

Worried SIMON touches his stomach.

GARY

You had malaria or something?

SIMON moves his hand away relieved.

SIMON

No, the doctor said it was just a midgy bite.

SIMON keeps glancing past GARY at LISA who is at the front of the bus trying to get the grumpy old BUS DRIVER to accept a five pound note. The DRIVER is having none of it. LISA has a lot of unkempt blonde hair with purple streaks underneath. She is as grungily dressed as her school uniform will allow. She wears a 'Kill the Bill' badge.

COLIN AND KEVIN *(chanting)*

Off, off, off, off

SIMON's attention in now completely on LISA. The other BOYS on the bus join in the chant. LISA tries to ignore the BOYS. She steps back off the bus somehow managing a smile.

GARY

So are you coming to the practice tonight? Oi? Simon?

SIMON is oblivious to GARY's question. GARY follows SIMON's gaze to LISA. She steps down off the bus. The BOYS cheer. The bus moves off. SIMON looks at LISA out of the window. GARY is put out by SIMON's interest in LISA.

10. INT. SCHOOL. BIOLOGY CLASS. DAY.

The TEACHER sits at the front of the class writing a letter. Except for some whispering at the back, the class are quiet, copying work from text books.

SIMON shares a desk with GARY at the back. They are looking out of the window at LISA who has been detained at the school gates by a tall TEACHER who is ticking her off for being late. He tells her to remove her badge.

GARY *(agitated, almost urgent whisper)*
...It's true. It was in the woods. Her and about ten of her freaky-deaky mates, all of them drugged up to here, chanting and rattling things. Proper Satanism. And she rips off her clothes and starts writhing in the grass, screaming sex, sex, sex. And in a shot they're all over her like a rash. Every one of them. Bang, bang, bang.

SIMON stares suspiciously at LISA who is walking away from the TEACHER putting her badge back on.

GARY *(cont'd)*
But it's not enough for her. Ten fellahs! and she's still panting for more. So. Well. There's this dog with them right.

SIMON flashes GARY an incredulous look.

GARY
It's true. It took a wild animal to satisfy her.

SIMON
Bollocks.

GARY
Ask anyone.

SIMON starts sniggering and shaking his head. A piece of chalk lands on his desk. SIMON looks up and sees the TEACHER staring at him sternly.

SIMON
Sorry sir.
SIMON starts turning the pages of the text book still smiling to himself.

GARY
You fancy her don't you?

SIMON *(defensive)*

Nah.

SIMON turns to GARY who is staring at him accusingly. Uncomfortable, SIMON turns back to the pages of the text book. He turns pale at the sight which greets him.

The pages are devoted to pictures and descriptions of tape worms: Enlarged photos of their hideous heads, cross-sections of their bodies, artists impressions of a tape worm inside a human intestine. But worst of all a picture of a tape worm at an early stage of developement which looks similar to the worms in the biscuit tin.
SIMON is startled by the school bell which shatters the silence.

11. INT. SCHOOL. TOILET. DAY.

SIMON leans over a toilet bowl vainly trying to make himself sick. He slumps to the floor exhausted.

GARY *(OS)*
Bacon rind's good. You attach it to a piece of string, swallow it, then yank it back up.

SIMON grimaces.

GARY is outside the cubicle scrawling something on the cubicle door. There is a malevolent glint in his eye.

GARY
What about shitting it out? That's what they did on my Uncle Billy's farm. Gave the cows laxatives. Massive ones. The shite came out like brown ale.

SIMON

Gary.

GARY

What?

SIMON
You won't tell anyone will you?

GARY puts the finishing touches to his work: Simon Wrigley-Worm Boy.

GARY

Oh no.

12. INT. SCHOOL. DINING HALL. DAY.

Prunes being piled on to SIMON's bowl. SIMON moves away from the serving area with his bowl of prunes. The dining hall is busy. Simon heads towards one of the tables where GARY is sitting with COLIN and KEVIN. There are two unoccupied chairs.

As SIMON approaches he sees the boys exhange glances. SIMON goes to sit down.

COLIN

It's taken.

SIMON moves towards the other empty chair.

KEVIN

That's taken as well.

SIMON looks at GARY who smiles up at him spitefully then sucks a wriggling piece of spaghetti up into his mouth.

KEVIN

There's some room on that table.

SIMON looks at where KEVIN is indicating and sees LISA sitting alone reading a book and eating a packed lunch. The THREE BOYS start sniggering.

SIMON's face fills with anxiety. He looks round the hall, the CROWD of CHILDREN is interspersed with CHILDREN who are staring at SIMON. The sound of whispering and sniggering starts to echo in his head. Frightened, he turns to GARY who is affected by SIMON's desperate look. GARY looks down at the table, ashamed. Then COLIN whispers something to him which makes him laugh. SIMON drops his plate on the slop-trolley and backs out of the dining hall.

13. EXT. SCHOOL. THE GATES. DAY.

SIMON stands alone. PUPILS leave the school. PARENTS pull up in cars to pick them up. A YOUNG BOY brushes past SIMON.

GIRL'S VOICE *(OS)*

Ugh, you touched him.

SIMON looks at his feet. He hears a car pull up nearby. He looks up hopefully but it is not KAREN. The YOUNG GIRL gets into the car pointing SIMON out to her PARENTS. SIMON watches the car pull away. When it has gone it reveals LISA sitting cross legged on the pavement reading her book.

14. EXT. SCHOOL. THE GATES. DAY.

It's quiet now. SIMON is still waiting to be picked up. So is LISA who is still reading her book. SIMON steals glances at her.

GARY, KEVIN, COLIN and SEVEN OTHER BOYS spill out on to the school grounds in football kits, chanting, jumping on each other, kicking the ball around. SIMON looks at them sadly.

LISA

What a bunch of animals.

SIMON looks at LISA.

SIMON

So you don't...You don't like animals then?

A van approaches. LISA stands up.

FOOTBALLER *(shouting to Simon)*

Wrigley worm! Wrigley worm!

SIMON turns to the FOOTBALLERS.

LISA

You shouldn't let them get to you. They just can't handle anything different.

SIMON

I'm not different.

The van pulls up. A scruffy VW driven by a BEARDED MAN. There are some other KIDS in the back, much less square than SIMON's peers at school.

The FOOTBALLERS chase the ball a little closer to SIMON. One of them stoops down and picks a bit of rubber tubing up from the ground.

LISA

Do you want a lift?

SIMON hesitates. He casts a nervous glance at the FOOTBALLERS. LISA shrugs and gets into the van. SIMON watches the van pull away. Suddenly a huge piece of rubber tubing crashes into the side of his legs. He jumps back, staring at the juddering piece of rubber. The FOOTBALLERS laugh at his reaction. SIMON backs away in disgust and horror.

15. EXT. THE ESTATE. DAY.

SIMON makes his lonely way through the deserted streets. He looks down at his stomach. He stops walking, pauses, then changes direction.

16. INT. CHEMIST. DAY.

SIMON stands in front of the counter almost dwarfed by a huge display of condoms. He gazes at them suspiciously.

The CHEMIST sweeps a large assortment of laxitives into a paper bag. The CHEMIST nods towards the bag.

CHEMIST

School dinners, eh?

SIMON tears his gaze away from the condoms and is greeted by the smirking face of the CHEMIST.

SIMON

No thank you.

SIMON grabs the bag of laxitives and hurries out of the shop. The CHEMIST is perplexed.

17. EXT. THE RAILWAY TRACK. EARLY EVENING.

SIMON trudges along the railway track taking the boxes of pills out of a paper bag and stuffing them into his pocket. A wind blows through the dark woods next to the railway track. SIMON glances anxiously at the woods then hurries on towards the house.

But when the house comes into view SIMON stops and stares. KAREN is helping TREVOR move his gear out of a car and into the house. On the roof of the car is a large plastic keyboard: written on the keys; Polyphon – An orchestra in your pocket.

18. INT. SIMON'S HOUSE. ENTRANCE. EARLY EVENING.

SIMON slams the door and scowls when he sees TREVOR's belongings cluttering up the hall. A few dry cleaned suits slung over a suitcase, many 'samples' of the streamline Polyphon synthesisers, mostly boxed up. One box is open. SIMON is startled when a black lead uncoils itself and slithers into the living room as someone tugs on it.
SIMON kicks the box and stomps towards the stairs.

KAREN emerges from the living room trying to look especially jolly.

KAREN

Hiya. Come and have a look at this.

SIMON ignores her.

KAREN

Hey.

SIMON stops.

KAREN

They've put him in a tiny bed and breakfast. I mean, with all this lot. Look, he's got to be back in London on Tuesday, it's not like he's moving in.

SIMON fumbles with the pills in his pocket. He sighs deeply and turns to KAREN and looks at her with big wet eyes.

SIMON

Mam, I've got a tape worm.

KAREN groans.

KAREN

Don't start. I've had you and your bloody diseases up to here. If you don't like me having a bit of fun. Tough.

KAREN slams the door of the living room behind her, leaving SIMON stunned, staring at the closed door. Tears fill his eyes.

19. INT. SIMON'S HOUSE. BEDROOM. EVENING.

SIMON, tearful, frightened, lines up a row of pills. He stares at the pills then takes the biology textbook from his schoolbag. He turns to the tape worm page and shudders. He snaps the book shut, takes a few deep breaths, then starts furiously popping the pills into his mouth.

SIMON stares down at his stomach. Suddenly a hideous high pitched scream rips through the whole house. SIMON jumps to his feet. The noise settles down into a supremely tacky version of "Viva Espana" whining out of the living room. SIMON hurls the biology text book at the bedroom door.

20. INT. SIMON'S HOUSE. BEDROOM. NIGHT.

SIMON is lying on the bed breathing very anxiously. There is a new song from the synthesiser. Something a little more sinister. The CAMERA moves CLOSER and CLOSER to SIMON. When his frightened face fills the frame the music suddenly stops.

SILENCE.
Suddenly an almighty rumble rises from SIMON's stomach. He clutches his belly then rushes out of his bedroom.

21. INT. SIMON'S HOUSE. OUTSIDE THE BATH-ROOM. NIGHT.

SIMON rushes to the door and tries the handle. It is locked. SIMON bangs anxiously on the door.

SIMON

Mam, mam.

TREVOR *(OS) (growling from the bathroom)*

What?

SIMON steps back from the door. He turns to the stairs. His stomach roars.

22. EXT. SIMON'S HOUSE. NIGHT

SIMON scarpers out of the house.

23. INT. SIMON'S HOUSE. BEDROOM. NIGHT.

KAREN enters the room with a plate of fish fingers and beans. She sees the mess in the room.

KAREN

Simon?

KAREN sighs when she sees the bedclothes lying on the floor. She picks them up and puts them on the bed then sees SIMON's envelope; 'To be opened in the event of my death'. *She looks up and sees the empty boxes and bottles of pills.*

KAREN

Oh my God.

KAREN drops the plate of food and rushes out of the bedroom. Meanwhile outside the window the small figure of SIMON rushes over the railway tracks.

24. INT. SIMON'S HOUSE. LIVING ROOM. NIGHT.

KAREN is on the phone, tearful, frightened.

KAREN

...Mousy brown...blue eyes. About half an hour ago. I was...

KAREN cries. TREVOR belches and turns on the TV. KAREN glares at him.

KAREN

I was downstairs. How do you expect me to keep calm? Hallo? Hallo? Bastards.

KAREN slams the phone down. SOUND of a train approaching.

TREVOR

Make us a cup of tea love.

Flabbergasted KAREN opens her mouth to speak but is too furious for words. She grabs a tea cup and takes aim...

25. EXT. THE WOODS. NIGHT.

SIMON frantically unbuckles his trousers then squats in the grass. SOUND of the train rushing towards him. He stares in terror at his stomach then covers his eyes with his hands.

BLACKNESS – The train screeches, whooshes past.

As the sound of the train fades away we hear peaceful forest sounds, bird song etc...

SIMON slowly draws his hands away from his face revealing a look of weary intense relief. He is surprised to see a dog looking at him, then even more shocked to look round and see a GROUP of YOUNG CRUSTIES staring at him in stunned silence. But worst of all for SIMON, there before him stands LISA, looking down at him with a bemused look on her face.

SIMON scarpers as fast as he can. The CRUSTIES start laughing. LISA flashes them an annoyed look.

26. EXT. THE RAILWAY TRACK. NIGHT.

SIMON runs along the track struggling to do up his trousers.
Worn out he slows down to get his breath back. He strikes his forehead in despair. He looks back at the woods and is surprised to see LISA standing there alone, lit by the moonlight, watching him.

SIMON looks at her. She waves at him. Slowly SIMON relaxes. A smile starts to appear on his face. He stands up straighter.

A huge crash briefly draws SIMON's attention to his house. A smile spreads across his face when he sees one of TREVOR's synthesisers crash on to the garden path. The SOUND of sirens getting nearer.

SIMON grins and takes a step towards the house. But then he stops and turns back to face the woods. LISA is picking her way through the trees. SIMON hesitates then sets off across the railway tracks to catch her up.

A police car and ambulance pull up outside SIMON's house just as TREVOR's dry cleaned suits are jettisoned from a top floor window.

SIMON catches up with LISA.

A train shoots into the tunnel.

THE END

Moriarty

Toby Litt

Toby Litt was born in 1968. He grew up in Ampthill, Bedfordshire. He studied English at Oxford. From 1990 to 1993, he lived in Prague. He is the co-recipient of this year's Curtis Brown Scholarship. He is currently working on a novel and a book of short stories. His piece, *Adventures in Capitalism,* is included in Malcolm Bradbury's UEA anthology, *Class Work.*

Toby Litt

Moriarty

Holmes had been pursuing Moriarty for almost three decades. (These, you must know, were not their real names and a decade, as far as they were concerned, lasted about five days.)

Holmes, like her pseudonymsake, was tenacious, melancholic and inspired; Moriarty, like his, was logical and depraved and always evanescent. They were both fifteen.

Holmes first saw Moriarty in the cornfield behind her house. It was three in the morning, August, and there was the fullest of full moons. Moriarty was gliding along one of the parallel furrows left in the waist-high corn by the tractor's wheels. In the pale cinematic of the moonlight, the corn looked like snow.

Moriarty had no legs.

He was like a mediaeval ghost, still walking along at the ground-level of its day.

Holmes, who had been standing naked at the bedroom window, dropped a light dress onto herself.

She carried her plimsolls through the house, only putting them on when she'd crossed the lawn.

The grass lisped coolly between her toes.

By the time Holmes caught sight of him again, Moriarty had reached the edge of the pond.

Holmes could hear Moriarty humming or singing or chanting, she couldn't tell which. She drew nearer, positioning herself behind the trunk of The Kissing Tree.

Above them, the moon was besotted with black clouds.

The wind blowing past smelt warmly of cotton sheets. There would be a dry thunderstorm before morning.

Moriarty cross-armed his sweater off over his head, heeled himself out of his shoes and palmed down his trousers. Holmes, still watching, plucked away her dress.

Moriarty moved forward into the pond, until only his head was above the water. Holmes clove to the treetrunk, pressing her nipples, her pubic hair, through the ivy, onto the bark.

Moriarty's head went under.

The world had changed.

•

The next morning, as she usually did during the summer holidays, Watson came round.

"She's still in bed, lazy cow," said Holmes' mum. "You just go on up."

Watson went in without knocking.

The curtains had been left undrawn and out the window Watson saw a tractor moving across the far end of the field.

"Are you awake?" Watson asked.

"Yes," came a voice from under the covers.

"Did you see *Top of the Pops* last night?" asked Watson, sitting down at the end of the bed.

"No," said Holmes.

"It was great," said Watson. "Morrissey was on."

Holmes stuck a hand out and batted away the sheets. She looked into Watson's eyes.

"I saw him last night."

"Who, Morrissey?"

"Moriarty."

"Which band's he in?"

"Don't joke."

"You mean you *really* saw him?"

"I saw him."

"But we've been waiting all summer."

"He was walking along through the field."

"What, out there?"

"He walked to the pond and then he undressed -"

"He never."

"- and he walked into the water." Holmes reached up and tugged at one of the curtains.

"Did you see his cock?"

Holmes stood quickly up. She was still wearing the calico dress. "I was standing behind The Kissing Tree."

"Did you see it?"

"Don't ask such stupid questions, Watson." Holmes stood where she had been standing last night, when.

"Sorry, Holmes."

"There was a full moon. I saw him in the full moon."

"So you followed him, did you?"

"Yes. I followed Moriarty."

"Down to the pond-"

"I stood behind The Kissing Tree."

"Did you speak to him?"

"Of course I didn't."

"What did he do when he came out of the water? Wasn't he soaking?"

Holmes went over to the wardrobe and started to go through her dresses. The hangers scraped lightly along the bar. Watson picked up the Mickey Mouse Alarm Clock. Mickey's little white-gloved hands pointed to twelve and to three.

"What did he do, Holmes? Did he have a towel? He did get out, didn't he? You didn't just stand and watch him drown."

Holmes spoke into the wardrobe: "I'm not going to tell you, Watson. It's too dangerous. Moriarty is too dangerous."

"But he's not dead, then, is he? He can't be dangerous if he's dead."

"No, Watson," said Holmes, turning round. "Moriarty never dies. Not at the Reichenbach Falls, not ever."

"That's a lovely dress, that," said Watson.

"Watson. You must not tell a living soul of what I've seen. Not a living soul, you understand."

"Yes, Holmes. Absolutely."

"Would you wear this dress for me, Watson?"

•

The two girls walked out the front door, down the concrete-slab path and swung through the gate. The Hound of the Baskervilles yapped at them through next-door's privet. They turned left, toward the village.

Holmes lived in the last house on the left: Number 8. Watson was at Number 5.

The houses were all four-square semis, ludicrous in 1940s Council House pink. From a distance, on a blue sunny day, the windows and lintels looked sparkly white.

Number 6 had a satellite dish.

Altogether (before Moriarty's family moved in to Number 1) the four houses in the road contained eight households: seven women, three men, fourteen children.

Holmes was the only only child. Watson had a big brother. He worked on the farm. Most of the other children were toddlers. Even so, there wasn't much babysitting.

Holmes and Watson walked down the road, toward the village. As they passed Number 1, Holmes said:

"Keep looking straight ahead. He's in the garden. Don't look at him. Come on, run!"

They ran till they were hidden by the hedge.

Holmes walked along the smooth 70s tarmac, Watson on the scrotty thick-leaved grass of the verge.

"That was a close call, Holmes," said Watson.

"We can't be too careful, Watson," said Holmes.

"They must have moved in yesterday when we were in town."

"Blast!"

"What is it, Holmes?"

"We could have seen so much about them, if only we'd been there. We could have seen what they meant."

"How d'you think he knew about the pond? D'you think he was just exploring?"

"Moriarty always knows his way around. He is never lost. He sensed the pond. It called to him through the night."

Up ahead they could see the church spire among its elms. A car went by, an Austin Allegro, small hands waving from the back window. Holmes and Watson waved back.

Holmes was the taller and prettier of the two: cream-pale skin, a precocious bob of black hair, dark green eyes. Only a slightly harsh profile threatened her present beauty, though it would later enhance it. Watson was a strawberry-blonde: plumpish, spottyish.

"Was he really trying to kill himself, do you think?" asked Watson.

"How can one ever know how Moriarty thinks? He is the greatest criminal mind the world has ever known."

"What does he look like?"

"It was dark."

"But you said there was a moon-"

"He is tall, pale, with dark hair."

"What – under his armpits and all?"

"Watson, you ask too many questions."

"I'm sorry, Holmes, it's just I sort of have to, don't I? Or else you don't tell me anything."

"You know all you need to know, Watson. Moriarty has moved into the road. We will never be safe again."

"But do we want to be safe?" asked Watson.

Holmes only looked at her.

•

During the summer holidays, they visited the grave every morning.

Watson hadn't thought much of her father till he died, just before Easter. Only during the summer holidays did she realise how important he had been. It was nothing to do with love, more her sense of human scale. The house seemed like a mansion without him in it. She would get lost for days, walking down the stairs. Her mother was still sleeping on the settee. Her brother was now the man of the house, but her brother wasn't a man.

Holmes was a man. Holmes knew about grief. Holmes' father had left home when she was only two.

Holmes always said her father was a soldier, but she didn't really know. The only clue she had was a picture of him, his head sticking out of a Chieftain tank. He was wearing a beret with a badge on it, but he might have borrowed that.

Her mother never talked about him, and she'd only found the photograph by accident. It fell out of her mother's copy of *Couples*. Holmes kept it in her Evidence Box.

They walked through the churchyard and down to the lower field. The old graveyard was full. They'd had to start burying people close together, in tight rows.

Watson's father's grave was no different from all the others.

"Hello, Dad," Watson said, before sitting down beside him.

"Hello, Watson's father," said Holmes.

From the lower field, you could look down toward the high brick walls of the farm. There was a rookery in the trees at the top of the next hill. The church bells rang for ten o'clock.

"Morrissey was great," said Watson. "I'm really sorry you missed him."

"Watson, what would you do if you only had a few weeks to live?"

"How many?"

"Three or four."

"I don't know. I'd like to go to London, to Baker Street. Just to see where we used to live."

"Where I used to live."

"Of course, Holmes."

"Nothing else? Isn't there anything else you'd like to do?"

"It's not really worth it, is it? I haven't got any money to spend or give away. I don't really know anyone outside the road and the farm and the village." She paused. "Why, what would you do?"

"I didn't ask you so you'd ask me back."

"But you must've thought about it to want to ask."

"Not really. Only since last night. I think Moriarty is going to kill me."

"Why?"

"Because Moriarty kills people. I feel doomed, just having seen him. I'm going to die."

"Stop talking like that, Holmes. Especially here. It's bad luck, I'm sure." Watson pulled a long hair out from the back of her head and blew it away off her palm. "Go on!" she said to Holmes.

"It won't work," said Holmes. "I can't be protected."

•

On the Market Square, they walked past the War Memorial kissing their thumbs and holding their breath.

In the shop, they bought two pints of milk each.

As they came out of the shop, they saw Number 4's Austin Allegro again. They put their cartons down and waved before picking them up and walking on.

About a hundred yards down the street, they stopped at a small house and rang the bell. Watson stood back, out of sight.

"Good morning, gran," said Holmes when the door was open. "here's your milk." She passed it through.

"Thank you, dear," came a voice from the warm inside. "Would you like some cake?"

"Not today, thank you, gran," said Holmes. "See you tomorrow."

"Bye bye dear."

•

They took the secret path back to Number 8, hoping that Moriarty hadn't discovered it yet.

Nettles stung their ankles and burrs stuck to their hems. The path went through inexplicable periods of heat and cold. Bees lunged heavily from one hedgerow to the other.

Just before it turned onto the road, the path ran along the far shore of the pond. Holmes and Watson stopped and sat down.

Holmes opened her milk carton, took several gulps and passed it to Watson.

"He was standing there," she pointed.

Watson looked across at the foot-smooth earth.

"It must've been lovely."

Holmes wiped her mouth with the back of her hand.

"Mum said we might be going into town this afternoon, d'you want to come?"

"No, Watson. I have to think about this. I have to think the whole thing through."

"Watson passed the carton back and Holmes finished it."

•

For the rest of the morning they sat in Holmes' room, talking. At about twelve, Watson went home for lunch.

She reappeared at the front door around one, her mum's Vauxhall buzzing in the road behind her.

"You sure you don't want to come?" she asked. "We're going to have treats."

Holmes waved over Watson's shoulder to Watson's mum.

"I'm sorry, Watson," she said, "this is more important than that. This is a matter of life and death."

"Shouldn't I stay then?" asked Watson, looking up the road.

"No. Go. You can't do anything here."

•

When Watson got back early in the evening they went over to her house and sat in the living-room, playing the Morrissey single over and over.

Watson sat in one of the armchairs while Holmes lay on the settee.

"He's magnificent," said Watson.

"I don't think it's as good as his last one," said Holmes.

"Maybe not," said Watson, "but he's still magnificent."

•

That night, Moriarty again walked through the cornfield and down to the pond and, again, Holmes followed him, watching.

Exactly as before, Moriarty, leaving his clothes behind him, moved into and under the water.

The following morning, Holmes didn't get up when Watson came round.

Two mornings later, Holmes asked Watson not to disturb her before twelve.

A week later and Holmes changed that to two.

•

"Did you see him again last night?" Watson asked, sitting opposite Holmes at the kitchen table.

"Have you been taking the milk round to my gran's?" asked Holmes.

"Yes, I have."

"Does she notice the difference? Does she know it's you and not me?"

"Of course she does."

"I just wondered." Holmes turned the spoon round in her cornflakes.

"Holmes, tell me what's happening."

But Holmes' mum came in with the shopping and they had to talk about *Brookside.*

•

"I'm getting worried about you," said Holmes' mum when Watson had finally gone. "It's not good, this lying in bed all the time. Get out and do something with your time."

"Mum," said Holmes.

"It'll be a good thing for you when school starts back up again."

"Mum."

'I don't know how you can stand it, up in that little room all the time, with all this lovely country to go into outdoors – and we've had such beautiful weather."

Holmes stood up.

"Aren't you going to watch *Coronation Street* either?"

"Not tonight, mum."

"It's not – you know – 'our friend' – is it?"

"Everything's not that, mum."

Holmes moved towards the stairs.

"And I want to wash that dress as well."

•

At the end of another week of watchings, Holmes went to see her gran.

"Well, we haven't seen you for a while, have we?" said gran." I was just putting a bit of Brasso over these here. They'll be yours, one day, when you're grown up. They were my mother's once."

"Gran, if I tell you something, you won't tell mum, will you?"

"Now, I can't make promises like that on nothing, love? If it's something awful, like a little baby, I'd have to tell her. It wouldn't feel right, not. You understand that. She'd have a right to know."

"It's not awful. Well, it is. But it's not really, not like what you mean."

"Let's sit down and get comfy and then you can tell it."

They moved through into the living room and sat down on the Velux armchairs on either side of the gas. Holmes looked up at her grandfather's collection of Toby jugs. Gran's eyes followed hers.

"Silly old fool he was," she said. "He thought they'd be worth a fortune, one day. Like on the telly."

"Perhaps they are," said Holmes.

"I suppose so," said gran. "Now what is it, love?"

Holmes felt the doily tickling the back of her neck.

"I'm sorry, gran, it's nothing. I shouldn't've said."

"How about some tea? We can talk after."

But, when the tea came, Holmes got gran onto the harvest and then the war.

•

Holmes spent the next three nights trying to sleep, trying not to follow Moriarty. That she failed in her resolution, going every time, finally decided Holmes on the correct course of action. Things had been turning very bad, recently. Watson had stopped coming round. School was only three decades away. Her Mother thought she was on drugs.

•

On the morning of the chosen day, Holmes wrote her will. In it, she left everything to Watson.

With the money in her savings account, Watson was to go to

London and buy a record player.

Special instructions were left about the location and disposal of the Evidence Box.

Holmes wrote special messages to her mum and her gran.

In the afternoon, Holmes went with Watson to the grave. Watson started crying almost immediately.

"What is it, Watson?"

"Nothing, Holmes."

"I have treated you abominably."

"I don't want him dead. I did, you know, when he was alive. I even prayed sometimes for it. And when it happened, I was really pleased for a while. I was pleased at the funeral, because I thought he was sort of pretending and would come back a different person. But then, now, I feel like it was me that killed him by hating him. If I hadn't've wanted it, it wouldn't've happened. Oh Holmes, I'm so horrible."

Holmes hugged Watson.

"Now listen to me, Watson – you are not to blame in this matter. I believe you are innocent of the murder of your father. His case is, indeed, a great mystery, but we shall solve it one day. Thinking that you are guilty isn't going to help. It doesn't help him and it doesn't help you."

"But you didn't even have a father! I feel so greedy that I did."

"Tell me, Watson, why have you never spied on Moriarty?"

Watson sat up and blew her nose into a tissue.

"Because you warned me he was the most dangerous criminal in the world."

"So you never stayed awake to see what he looked like?"

"I drew the curtains before it even got dark."

"Oh, Watson," said Holmes, sniffing, "was there ever a truer more loyal friend than you?"

"I'd be very sorry if there wasn't," said Watson, "I'm such a wet and a weed."

They laughed at eachother for a while.

"Tonight – can you meet me tonight, at three o'clock, round on the secret path side of the pond?"

"Of course, Holmes."

"Dress in warm dark clothes and don't bring a torch or anything. There will be a moon. The last one, I think, probably. The last moon of the summer. Tomorrow they cut down the corn and kill all the animals. Tomorrow is the real end of things."

•

When she got home, Holmes tore the will up and flushed it down the loo.

She watched *Coronation Street* and *Brookside* with her mother.

•

Holmes had been right. The moon, though partial, gave enough of the edges of things.

Watson shivered with the excitement of sneaking out of the house and then with the chill of the air.

Number I had a light on, downstairs.

The graveyard as she passed it was full of believable ghosts.

Stumbling down the secret path, spiderstrands tickled up her nose.

When she got to the pond, Holmes was there waiting.

"He hasn't been, has he?"

"Three o'clock – every night."

"What's the time now?"

"Two fifteen."

"I've never done this before, Holmes. Sneaking out, I mean."

Holmes was looking in the direction Moriarty would come from.

Through the branches of the Kissing Tree, against the glow of the town, she could see the tv aerial of her house.

"I hate it when they cut the corn and you can hear the mice squealing."

"Can you really, Watson?"

"I don't know. Perhaps they never really stop. If you listen closely enough, they're always there. Even in winter, when they're really not. Holmes, what are we going to do? Are you going to tell me?

"Yes, Watson, I am. You are my best friend of all, Watson. I have been very mean to you over the last few decades. I haven't let you in at all. There are more important things than just – "

"Then what, Holmes?"

"You are very important to me, Watson. But now I must tell you what we are going to do."

•

Moriarty came through the cornfield, as he always did, just before three o'clock.

The moonlight was fluttering out.

He walked a little faster than usual. It was cold and the water would be colder still.

An upstairs light was on in the house at the end. Usually, all the lights in the road were out, except for the tv in Number 6.

Moriarty stopped for a glance up at the window. A tall figure moved across and back, once, twice.

As he moved toward the pond, Moriarty rode his hands, palms down, over the surface of the corn.

He felt the ripe heads knocking against the knuckles of his thumbs and the bristles flicking between his fingers.

He began his ritual song: Father-Mother-Father-Mother-Father-Mother.

The ground swung down to the poolside.

He positioned himself correctly and began the undressing. Jumper. Shoes. Trousers.

The coldness of the air was a new kind of difference.

He moved towards the water less openly than before.

He wanted to cup his palms over his nipples, but knew that wasn't allowed.

The water round his ankles was molten.

He sang louder and slowly forced himself on, in, under, again.

He opened his eyes, though there was nothing to see except the chance of moonlight. His eyes would sting tomorrow, but that was part of the honesty. Like the clothes. Like the cold.

He let his legs float up behind him. He looked down into the water. His buttocks were now the only part of him on the surface. He felt them pimpling against the air.

For as long as he could, he held. Then five counts more. Then another five. Then five. Then another. Then ten.

When he burst up out of the water, he saw immediately that something had altered.

The usual composition of pond, trees, sky, moon, clouds, had been disturbed.

There was an extra square of whiteness.

He looked towards it.

Standing by the pond on the opposite side were two naked women, looking at him, holding hands.

A Sprig of Basil

Sue Hubbard

Sue Hubbard is a poet and an art critic for *Time Out* and *The New Statesman*. Her poems have appeared in such anthologies as *Klaonica* and *In the Gold of Flesh*. She has published two pamphlets of poetry and her first full collection, *Everything Begins with the Skin*, is published by Enitharmon. She is working on her first full novel.

Sue Hubbard

A Sprig of Basil

Stray leaves from the overhead vine cast serrated shadows on the white-washed wall. It is mid-day. It is August. The heat is unrelenting.

Sally takes a sip of iced *retsina* and leans back into the coolness by the door of the taverna as she doodles on the paper tablecloth a quick approximation of the little girl in a yellow sun-washed T-shirt, playing beneath the table with a moth-eaten cat. It is something to do. A tool against her self-consciousness. She has still not got used to this eating alone. Strange, when you are married, what you take for granted. A body to wake next to, a ready ear at the end of the day, someone to eat the other portion. All around her on the terrace, shaded by three oleanders, groups at the other tables chat, pour wine, share plates of black marinated olives and portions of fried calamari. She is cross with herself for feeling uncomfortable. This whole experience of solo travelling is something new. But she's learning. That's why she came. Divorce, she is discovering, is a great educator.

The kitchen door is open. In contrast to the fierce sunlight outside, the interior is cool and dark. Lace curtains billow in the heat, shading the heavy carved furniture, the hand embroidered cushions. A woman is standing by a white marble counter. Sally can see her through the doorway without herself being seen. The woman is standing with her hands placed in the curve of her back, her swollen belly in silhouette. She must be about seven months. Sally watches her stretch, freeing the tension trapped in her shoulders and spine before returning to the marble counter to place two fish in a pair of kitchen scales.In front of her a group of chattering Italians, just escaped from the heat of the beach for lunch, poke the pile of red mullet lying in a silvery-pink heap on a painted dish, picking up each fish by its tail fins for inspection. The fish, it seems, are sold by weight.

Sally sips her drink, watching with a detached concentration, before turning back to her doodle. She has time to spare. The office, her last article, are all behind her in London. Three weeks. They spread out in front of her like an assault course. Her drawing is interrupted by the small girl tiring of the cat, and running into the kitchen to watch the woman weighing fish. She pauses momentarily from the scales, and leans to kiss the child. Sally notes the grey rings under the young woman's eyes, the fine lines dragging down the corners of her thin mouth, her blond sun-bleached hair and limp floral dress exposing brown limbs, her bare feet... She hears her call in Greek to the old woman in the corner of the kitchen chopping tomatoes. Then, "What fish do you want?" in English, tinged with a German accent, as she turns to serve the next man in the queue. *Three languages. How come?* Above the marble counter, hangs a collection of photographs. The woman and the little girl on a makeshift swing. Another of the woman with her hair up, in a smart suit, standing between two moustached fishermen in heavy sweaters, her arms around their waists, as if just arrived or about to depart on a journey. *Winter perhaps? After the tourists have gone?* The largest, a group meal, possibly a celebration, at the long kitchen table, is inscribed with a flourish of greetings. Snap shots of a life, thinks Sally.

The man who had brought them over to the island on the boat brings Sally her lunch. Tomatoes and basil with *feta* cheese, dribbled with a signature of green olive oil, thick slices of coarse bread in a basket. He wears faded shorts, a vest and battered rubber flip-flops. His black hair curls at the neck, luxurious as his full moustache. He nods as he places Sally's lunch in front of her. *The man in the photo? The woman's husband perhaps?*

The Italians eat noisily at the next table, picking fish from the bone with their fingers, laughing and drinking with a sensual panache as if part of a piece of theatre.

Sally mops up the last glistening pool of olive oil and tomato with her bread, eyeing her notebook lying open beside her on the table. She has written nothing except. "Leave Heathrow Tuesday

14.40. Arrive Athens. Boat from Pireaus Wed. morn. early am." She looks back into the kitchen where the woman has kicked off her shoes and is sitting on a stool by the counter, massaging the small of her back. I could, thinks Sally, make her do whatever I want. I could be the one to change the course of her life...then she picks up her pen and, as she breaks the rest of the bread into absent minded pellets with her free hand, she slowly begins to write... "Ingrid's foot...

"...slipped from underneath her as she struggled with her battered suitcase. Waves split on the concrete jetty, rocking the red and white fishing boat like a cork. It was March and the sea was choppy with white horses. In one arm she balanced the baby against the angled jut of her hip, while the little girl buried her face in her damp billowing skirt. Ingrid tugged the small child across the slippery gang plank.

" 'Come Katrina, come quickly now.' Her voice was flat and strained.

"She hoisted the baby over the railing, handing the whimpering bundle to the stocky fisherman already on board. Like all the men in the area, he had a thick moustache, black and bushy as a small ferret on his upper lip, and a heavy growth of stubble. He held out his large hands for the baby; calloused working hands, their broad nails engrained with rims of black engine oil.

" 'Yanis was going to take us, Kristoph,' she explained, holding up a small bag to follow the child, 'but he had to go off and see about the new outboard. I have to take the children for their check-up at the clinic. Then we are staying over with his sister Anna.'

"Would he, she wondered, guess at her lie? The baby continued to cry fretfully as if detecting change. Yet they had made the crossing a hundred times before, to the small port on the main island, from the concrete jetty that Yanis had built with the help of his cousin, her first winter.

"Ingrid bundled Katrina and the baby into the hold among the nets and fishing tackle, climbing over a heap of empty *ouzo* bottles, shifting cans of diesel and coights of rope to make a nest for them among a pile of rugs on the bunk. Then she turned the battered portable radio, tied with string onto the life-buoy, to a crackling station and a distant wail of *bazuki* music. Along with the rocking motion of the boat it seemed to quieten them. The dusty bottles and glasses were left from summer when the boatmen carried tourists between hotels and beach and offered them a tot as they returned at sunset, drunk with too much sun, skin red and tingling, ready for an evening on the town. During those months, the men hardly fished. She took the twist of paper from the neck of one of the bottles, releasing the pungent aniseed smell. The clear fiery liquid hit the pit of her stomach.

"Courage. For courage, she thought.

"While Kristoph was rolling the heavy blue cylinders of Calor gas up the jetty, she climbed onto the bow of the boat which had swung round in the wind to face the tiny island. She stood there, her mac wrapped tight around her, her wispy blond hair plastered against her face by the salty spray, like the carved figurehead of some ancient prow.

"She tried to cement a final picture of the island in her mind. The island that had been her home for seven years. She loved the place. It had been love at first sight, perhaps, she realised wryly, the great love of her life. Just as it was every summer for all the tourists that Yanis brought back on the boat, daily, from the town to swim naked from the rocks and empty beaches, snorkeling amid cerulean shadows and pellucid pools looking for striped angel-fish and squid, before coming up to eat her charcoaled mullet in the shade of the vine.

"She had brought very little with her. Just some bread, *feta* and green olives, wrapped in a coarse checked cloth; the photo that had stood beside the bed, of Yanis with the children; a change of clothing for the baby, and some sprigs of basil from the pot in the kitchen window. She had wrapped the roots in damp newspaper and placed it inside a plastic bag. Would it grow wherever it was they were going, its sweet pungency catching in her nostrils, drawing her back to this place.

"She had tried to write a note. She had tried several times, screwing it up and throwing it frustrated and angry in a scrunched ball into the stove. What could she say? She knew he would never understand.

"She was his wife. They were his children. That was all he understood. That was all he had really ever understood. For him it had always been that simple. Perhaps he was right. Perhaps she was the one who complicated things.

"In the end she simply wrote I'M SORRY, in capital letters, on a piece of paper and stuck it, with a bit of old chewing gum, to the bedroom mirror. That, at least, was true.

"And what of Mama in her white-washed room at the back of the taverna? The little room, with the camp bed and kerosene lamp that, in winter, cast huge flickering shadows, like strange silent gods, against the rough-caste walls, where she knitted and crocheted all day, fine white webs, like some ancient spider. Ingrid loved her without ever having meant to. Would she understand? Soon her dim eyes would be so bad, she would have nothing to occupy her.

"How would they cope without her? How had they coped before? But she couldn't take anymore. There was no common language, nor had there really ever been, except for the language of touch and her deep love of this wild remote place. For a time she thought it might be enough, might be what she was looking for. Though she wasn't sure now if she had ever really known what that was.

"But not this. Not this.

"Leaning down to cover the children with a rug, she caught sight of herself in the cracked mirror, hung with a garland of plastic flowers and a St. Christopher medallion, above the boat's engine. There were smudged black rings under her eyes where the skin hollowed and thinned. She looked ill and old. She was still only thirty-two. She had never had a proper chance to recover after the haemorrhage. She had nearly died, nearly lost Katrina. They had only just managed to get her to the clinic on Samos in time. Drunk with pain and soaked in blood. The nurses, in their stiff white dresses, at the hospital of the *Beatific Virgin,* had mopped her brow with a damp cloth while Yanis had paced up and down on the balcony, clicking his worry beads and working his way through two packets of Camels.

" 'Is she alright? She will be alright?'

"If she had been in Germany, he would have been with her holding her hand. But not here. This was woman's work. And then, as soon as she was better, she was back in the little kitchen cooking thirty, forty lunches a day. The season was so short, they couldn't afford for her not to.

"She stood there in the wind, damp wisps of hair clinging to her face, watching Kristoph, his back bent, rolling the heavy gas canisters up the hill. A mist hung over the island, a thick mauve fog that blanketed everything beyond an arm's length. In winter the gales were often so strong that the waves swept right over the jetty and it was impossible to leave the island, sometimes for days. Then she would wrap a heavy woollen shawl round her head and lean out against the salt wind to carry bundles of hay up to the sheep and goats on the barren rocky outcrops under the arthritic olive trees. This was a Greece the tourists never saw. Cruel, pantheistic, vengeful.

"And in the evenings she would sit with Mama as she did her knitting, trying to tune in the TV, but often the reception was so bad it wasn't worth it. She thought of the nights the generator had failed completely, when she had sat making a dress for Katrina by the light of the oil lamp, an elaborate patchwork cut from her old skirts, while Yanis mended his nets. Sometimes she would read her battered school copy of Rilke: *For Beauty's nothing but beginning of Terror we're still just able to bear...*

"Those silent evenings were among some of her happiest. Out of time, beyond time. Cocooned against the night in the shadowy, whitewashed kitchen, with the sound of the wind in the pine trees, she was back, for a moment, a child, listening for ghosts at the window, safe under the heavy quilt in that carved bed in her Grandmother's Bavarian house. The regular click-click of Mama's needles comforted her. It was as if each stitch caught up on her wooden needles was a second ensnared, time tamed into shape in a series of sweaters and waistcoats. Outside the hay loft door banged on its loose hinge. It felt, on this tiny battered island in the middle of the Aegean, as if they were the only people in the world.

"When the weather was really rough, Yanis would often be gone for several days, unable to get back across the narrow strip of water. There were always things that needed to be done, like taking the spare engine across to the boatyard in town. He might do some mechanical work for a few *drachmas* and get drunk in the bars, play a bit of backgammon with his old school friends, drink thick sweet coffee and *ouzo*. When he returned, taciturn, restless, there would be the same strained silence and Mama's sad reproachful face.

"Her mind coiled its way back to that first summer. It seemed now like someone else's life. She had been twenty-five. It was a spur of the moment decision. She was fed up with the other *au pairs,* babysitting on Saturday nights, afternoons off spent aimlessly wandering down Oxford Street. So she packed her rucksack and headed for Greece. She had no idea where she was going or for how long. She would call her father sometime when she got there, promise him she would come back and enrol at the University in Hamburg in the autumn for a – she smiled at the irony – business studies course. Her mother didn't care what she did, she was too busy with her own life. Her students. The lecture circuit. They had only sent her to London to get her away. A last chance before it all broke. Anyway the struggle was more or less over by then. There had been too many splits and factions. Daniel Cohn-Bendit had already left. He had, she supposed, been her inspiration, if inspiration was the right word. She had been too young for the great days when they planted bombs in the banks in Stuttgart and Frankfurt. The fervour was going. Maybe they were becoming too complacent. After all there was a boom. She thought of those meetings when he had come back and addressed them, spoken of the struggle, his flame-red hair shimmering like a beacon.

"Had she ever really cared, she wondered? Or had it all simply provided her with an identifiable space to inhabit beyond the predictable perimeters of her day to day existence, a place she could mark out and name as her own. She had enjoyed the squat, the sense of being deliberately beyond some indefinable edge. No one had known where she was. She had been born Heidi. But that sounded fey, childish. So she had become Ingrid and, in so doing, shed her past, her parent's expectations, their preoccupations, like a lizard sheds its skin. She would recreate herself, not in their chosen image, but her own. She tested out various poses. Intellectual, vamp, comrade. Her wardrobe changing accordingly like props in a play. Anarchists from all over the world, from the other side of the Wall, from Ulster, from the Lebanon would stay for a few days sharing a network of underground information. For a while they hoarded a stash of arms destined for the Palestinians. Deiter had shown her how to make bombs. Fertiliser from the downtown garden centre, a broken clock, some sticks of dynamite. 'Steady hand, steady heart *leibling*.' She only went on one lot of plants, the spate of bombs that went off just before the local elections. But then things started to fall apart. Someone who worked for her father found out where she was and tipped him off. There was a show-down. Shouting and tears. Things were hotting up anyway. So she accepted his ultimatum to go to London before everything broke.

"Midnight. Victoria station. Empty apart from the regular drunks and small groups of sleepy backpackers. She took the train, then the ferry, watching the sunrise on the port as the moon faded on the starboard. After that she hitched. She simply stuck out her thumb and headed East, down through the flat spine of Yugoslavia to Greece. Finally she reached Athens in the middle of the night, crammed in a mini bus full of Norwegian students. She stayed with them for two days wandering around Plaka trying on the cheap silver jewellery, leather jackets, drinking beer till the small hours in the cobbled back streets. Then she bedded down with them, a pile of bodies in the back of the bus. She and Tobias made love all night, trying not to make a noise and disturb the others. Next day she moved on. They were headed for Crete. She didn't fancy Crete. That was how she liked things. No commitments. One day at a time.

"She caught the first ferry sailing out of Piraeus. Twelve hours later she was in Samos. She liked the feel of being on the edge. Across that tiny gulf of water was another civilisation, a different world. The Ottoman Empire, Asia: minarets, carpet bazaars, blanketed women, the sacked library at Ephesus.

"She spent several weeks bumming around on the beaches, naked and oiled, turning a golden brown, her blond hair growing brittle in the sun, only retreating to the shade of a tamarisk tree with her plastic bottle of Evian and brown paper bag of figs and olives when it got too hot. She drew a bit, slept on the beach, was chatted up by the local boys. Sometimes she slept with them under the shooting stars after they had taken her on the back of a motor bike down to the local bar and bought her beer. She would lie in the velvety night searching for Orion's belt, the Milky way. She had nothing else to do.

"She was restless, as if she were waiting for something. For what? It had always been like that, this sense that there was something important just around the corner, just out of reach. That's what kept her on the move. Before the squat in Berlin, she had tried Paris, Stockholm, Amsterdam. But there never seemed any point to it all. No reason to stay long anywhere. She had wanted the Cause to be enough. But she had never felt really sure. In the end, one way or another, she always moved on.

"She had been on Samos nearly three weeks when she met him on the quay. She sat there in the evenings with her beer, among the fishing boats and the gleaming white millionaire yachts, dipping her brown legs into the green water as the holiday makers paraded themselves, tanned and perfumed, in their summer cottons, along the water front. He always moored in the same place. He chatted to her as he moved about the deck, coiling ropes, scrubbing down paint, fiddling with the engine. One evening he asked her on board for a drink, then invited her back to the island. It was four, five miles out of the bay. No one lived there except him and his mother. His brother and sister and uncle had moved across to the mainland. Another family had lived there when he was a boy, but they too had gone across to open a bar on Samos.

"A small holding. A herd of goats, a few hens and vines, some beehives. They scratched a living in the winter, fished and made money on boat rides and meals for the tourists in the summer. Sold lace and honey. He was building a house. It had taken five years already and still the stairs led nowhere. In the summer he was too busy. The tourists would go swimming in the clear water or lie all morning sunning themselves naked and oiled on the rocks like lizards until it became too hot and they sought refuge under the mauve shadows of the vine outside his kitchen. They would eat grilled fish – whatever the men had caught that day – stuffed aubergines and Greek salad. He would chat-up the sunburnt English girls, sometimes arrange to meet them in the bars of Samos. His mother was getting too old to manage the cooking alone. Every morning she was up at five, chopping onions, washing tomatoes. Sometimes his cousin came across and helped. But he was married and busy with the bar in town.

"He needed a wife, he laughed, throwing his head back to show a row of gleaming white teeth beneath his thick moustache. Every evening after that, he would come and find her on the quay. 'Come dancing with me, come swim with me tonight. Come with me, come with me, you are so beautiful.' His words were like warm syrup, liquid and sweet. She didn't believe him but she went anyway.

"One night they swam together from the boat. The air was soft as silk. They stripped naked in the moonlight, plunging into the warm water. His body was taut, compact, the muscles knotted from hard physical work. His buttocks shone white in the dark. Unlike her he never sunbathed, his torso was mahogany simply from working outside. They swam like a pair of dolphins, neon with phosphorescence, circling each other in the water. Back on board they knelt facing each other in the dark as he gently rubbed dry her hair with a towel. Leaning over he suddenly licked the salt from inside her ear with the tip of his tongue. She gave a tiny gasp, felt herself grow wet, her knees soften. She clasped his dark curly head, pushing it downwards. His breath was warm, his damp moustache like something alive.

"It was so easy to say yes. He wanted her so badly it seemed churlish not to. She grew bright red geraniums and basil in white-painted olive-oil drums outside the kitchen. She kept the accounts and filled in the boat registration forms, the income tax.

"Not only beautiful, but also clever, he would say, grabbing her from behind around the waist and dancing her round the kitchen in a bear hug. He had gone to school, but had skipped days to go out at night with the men, helping them trawl their nets under the bobbing fishing lamps. Numbers and words made him angry. But soon it was her, with her schemes and organisation, not the accounts or the perplexing official forms, that made him smash his fist against the rough table.

" 'You think you're so clever, ugh? You don't forget, you bloody foreign bitch you, who is boss here. No one make me look stupid.'

"Then, in the distance she would hear the hiccup of the outboard. In the corner, Mama sat in silence chopping tomatoes, her eyes full of tears.

"For a while things would get better. A friend on Samos gave him a broken cassette player. He brought it home and took it to bits on the long kitchen table, carefully rewiring and soldering until it worked. For you, he said, handing it to her like a triumphant child. For a while they had music. She knew he thought of that as man's work, mending things. Something she couldn't do. But still he wouldn't listen to her. She wanted to tell him of her loneliness during the long winters, of her need to talk to her old friends in Hamburg, for the voices and chattering comfort of other women.

"Deep under the starched cotton sheets of the iron bedstead, with the first autumn winds banging the shutters, she tried to explain, tried to tell him about her life in Germany, what it had been like for her as a child, alone in that flat for hours, waiting for her parents to return from some seminar or lecture in another town; to tell him about her life in Berlin, about Deiter, what she had planned to do at the university if she hadn't dropped out. She knew everything about him, how he had stayed with his Uncle in town during the week when he went to school, how old he was when he had caught his first fish. But he never wanted to know about her life before him. Sometimes he would sit bolt upright, throw the covers from the bed, light a cigarette and march out of the door down to the windy beach and she would stand at the window, watching him, a glowing red dot in the distance. Other times, he would simply take her tongue between his white teeth, kneading her small breasts in his rough hands to silence her. These were the only ways he knew. Eventually, all that was left was the space between them. Frozen, white as a glacier.

"When she thought about it, as Kristoph cast off the painter from the pier, it surprised her that she had lasted seven years. What would she do now? Go to university? It was too late. Run a Greek restaurant? She smiled. She wouldn't decide. She would just see what happened. That's how she had always done things in the past. The children were still little. She wiped the wet strands of hair from her face and turned to take one last look at the island as the engine hiccupped and the boat's prow turned into the wind..."

Through the kitchen door Sally can see the woman flopped in a chair, her legs spread out in front of her, her skirt pulled carelessly up around her brown thighs, her head thrown back in exhaustion. Her hands rest heavily on the mound of her stomach. She has finally finished the lunches for the day.

As Sally watches her get up, straighten and go to the door to call in the child who is back playing with the cat, she flips over the pages of her notebook. *Does it, she wonders, sound credible? Could she, would she, just up and leave like that?* Or does she, herself, for some reason, some working out of her own, need to make her to do it? Shadows lengthen across the terrace. The taverna has nearly emptied. It is mid-afternoon.

From the jetty, a hooter sounds. The boat is about to return to Samos. Hastily Sally gathers up her things, notebook, sun oil and glasses, into her straw basket. The Italians are already heading down to the pier.

"Vieni Paolo, Vieni," a woman laden with beach towels and flippers calls to a small boy chasing a darting lizard across a rock. On the way back to the boat she will have to decide how she is going to spend her evening. Maybe, after she has eaten, she could take her book down to one of the cafes in the harbour. Maybe she might even start chatting with someone.

In the dark kitchen she can still see the woman. The little girl has climbed onto her lap. They are playing a game, the child squirming with delight as the woman pulls up her T-shirt and blows raspberries onto the small girl's bare brown tummy. In the corner the old woman sits watching them, laughing encouragement, as she knits.

Maybe she has got it wrong, misread things, the dark rings under her eyes, the apparent disparity in education. The boat's hooter blows again warning her they are about to depart. She picks up her bag and hurries down the track, the child's laughter echoing behind her. She is the last to arrive. The boy is already casting off. She jumps aboard and tries to find a free place among the Italians who have spread right over the deck. Perhaps, she thinks, laying out her towel and leaning against a whitewashed buoy, her face turned towards the golden evening sun, things are not always as they seem.

Perhaps, after, all she won't stay in her room this evening, she might go down to the port. She could wear her new, long linen skirt, her cream camisole top. Maybe she would take her notebook, try a different beginning – something along the lines of: *After seven years, as Ingrid woke in the little white-washed room, she still had no regrets....*

The engine starts its low putt-putt as the boat turns from the jetty into the evening sunset, the sun a ball of red fire slipping down behind the horizon. She will have time to think about it over the next few days. To make a choice. It's her decision. It is, after all, her story.

The Nihilist Evangelist

Bo Fowler

Bo Fowler was born in 1971 and studied Philosophy at Bristol University. He has written three novels: *323*, *The Boy with the Halo Blues*, *It's Wallows All the Way Down, Stupid!*, and a collection of short stories. He is currently writing and directing a short film and is finishing the novel, *The Nihilist Evangelist*. He is a devout agnostic.

Bo Fowler

The Nihilist Evangelist

"Machinery is the new Messiah."
-Henry T Ford

"There is not enough religion in the world even to destroy religions."
-Friedrich Nietzsche

"Why do you torture your poor reason for insight into the riddle of eternity?"
-Horace

(Most of the names in this book are actually names of Midland Bank's Financial Planning Managers. A list of their names appeared in an advertisement in the Sunday Observer on 4th December 1994. The ad reads, "I am Mike Lindup and I'm a little indisposed, but if you call 0800 65 65 65 one of my colleagues will be in touch." Then the ad listed the names of all Midland Bank's Financial Planning Managers. You may have seen it. There are 800 Midland Bank's Financial Planning Managers on the ad. I have only used a few.

No offence intended.
Midland Bank plc is a member of IMRO

•

My old comprehensive school also appeared in a feature in the Observer Magazine on Sunday 4th December 1994.
Imagine that.

•

This story is in part about porcelain art at the end of the 20th century. Porcelain art is rarely central to a work of prose and the following novel should be seen as an attempt to rectify matters, at least in relation to porcelain art at the end of the 20th century.

•

This is the moral of the story: People matter more than the truth.)

Fifty centuries from now the dark side of the moon will have turned into one giant radio telescope.
Eighty centuries from now the giant radio telescope will pick up an ever so faint message emanating from the Dwingeloo Galaxy, millions of light years away.
Decoded the message will read as follows:

60UEJ5RT*RQ"

No one will ever know what it means.
One hundred centuries from now the giant radio telescope on the moon will pick up another ever so faint message emanating from the star system Epsilon Eridani ten light years away.
Decoded the message will read as follows:

ACKNOWLEDGEMENTS

This long and winding electromagnetic transmission, broadcast on the wavelength of 21 centimetres and sent in the rough direction of Earth, would not have been possible without the help of many people and electrical appliances – too many to name each individually. However, I must express my heartfelt gratitude and love to Kitty Fitzgerald for introducing me to the universe, giving me my sex and giving me a piece of helpful advice.
I must also thank Jonathan Rowley, the founder of the third largest chain of supermarket stores in Europe, and his sons. I also wish to acknowledge my debt to George Milles Jr, the wealthiest man ever to live, a man I no longer believe to be God. I would also like to thank Graham Shipton who told me the first joke I ever heard. It goes without saying that I will always be indebted to Mrs Lindo who showed me the more memorable parts of Earth, gave me my freedom and suffered from the delusion that I was her husband. I must also thank Walt Unsworth whose classic text on Everest, "Everest", I quote in this transmission without permission often. I would also like to thank NASA and the fifteen thousand people that placed me in low earth orbit. I feel I am a brother to each and every one of you.
Of course all of these people are long since dead. As is Edgar Malroy who was my patron and closest friend on Earth. So I once bet five hundred thousand pounds that God existed, doesn't everyone make at least one mistake?

PROLOGUE

Florida is the largest producer of tangerines in the world. Production in the late 1990s reached 20 million boxes annually.

Tangaroa, which sounds a bit like tangerine, was the name of the supreme deity of most Polynesians. The Hawaiians called Tangaroa Kanaloa which doesn't sound anything like tangerine. Tangaroa was said to be the origin and the personification of every fish in the sea.
Imagine that.

Orange City, a town in the south of Florida, had a population in 1998 of just 2,795. One person who lived in Orange City at that time and had occasional involvement with the tangerine business was Daphne Stevenson.
Daphne Stevenson was a check-out girl in one of Orange City's two supermarkets that had been owned by the Davies family for nearly forty years. This was of course in the days before supermarkets were automatic.
Daphne Stevenson had gone to school with Bob Davies. Bob Davies would inherit the two supermarkets in Orange City in 1997 when his father died while travelling to a convention in Dallas, Texas. Bob Davies' father's plane crashed in Death Valley.
These are the final entries of Bob Davies' father's diary:

14th January – our plane came down in bad weather. There are six survivors. We are setting off to find help. It is very hot.
15th January – We headed in a straight line all day. I argued with the pilot about his plan. He refused to listen. Food is running low. It is very hot.
16th January – Argued again with the pilot. We have been going in a straight line now for nearly three days. It is getting us nowhere. It is very hot.
17th January – Myself and two others, Moss and Reaney, good men, have left the group. We intend to walk in a circle. The pilot is a fool. It is very hot.
18th January – Feel good. Moss is a composer. His humming is driving us mad. Reaney wants to be a professional baseball player. It is very hot.

19th January – Moss found our earlier footprints, we are now going around in circles. It is just a matter of time now. It is very hot.
20th January – Wonderful weather. Things are definitely looking up. It is very hot.

Bob Davies' father's body was never found so how anyone got hold of his diary beats me.
They had necked once behind the gym, Daphne Stephenson and Bob Davies, in their youth. Daphne's jaw would dislocate.
Pop.
Three times she had to break away from Bob Davies' amorous embrace and push her jaw back into place with two fingers.

Daphne Stephenson sometimes had epileptic fits too.
So did St Anthony, the patron saint of skin rashes.

On the 16th of June 1998, she had a fit while at work. Bob Davies was then the manager, because of his father's disappearance. Bob Davies didn't phone for an ambulance. He called over his priest who, as providence would have it, was in the frozen meats section.

The priest, a man by the name of Stephen L Jones, had a theological degree from Zephaniah Bible School in Portland, Oregon, where the most exciting thing to do on a Saturday night was to listen to Professor Watmough snoring in the vain hope that he would utter something interesting in his sleep. Stephen L Jones decided that Daphne Stephenson was possessed by a devil. A medium sort of devil. Say. He proposed a tried and tested treatment.
First, prayers were uttered as Daphne Stephenson, foaming and shaking wildly, fell off her check-out seat.
The till was closed.
Daphne's jaw went pop.
As Daphne's condition deteriorated, more drastic measures were taken.
The priest rolled up his sleeves and hit her about the body with a frozen ostrich leg.

The post-mortem examination of Daphne Stephenson's body showed that she had suffered four broken ribs, a broken arm and a

fractured skull. It was the fractured skull that killed her.
Daphne Stephenson's body was untied. The priest left with four bags of shopping. The body was hidden in the supermarket deep freeze by Bob Davies.
The till was opened.

The police found the body. They got confessions. They went to arrest the priest. But by then the priest and his followers, including Bob Davies, the manager of the supermarket, had barricaded themselves into the church. As people do.
It was a little church built on a small knoll and surrounded by a white painted fence and poplar trees. There were thirty-five different species of wild flower growing on the grass around the church. Although no one had ever counted them.
Inside the church huddled twenty-six people who had decided to dedicate the rest of their lives to protecting Stephen L Jones, the priest who was becoming known on the TV and in the papers as the Ostrich preacher. Most of the twenty-six faithful were tangerine pickers or retired tangerine pickers or would be tangerine pickers. In fact just about everyone huddled in the church had in some way or other occasional involvement with the tangerine business.

They also somehow had guns. Big old Chinese guns.

When the police arrived they were greeted with a hail of fire. They had expected this. The police had got used to being greeted with a hail of gun fire when they went to churches on business, what with it being nearly the end of the millennium and all that. The holy were trigger happy.

The holy were always blowing themselves up, or poisoning themselves or entering into suicide pacts, or burning their churches and temples down, filling undergrounds with nerve gas, or shooting themselves in the head in the proper way so that they didn't turn out to be vegetables, or getting the police to shoot them, what with it being nearly the end of the millennium and all that.
"It don't seem right," some folks said.

Things didn't get much better after the millennium either.

By and by a siege got underway. Billy Adams, a local entrepreneur, set up his hotdog stand just outside the police line and made a fine American profit feeding the police, the federal agents and the press. There was also a fair number of tangerines eaten.
Things started nicely.
The local sheriff got to use his loudspeaker which was something he really liked to do. He said things like, "Err come on now" and "This is silly Stephen."
Stephen L Jones got to go on live TV telling everyone who would listen that he was God's messenger etc etc.

At night you could hear the little group of people huddled in the little church sing.

The church was called Riverside and it would soon be on the minds of most people on the planet for a brief while. About the time it takes for a carton of milk to go off. Say.
You see what happened was this: there was an attempted break-out. Stephen L Jones and his followers ran out the great big white doors of their pretty little white church, guns a-blazing.
The police dropped their hotdogs and tangerines and fired back.
It was hell.
The twenty-six Stephen L Jones followers surged towards the police cars, parked across the drive, firing their weapons from their hips, screaming and praising the Lord. Stephen L Jones, bible in hand, pushed his followers on from behind.
By the time they had got half-way down the little winding drive, most were dead amid the thirteen or so species of wild flowers that no one had counted.
By the time they had reached the police line, only one follower of the Ostrich preacher was alive.

She was alive because no one would shoot at her.

A funny thing happened that day in Orange City when the followers of the Ostrich preacher tried to break out of the siege. A bullet fired by one side hit a bullet fired by the other. They met in mid air, decided to forget their differences and kissed, sort of dissolving into each other. The odds for something like that must be a billion to one. But it happened.

At least twice. Once in Orange City during the siege of the Riverside Church in 1998 and once at the battle of Gettysburg in 1863.

Billy Adams the entrepreneur found the copulating bullets amid the wild flowers and put them in the museum of the Riverside Siege, which he set up in an abandoned school just outside of Orange City.
Billy Adams also somehow managed to get hold of a Chinese rifle used by the Riverside faithful that day. No one knew how he did it.

Policemen just lowered their guns. The woman was armed with a Chinese assault rifle built when China was officially atheist and the largest producer of soybeans in the world. The rifle was modelled on the Soviet AK47 and had been used for a time by the IRA. It was accurate when fired in single shots but was difficult to control on automatic. The woman fired on full automatic or "rock and roll" mode. The reason policemen lowered their weapons was because the woman had strapped her three babies to her body.

In the end she killed four policemen and wounded ten before Sergeant S Gillham fired six rounds at her. Three of the rounds hit the woman, one missed altogether. One of the bullets hit one of the babies in the head and the baby, whose first name was Elgia, died instantly. The other bullet punctured another baby's lung. The wound made a ssssssssss noise as the baby's right lung collapsed. That baby, whose first name was Robert, later died in an air ambulance.

Gettysburg is in south Pennsylvania and was well known in 1998 as a centre for the production of paper cartons. James Mease had written in 1804 that soybeans would do well in the climate of southern Pennsylvania.

Sergeant S Gillham had four children. His wife was shopping in one of the two local supermarkets at the time of the attempted break-out. Sergeant S Gillham died in his sleep four years later. His last words mumbled in his sleep were these: "be careful out there."

The woman who strapped her three babies to her body's name was Mary Malroy and she died following the orders of a man who claimed to be God's messenger etc etc.

Was he?
Who knows?

China was at one point the largest producer of porcelain in the world.

I

I climbed Mount Everest 80,000 years ago. I am a supermarket trolley. Hallo-ha.

On November 3rd 2022, at 11.30 am, in Chelmsford, I, RT32, was produced. I was the 100,001st trolley off the production line and a Scorpio. The celebrations for the 100,000th model had finished by the time I was activated. The 100,000th model had a green plaque welded on to it.
I had a faulty front wheel that had to be replaced.

After I rolled off the production line I was greeted by a technician with a friendly face.
She tapped me on my push-bar and said the first words I ever heard.
"Who's a pretty boy then?"
Which was how I discovered, or rather was allocated, my sexuality.

The technician modified my voice synthesiser accordingly.

Why argue, I thought.

For a time I considered the technician with the friendly face a mother of sorts. We all did I suppose. Later I would hold the irrational belief that Ron and Anne Jenkins were my real parents. I would visit them in the Shetland Isles. It was a very tense occasion. I told them about my work at the supermarket and they denied all knowledge of me.

Of course some time after that I would have a very clear idea of who my father was; George Milles Jr, the wealthiest man ever born.

The technician who gave me my sex and tapped me on my push-bar was Kitty Fitzgerald. She earned £9.50 an hour in 2022. She was not incredibly enthusiastic about my existence. She said "Who's a pretty boy then?" casually, as if she was disinterested. And she probably was.

The reason why Kitty Fitzgerald was so apathetic towards me and the other fifty or so trolleys in her care at that time was due to the fact that three weeks earlier she had come home to find her husband having sex with the family vacuum cleaner.

They got a divorce and she never spoke to the vacuum cleaner again.

Now I don't blame the corporation for letting an emotionally unstable person near young and highly impressionable supermarket trolleys. After all, how were they supposed to know?
I also hold no grudge against the vacuum cleaner, which was after all just doing its job.

Anyway, my technician, poor Kitty Fitzgerald, never consciously (as far as I am aware) acted spitefully towards us. She just couldn't show us any warmth – it is my experience that technicians who find their husbands having sex with the family vacuum cleaner can't.

This is how I climbed Mount Everest: Slowly.

2

Memories of my time with the other newly created trolleys are crystal clear, thanks to my near faultless memory system. The computer firm that designed it had a slogan about the ZEml2000 Nexus, the official name for my memory, which was this:

"It's so good it will even remember events it wasn't at."

I can't vouch for that claim, of course.
We were a talkative bunch. Mostly we repeated what Kitty had said to us over and over again.
"Who's a pretty boy then? Who's a pretty boy then?" etc etc.
Or we would read out loud the various words taped to the walls

of the kindergarten-cum-repair pit we were taken to directly after production.
"Customer" "Till" "Money" "Poultry" etc etc.
I was something of a late developer. I got my first words out about two minutes after the first trolleys did. My first words were "Frozen meat section".
By this stage it had become increasingly obvious that some of us had some major errors in either our software or hardware.
Some trolleys were saying everything Kitty had told them backwards. Others waved their manipulator claws about madly, while the odd one or two drove around erratically, colliding into better functioning trolleys.
It was, I remember, a bit alarming.
Technicians removed those erratic individuals. Some came back to the kindergarten after only a few hours; others were never heard of again.

And then we were told about the concept of sleep.
Kitty explained that we all had to go to sleep so that all the new data we had absorbed could be assimilated into our infinity chips.
She told us she was going to switch us all off.
Some trolleys started to protest.
Why argue, I thought.

Kitty Fitzgerald told us not to be afraid of the "off."

That was when some of us started crying. Some of us kept on crying all the way to the point when she flipped us off as she moved amongst us saying "It will be alright," looking at her nails as she did so.

It was only natural to cry.

I prayed.

I have loved three women. One was Kitty Fitzgerald, one was 1898 and one was Mrs Lindo. 1898 was a check-out machine.

I would visit Kitty Fitzgerald in 2025 but she would refuse to let me into her flat. I was with a Ding Dong 7 at the time. Kitty Fitzgerald was convinced that I was a Jehovah's Witness and she was right, I was.

1898 was the year that Maurice Wilson was born in Bradford, Yorkshire, the son of a jumper manufacturer. During World War One he was shot twice by a German machine gun in the third battle of Ypres.
One bullet hit his arm, the other bullet punctured his lung. The wound made a ssssssssss noise as his right lung collapsed. Blood bubbled over his uniform.

He got better.

The inventor of the machine gun, Dr Richard Gatling, also invented a machine for sowing rice, and it was from this rice-sowing machine that he got the idea for the machine-gun.

Maurice Wilson came to believe that if you fast for thirty-five days, subsisting on sips of water, and pray to God, then you could do anything.

He attempted to climb Mount Everest to publicise this belief. He was a nut.

Kitty Fitzgerald would be brutally murdered during the Great Mania by her electric toothbrush. I have been to her grave three times. Hallo-ha.
This is what it says on George Milles Jr's grave, the wealthiest man ever:
"A state for dirty stories may be said to be inherent in the human animal."
George Moore (1888)

1888 was 1898's best friend. 1888 never approved of me even when I became a special representative of Pope John John.

My childhood was not all that long, about twelve hours not counting switch-off periods. That my youth was so short, is really not all that remarkable; some butterflies are born, grow up and die in the space of a special offer.

In the few moments between programming we were allowed to play. We played "Shoppers and Trolleys", where one trolley would pretend to be a human and push another trolley around in a

make-believe supermarket.
I didn't like the game much but I played it just the same.
I normally played the human pushing other trolleys around the room. It was not the preferred role; everyone wanted to be supermarket trolleys.
Which was a good thing really.

We were programmed with things the company, ShopALot, decided we should know; things like the time yogurt took to go off normally, how late ShopALot supermarkets stayed open, the history and interesting asides about products the supermarket stocked, human biology, human psychology, human humour, why people needed to buy things, why though we should never simply give people things without expecting them to pay and why if they did want to take things without paying we should always be polite. (I would later, for a short while, become a Marxist.)

Such programming took place using a direct-feed interface and in all lasted only six hours. Programming was an efficient way to fill our infinity chips with information and much more efficient than a lecture.
Although we did have one lecture, of a sort.

We had been told that shortly before we were due to leave for the supermarkets, we would be given a few words of support and advice from a high ranking member of the company.

We were very excited. The high ranking member of the company, whose name was Graham Shipton, earned £42 an hour at the time and was not married.

Maurice Wilson never married, though he had the names of his sweethearts on the small Union Jack he planned to place on the top of Mount Everest.
Maurice Wilson froze to death in his sleep at the base of a forty foot ice wall a fraction of the way up Mount Everest. Hallo-ha.

George Milles Jr had fourteen hundred wives. He called them all Sarah to avoid confusion.
Each night one of his fourteen hundred wives would be sent a

card inviting them to his bedroom.
There they would watch TV for a bit, eat popcorn and then make love.

George Milles Jr had three thousand children, all of whom he called Tom or Jane, depending on their sex, to avoid confusion.

This is what Graham Shipton, the high ranking member of ShopALot said to us in his lecture of sorts.

"Hi. Are you all comfortable? Obnoxious morning, isn't it? Looking forward to your future with us at ShopALot?

You know before I came to work here I had done a number of different jobs. I had accumulated a modest fortune in used boxes That's right, used boxes. I recycled them you know. Largest used boxes, cardboard mostly, recycler in the country. I was rolling in it. I had all the money a guy could use but there was something missing. I didn't know what I was supposed to do. And you know what? I still don't. My entire life is spent trying to convince myself that I am doing what I am supposed to do. That I am following "the plan", that I am fulfiling my purpose. Am I supposed to be telling you this now? Was I supposed to shave this morning? In my office I sit there and wonder whether I ought really to be in the office building across the road that make, I don't know what. Maybe I am meant to be there. Maybe that's my purpose. Maybe I'm not doing what I am supposed to do. Take my brother, he makes curtains, even makes the funny little rings. Maybe that's what I should be doing, making curtains. Let me tell you something; when I was a kid I wanted to be a dental technician more then anything else in the world, but something happened. An uncle took me for a ride in a hot-air balloon and I lost interest. I grew out of it I guess.

Now I just don't know. Not knowing your purpose is a terrible fate, believe me, it's a terrible thing.

You on the other hand, you spanking new supermarket trolleys, you have been blessed with a clearly defined, easily grasped purpose. You are and always will be supermarket trolleys. "The plan" of your entire lives is crystal clear. Your destinies are as predictable as can be. You have purpose. You have certainty. Security. Peace of mind. I'll admit it, this guy is jealous, sure. Who wouldn't be? Why I'd give everything to join you guys. But of course it isn't possible. I mean for one thing I can't carry as much as you, and well, there are other reasons I could think of, but I can still dream."

Then he told a joke. It was the first joke I ever heard.

Do you know what Edgar Malroy would have done had he heard that speech by Graham Shipton, the high ranking member of ShopALot?
Edgar Malroy would have dropped his pants.

3

"There was this man who worked in a Nuclear Power plant and every day he would leave the plant with a wheelbarrow full of rubbish.
The security guard at the gate became suspicious. Becoming suspicious was, after all, his job.

He watched the man who, every day, would leave the nuclear power plant with a pile of rubbish.
Then one day the security guard confronted the man and accused him of stealing.
The man confessed.

He had been stealing wheelbarrows."

Life, according to Graham Shipton, we would find, was like that.

Then Graham Shipton told us that he had a golden rule, a rule that would make our time on Earth more worthwhile.
His golden rule was this: always always always say to your customers when you meet them for the first time or when they leave, "hallo-ha."
He told us it was spelt "H-a-l-l-o – h-a."
He told us it was the Hawaiian word for "Hello" and "Goodbye."
That little expression was etched into our ZEml2000 Nexuses.

Mr Shipton made us say it out loud five times, then he had different trolleys do each of the sounds, then he divided us into two groups so that one group said "hallo" and the other group said

"ha". I was in the "ha" group.
Mr Shipton seemed as excited about this as we were.
He said he wanted to get one other thing clear – as far as any higher thoughts went, he advised against it. It had only got man into trouble.

I think Mr Shipton was something of a mystic.

Then he looked at his watch, waved at us enthusiastically and said that he thought he was supposed to be somewhere else, although he wasn't sure and left.
We all said "Hallo-ha."

Incidentally, I was for a period a mystical writer and wrote three mystical books, *The Circuit of Unknowing*, *Beans and Time* and *World Travel With The Consumer God*, all of which I have subsequently disowned. Hallo-ha.

Then my childhood came to an end. We were told by Kitty to wait for our names to be called out and then we were to leave the kindergarten.

Just before she read out the first name, Kitty Fitzgerald gave us all a piece of advice.
She told us to be careful out there.

When the first trolley had his name called out and promptly disappeared, we all said, "Hallo-ha."
We said "Hallo-ha" a lot that day.

Here is a passage from one of my books on mysticism:
"Whosoever has felt the reassuring unseen hand of God turn and direct him down the many and varied aisles of life will never knock over or even scratch the tins of sin. For such a person knows He that is the invisible customer. Whosoever has queued with God does not despair at the length of any queue, does not despair at one's sell-by date. God has infinite credit. God the all perfect never goes off. What are we but products in God's glorious store, this great and vaulted universe? Open twenty-four hours a day. We cannot hide from God, for he reads our bar-codes instantly.
Everything has its place and packaging. What is one bag of peanuts under the

floodlit gaze of God? Oh Lord we are your humble groceries!"
- ***The Circuit of Unknowing.***
One critic called it supermarket theology. It became something of a catch-phrase.
Most critics called it crap.

Edgar Malroy, quoting Oscar Wilde I believe, used to say of critics that they were like eunuchs in a brothel.
I have sometimes felt myself to be a eunuch in a brothel, a non-consumer in the consumer paradise of the supermarket.
One critic compared *The Circuit of Unknowing* to a passage in David Hume's final work, *Dialogues Concerning Natural Religion*, in which Hume, in order to illustrate the point that the universe could be just about anything we cared to imagine and more besides, said that it might be a ship or a giant cabbage.
Hume said that he castrated *Dialogues Concerning Natural Religion* of its nobler parts.

ShopALot, the chain of supermarkets I had been built by, had been created by Jonathan Rowley who had been born in 1898. Hallo-ha. He was not, nor to my knowledge did he ever become, a eunuch. To say his father, Jospef, was an enthusiastic ropemaker was to understate things. At the age of just nine months, Jonathan Rowley had been taught to twist strands of hemp, flax and animal gut. Before the age of two he graduated to wire.
At the age of four Jonathan Rowley wasn't allowed to go to bed until he had made his shoelaces for the next day.
In the morning he would find himself tied up by his father. Once he had freed himself Jonathan had to turn the rope into a rope-ladder to climb down from his bed which Jospef had suspended from the ceiling. "It got really tedious," Jonathan recalled once.

Edgar Malroy said once that it was possible that the universe was shaped like a vagina.

Jonathan's mother spent twenty years of her life with a piece of greasy rope tied around her waist because she never learned how to undo a reef knot, and because Jospef, so disgusted with her roping ignorance, refused to undo it. He also forbad Jonathan

from helping his poor mother.
Jospef allowed only spaghetti and noodles to be eaten in his house. Even then Jospef would allow members of his family to put spaghetti or noodles in their mouths only if they had been tied in interesting knots beforehand, and the particular knots named correctly. Dinner in the Rowley household was a laborious affair.
On weekends Jospef would take his son to the park and teach him to lasso ducks and small children.
"Always carry a length of rope, Jonathan, a length of rope saved my life many times. A piece of rope is a man's best friend, Jonathan."
Jonathan's father recommended a length of rope six yards long.
As Jonathan grew up his father's obsession became worse. Jonathan became his father's official apprentice at fourteen and helped make ropes for Russian tight-rope walkers, a growth industry at the time.
Though he became an especially skilled roper, Jonathan found the work tiresome.

In 1913 Jonathan's father started to communicate with his family by manipulating a length of rope, twisting it into the shapes of letters.
A year later his father was communicating exclusively with his piece of rope.
Something in Jonathan snapped. After untying his mother he left home and joined the Royal Flying Corps where he made rope for observation balloons.

Spaghetti means little strings in Italian.

Jonathan returned to London in 1920. Unable to get an office job in the city and determined to avoid the rope business, he bought a hundred tins of condensed milk.
He sold them on the street. On his first day he made a profit of six pence. Jonathan soon discovered his natural ability for selling: self-confidence, cheek, a loud voice and a body odour problem.

Jonathan ventured into the wholesale business, buying six tonnes of uncut soap off a ship from Rotterdam.
But it rained and the massive block of soap slipped over the side of the ship.

A crane was used to try and retrieve the soap from the bottom of the Thames. Sixteen times Jonathan watched the giant bar be brought to the surface, only to slip from the crane's grip and plunge into the water again.
"I had two grand running on that bar of soap. The money went up in bubbles," recalled Jonathan Rowley.

During the Middle Ages soap production in Europe virtually ceased altogether, because the Church warned of the evils of exposing the flesh.

Subsequent investments proved more successful. In 1922 Jonathan bought into popcorn.
In 1930 he opened his first retail store in Watling Avenue, in East London. This was immediately followed by one in Green Lanes.
In 1923 Jonathan met his wife – she was having difficulty tying her bonnet. Her name was Sarah McGuire. It was a whirlwind romance. It had lasted the ten minutes it had taken them to find a church. They had two children. Hallo-ha.

4

By 2022 there were 38 different brands of popcorn in any branch of ShopALot.
Aztec priests used to wear amulets of stringed popcorn in religious ceremonies. They really did.
American Indians were said to have brought bags of popcorn to the Plymouth Pilgrims for their Thanksgiving dinner in 1621.

Edgar Malroy used to say that the Old World should celebrate Thanksgiving too, because we had got rid of so many religious nuts when the American colonies were set up.
Towards the end, Edgar Malroy confessed to me a great fear. Edgar Malroy's fear was that the first Aliens to visit Earth might be missionaries. This worried him a lot apparently.

One brand of popcorn we had on sale in the supermarket, was called Popecorn and was distributed by the Vatican.
The information on the packet stated that each piece of Poped corn had been individually coated in sugar and blessed by a Bishop.

It also said on the packet that Popecorn could be eaten as a snack anywhere but was best eaten when watching one of Pope John John's many films.

In 2022 an airplane carrying catholic missionaries and the last Panda Bear in the world crashed in the Brazilian jungle. Father Philips, stranded in the jungle for six weeks, used Popecorn as a substitute for wafers during mass.

The ten thousand wafers on board the plane had been burnt to a crisp.

Father Philips and his fellow missionaries were discovered eventually and told the world their harrowing story.
The boys in the Vatican saw it as an advertising coup and sales of Popecorn doubled.

In 2022 300 million pounds of popcorn were popped world wide.

As his company grew, Jonathan Rowley acquired a number of horse vans, these horse vans were unusual in that they didn't use reins. Jonathan had forbidden them.
Just as he had forbidden the use of string to wrap up items. A leg of lamb, say, was wrapped up in thick waxy paper which would slowly unwrap itself.
Jonathan Rowley's unconventional solution to this problem was to employing re-wrappers.

In 1965 Jonathan Rowley was awarded an honorary degree by the University of London. His acceptance speech lasted over an hour and focused on cold store technologies.
At the ceremony the vice chancellor expressed the hope that some graduates would soon be leaving the planet.
Jonathan Rowley had his degree framed.

I have a degree in Agnosticism. I also had it framed. Its in a bad shape now. Its been hit by mirco-meteorites.
Most have been the size of garden peas.

In 1928 Jonathan Rowley acquired four new shops on the outskirts of London just before he went on holiday with his wife and

children to Easter Island.
While on the island Jonathan worked on a paper which he never finished, in which he tried to show that the giant statues found on Easter Island could have been put in place without the use of fibres of any kind.

George Milles Jr, the inventor of the infinity chip and the wealthiest man ever to live, was buried on Easter Island, along with six hundred of his favourite wives. Hallo-ha

Edgar Malroy has a grave although hardly anything of his body was ever found. The scientists said if you picked a pile of gravel within the blast zone there would probably be an atom or two that had previously been part of Edgar Malroy.
So that is what I did.
Edgar Malroy's epitaph reads:

Not sleeping but dead.

The same inscription was put on the graves of other the six thousand of Scepticism Inc. that perished that day from Red Mercury.

Edgar Malroy always misspelt Scepticism. Whenever I pointed this out to him, he would say, "How do you know?"

By 1932 Jonathan Rowley had a hundred stores in the London area.
In 1934 Graham brought his brother in law Hyman onto the board as executive director.
Hyman was a south American tree frog specialist.

Meanwhile Jonathan Rowley's marriage broke up, as Sarah Rowley, experiencing a new sexual freedom, confessed to her husband that she was a bondage freak.

Edgar Malroy fell in Love in 2032. Just like that.
He asked me once whether it was possible to disagree with someone violently, absolutely, to consider them immoral and nuts and yet still love them.
I told him I thought it was a long shot.

Music Practice

Claire Hamburger

Claire Hamburger was born in London in 1957 and now lives in Lowestoft, Suffolk. She has two daughters and has trained as a painter. She has been employed in many jobs, including teaching Creative Writing. She has been published in various poetry magazines and by *Sheba Feminist Publishers*. The following is an extract from a novel in progress.

Claire Hamburger

Music Practice

Leah

We are looking for homes for people with holes in their hearts.
It is not a gesture of charity.
When we were dutiful daughters, we thought that charity was love.
Now we know it is far from love.
Live Aid, Band Aid. Stick a plaster on a festering wound.
Later, we tried to pull it off,
 surprised the wound was more infected than ever.
The more we tried to wrench the plaster off,
 the more pain we caused.
Skin. Blood. Pus.
We reached the bone.
Now we are searching for air, for light, for space.
Two balls against a wall.
Pirouetting in a circular skirt.
Drum-roll of victory resounding through sweeping hills.
No more heads against a wall, pebble-dash marked out
 for being different.
There is heat in the air. Streets are shimmering.
A Hackneyed ghetto-blaster thumping out a bass line.
Sea gulls screeching, people dancing ska at a carnival.
Babies bash with wooden spoons on dustbin lids.
We will run through a field, lifting up our skirts.
We will run through glass but remember not to tread on it,
 remember not to look through dazzling diamonds in the sun,
 dazzling dreams that churn.

There will be no arguments, storms, thumpings
In our heads. At our doors.
We will not fear the thumping at the door.
We will ask "Are you in our house?"
We will know whether to let you in.
With obsessive meditation, strident striving on a theme,
  we will break the glass and cross the room.
Our flying, billowing hands will squat in self absorption
  on piano keys
Playing melodies that jar.
Chords that harmonise.
Perfect cadences.

We will find our mothers, the place where we were born, our grandmother's ballet classes where we will whirl in a ball-room filled with mirrors, spring garden breathing magnolia.We will hug a tree; bury our heads in flowers, find a hiding place and perfect the art of hiding.

We will remember the boy without an outer layer of skin who tried to play a triangle, the metal sticking to his fingers, his head askew, off-beat with pain. That boy without skin, who died of exposure.

There's games some of us can't play, won't play,
Worlds we can't enter, won't enter.
But a call in the morning can waken a village
  from insolent slumber.
Can lift mountains. Can send birds soaring.
We will paint a landscape onto silk, delicate, poised...
Space.
Air.
Two balls against a wall.
We will bear witnesses.

You, Jocelyn
Are you going to find your mother, Jocelyn? Did *she* name you "Jocelyn" or did *they*? Does the colour of your lips, your hair, your skin, resemble hers? Your shape? Your aura? Do you love and hate the

same things, the same people, the same places?

The sky was grey that November the Fifth, wasn't it? The rain hadn't ceased beating against the cracked walls all day in that East End community, street, estate, flat where you could be *born and bred* and never know what a community is. You stooped over the bath you'd scrubbed clean only hours before, to retch and vomit, your throat a cheese-grater gullet, things you'd put in your mouth, things other people had put in your mouth, that you didn't think should be there. Your skin itched, didn't it? The effect of grime and decay, the grime and decay of the community and the grime and decay of other people's unwashed bodies creeping inwards towards your skin.

Your daughter, Amy, watched you retch, the door bolted to lock both you in and Dean out. She took her potty down from the low shelf next to the bath, stuck her tiny fingers down her throat, mimicking you and then she laughed.

In a frenzy of gut ache, saliva and shame you pulled her hands, hard, away from her mouth and attacked her with the plant spray, cool drops cascading down her warm cheeks and tickling her. She giggled as she caught the drops on her tongue. You turned the spray on yourself, forcing water into your sickly mouth, chasing Amy into the passageway finally, liquid flying everywhere

Dean was standing at the living-room door; a guard, hips jutting, keys dangling on his belt.

You imagined the worm wriggling behind his sparkling eyes and decided to ignore the purse of his thin lips.

"Why are you so fucking happy?" he'd asked while you were making breakfast, because you were singing.

You stopped singing. Your eyes were anxious as you dropped toast onto his plate and whispered, "I don't know." What you wanted to say was, "I've forgotten."

Fireworks night. *You knew there'd be fireworks, didn't you, Jocelyn?*

You knew that you, Dean and Amy would walk to the park; stand, penned-up against a fence with thousands of strangers, watching the execution, a man on a chair being set alight. You knew you'd watch intently as each part of his body dissolved, leaving only a skeleton of a chair, barely visible within the flames.

People were going to shout *ooh* and *aah* at the Catherine wheels pinned to trees, crane their necks to watch stars shoot across a blazing sky.

You thought Amy might scream with fear, turn her head away from the flames, cover her eyes, her ears, to escape the banging and the slow death of the stuffed man and you knew Dean would force her head back towards the execution. *Don't be a baby. A few fireworks won't hurt you.* And if Amy didn't stop screaming he'd lose his temper and shout, "Stop making that fucking racket."

Then he'd swill another can of beer, crush it beneath his feet with a boyish pride, and the three of you would walk home in silence, your muscles tightening with tension at every step nearer.

People would whisper behind you, *It's a nice family occasion, ain't it? Oh, don't they make a lovely couple and that pretty little girlie too?*

You'd want to turn round to them and tell them the truth. *I'm not going home to sit curled up on the sofa with him. I'm going out on the streets for him. What do you say to that, eh?*

You loved him once, didn't you? How he said he'd be Amy's dad, how he said he'd look after the both of you, how he made your body talk, an intimate conversation in touching, how you buried your hand, your head, in the mane of curly brown hair and thought he might be that shining knight you'd been waiting for?

As you cleaned up the mess from the plant spray under his sullen gaze you asked, "Shall I make the tea then?". He slumped back in his chair in the front room, eyes glued to the test card, bottles decorating the area around his feet and Amy almost rolling in them. She was singing to a book and staring at you with wistful eyes. You always hated that look, didn't you? Pleading, chocolate-box spaniels, starving children.

Your guilt pursued you. "What can I do? What can I do? it's all my fault, isn't it?"

You took Amy up in your arms, away from Dean's bottles,

hugging the breath out of her. But her body was rigid.

"Well, what are you waiting for, woman? Yeah, go on, make the bloody tea."

Dean didn't like you to relax, to have time to think. Thinking is a dangerous occupation for a gal like you, eh? "You are a working gal, ain't yer? Hot to trot, like," he joked sometimes, squeezing your bum as you walked past, working...

He was angry that day because you weren't paying attention to him. When you'd come back from work in the early hours you hadn't got into bed with him for his morning fuck. You'd sat in the front room, doodling pictures of the seascapes in your head.

You took Amy into the kitchen and she carried on humming. You took stock of the available food – a tin of beans, four slices of bread, two tea bags, a half pint of milk, a tin of custard powder, two bottles and four cans of beer, and a line of speed in the fridge.

It would have to be beans on toast again.

You peered out of the window at kids dismantling a car in the yard. One of them saw you and stuck his tongue out. The plants on the window ledge were dry. Your mouth was parched. You took the cracked china cup with bluebirds flying away from out of the sink and watered the cactus, in bloom, blood red. Then the fern. You brushed your face against it to feel its soft lushness.

Dean said houseplants were messy. He said Amy's pictures, and yours, should be put on a fire and burnt. "Tatty scribbles. What's the point of 'em? Don't they teach kids nothing these days? Bleeding waste of time..."

You thought, "I am messy. I am a tatty scribbler. I should be put on a bonfire and burnt."

In the kitchen you had sanctuary for mess and scribbles, the shimmer of celloes playing in a symphony on the radio you'd found in a skip and was stunned to find actually worked. The fern was spreading, blossoming in condensation, the walls constantly damp and, starting at the skirting board, fungus growing up them. Black, squashed spiders for the white witch. *You imagined yourself as the white witch, didn't you, Jocelyn?* You wanted to hold on to magic.

There was a woman who smiled at you, who lived across on the opposite block. You thought maybe she could join your coven, the black witch. "Bitch," Dean called her.

You'd sat down with Amy on your lap, doodling again – a petrified forest on a vast beach, two little figures.

"Jesus! What's that smell?" Dean yelled.

A scorching smell joined with the boozy, fag ash air. Another burnt saucepan. Another slap in the face. You listened to his footsteps. *Footsteps, heavy and insistent, have always frightened you, haven't they?* He had a hard-on, showing through his tight jeans. You couldn't help laughing and the next minute the saucepan was in his tattooed hand and he'd thrown it at you. It hit the side of your face.

Amy stared at the blood trickling down, sucking her thumb and rocking. You just carried on laughing, the room swimming, your skin as taut as cardboard. You couldn't remember who you'd been cooking for. Not for Amy. She'd just squash the beans between her fingers and flick them across the table. You never ate a meal anymore.

You stared out of the window, blood drying on your cheek, your laughter reduced to nothing, thinking about identical bricks, identical windows, identical paintwork; the lack of green, growing.

"I'll go and get some more beans," you murmured absently. "I expect the shop'll still be open."

"We ain't got no money, you stupid bitch. Forget the dinner."

Amy had run into the front room and curled up in the curtain, her hiding-place, and you thought how everything was hollow as you felt Dean's glare behind you.

You went into the front room, hoping to catch a glimpse of *enough blue sky to make a pair of sailor's trousers,* as you'd described it to Amy. You thought the rain might lift and fluffy, care-bear clouds might miraculously appear, even a rainbow you could show Amy. You opened the window wide, the sky calling you, rain cooling your sweating body, wetting your t-shirt and showing up your shrunken breasts with big, breast-feeding nipples. You turned back into the room, scooped Amy up under your arm, animated now. "There's a rainbow. Look, baby, a rainbow!" You saw the black witch wheeling her buggy across the yard. She had the kind of face that strikes a chord – tranquil, kind but not dead. You wanted to be like that, just like that, but you weren't.

Suddenly Dean was behind you, gripping your waist like a vice, pushing into you.

"Don't! Stop..."

Amy was limp in your arms, dangling out of the window. Everything was slippery to the touch. *All fall down. Bye bye baby. All fall down. Bye bye love, Bye bye happiness.*

The Blue Peter theme hummed merrily from somewhere in the background. You watched her fall, weightless, rapidly...and you saw slow motion, slow motion time...flying, flying, galloping...trying to find a way to catch her.

A muffled scream. Rain flecked with pink, red...A rag doll in the gutter below. You lay down in a pool of liquid, an insect left on its back to die. The ends of the curtains were hanging down outside the window making a flapping sound against the wall. Flip-flap, flip-flap.

A pounding on the door, the scent of urinals. Dean knelt in the middle of the room. You thought he might be praying but when you peered at his face you realised he was crying.

"I want to jump. I want to jump," you muttered, trying to get up but someone forced you down again. Did she fall or was she pushed? Can you fall through iron bars? Did you mean to drop her, Jocelyn?

Jocelyn

It's a way of life, living on the edge. You see, if I look back and inside, there's a whirlpool of dreams, what might have been choices. But I don't know if there were any choices, really. False hopes, maybe, head banging against an impenetrable wall, whirring noises. There was a kind of clarity just knowing how to stay alive.

If I look forward, outside, there's an abyss, what might be choices. But if I make the wrong one, I'll fall, die, things I think I want beyond my reach, so I'm in danger of toppling over when I try to grab them.

I keep saying I'm going to go away somewhere, sometime when I get out of here or there. I want to get out, get away from the edge but I'm paralysed, standing between...

What I hold inside me is Amy, her birth, a piece of knotty coral in a fantastic, ultramarine sea. That has never come adrift.

I don't know how to explain how much I wanted to jump and how much I couldn't. I lay in a white, dazzling box, a light beating down, burning my eyes if I opened them, drumming my eyelids if I shut them. I was curled up in a pink nylon dressing gown which wasn't mine. Dean used to buy me sexy underwear. I'd wear that in bed if I wore anything. Sweat poured profusely from under my armpits and I drooled at the mouth, a clamminess dousing me from the plastic protected mattress on which I curled foetally. I shivered, my limbs blue, numb, my belly swollen, obese, pregnant and aching, my hands tight around it.

I thought I might be in the labour ward but where was the machine with the zig-zag lines to measure the rise and fall of heartbeats? Where was the transparent box with tags, blue or pink, for the baby?

The box Amy was put in when she was born reminded me of tupperware. I was frightened that a lid would be placed on top of it, making it airtight to keep the freshness in. Tupperware parties. My adoptive mum used to hold them. I suggested that Ann Summers parties might be more exciting. She wasn't impressed.

"You'll come to a bad end, you will, Josie," she exclaimed, hitting me round the face with a tupperware box.

I made a list of all the things you could put in tupperware boxes, babies not included, and another list of things you could put in jars and label obsessively, as she did, to pass the time away.

I kept dreaming, while I lay in the dazzling box. I dreamt that I gave birth to a doll, one of those soft, stuffed bodies and lurid, hydrocephalic heads. It loomed into focus, a monstrous, immobile face on the scan, then faded away amidst vast waterfalls halfway down snow-capped mountains. My teeth clenched a bright red blanket and I buried myself, making a cave of ultra-red light. But it didn't stop the dreams from pursuing me.

A witch, wild-haired, towering, appeared out of a clumsy Edwardian wardrobe and I was a child, petrified that the night-light had burnt out, that the adults' voices downstairs had ceased. The witch fought with a woman I knew was my real mother, an angel with flowing, golden hair, dressed in a lacy, bleached, starched nightgown, blood from the scratches caused by the witch's claws spluttering over a dazzling bodice. The two women dissolved into one person. As I woke up, panting, I felt myself for blood, for claws, for golden hair.

In between the dreams were flashes of lucidity.

"Amy, where have they put you? Are you still alive? I can't move to come and find you. Wait until our ship comes home darling. Then we can sail away."

I lay there in the madhouse, a hollow carved out of my belly, a sandpit, a vast, water-logged hole. The jab of a spade was unmerciful, gouging me out. I clung to myself, held my nipples, twisted them with gripping, pincer fingers. There was still liquid in them, nourishment, gone from blue-white to yellow again. I licked it off my fingers. It was so sweet. Oh, Amy. So sweet. I pulled the curly hairs from around my cunt, one hair after another, to stop myself slipping, becoming the dark, the nothing I was afraid of.

I saw an image of Amy, smiling up at me from her cot in the morning, gurgling to her teddy bear, Baa, with a chewed-up ear. But when I re-entered her room, the cot was empty, dusty. Baa was on the floor with insects crawling over him. A row of animals on the chest of drawers stared at me intently with beady, sinister eyes. Amy's first pair of shoes, red patent leather, fell to the floor from a high shelf decorated with peeling transfers and the mobile of clowns made violent, jangling shadows on the wall.

Jars, rows of them. Good mothers made jam. Fairies lived

under the mulberry tree, underneath toadstools. It was simple once.

I made no jam for you, Amy. I wanted to climb in my mother's hair, full of light, Rapunzel's prince climbing up her hair. My hands wound through your hair, Amy, your tangles, and you pushed me away, wincing. Then I wanted to squash you into my fist, a ball of pink, gooey dough to fill my gaping mouth and yours, waiting...The tangles in your nest caught my hands, bound me to you so tightly that I couldn't let go. I wanted to give you trees, dazzling silver sky caught between branches of sweet magnolia but all I gave you were ghosts. Ghosts up draughty, graffiti-covered stairs which I tried to fly down so that the ghosts couldn't catch up with me and stab me in the back. I wasn't fast enough to fly, as you do in a dream, jumping from the top of a tall flight of stairs, air churning through your body as you land effortlessly.

A blind woman ghost on icy nights shuffled with soft footsteps in woollen slippers, her stick gently tapping against walls, stairwells, corridors. She was a lullaby, whispering the silence, protecting mothers from nightmares.

"I could never give you enough."

I only wanted Amy to be released from the tower, the concrete, the grey, a wordless brutality. I thought I could send her soaring, like the bluebird on the chipped cup I filled with water for watering my plants.

Blues (Later)

A Salvation Army hostel takes Jocelyn in, a frozen chicken, for Christmas. She plucks her own feathers , borrowing a man's razor after he's told her his life story over a bowl of lukewarm chicken soup. Then she's shaved her head, leaving a sea of matted hair in which she buries her hand before sweeping it up into a carrier bag.

"A woman's glory is her hair," her adoptive dad used to remind her. Jocelyn doesn't want a woman's glory. She has tried to starve the woman out of herself. Now she tries to eat the soup, dished out to her from a witch's cauldron, in her newly-born hairless state.

She asks to borrow clothes and is given a man's tweed jacket, a white skirt, some baggy blue trousers, from a bin bag. They accept her robes in exchange, smiling warily. She says, "Burn them if you like."

They are afraid of her, perhaps more afraid of her now that her veil has been lifted, her bald head and her face exposed for the first time. She wants to get her head tattooed when the shops open again after Christmas.

She sits in front of the bowl of soup, waiting for a lull in activity. There is something she must do.

•

Jocelyn uses the razor to open a "Crisis at Christmas" box at Reception whilst Reception is unattended due to a crisis, a fight between two hotel dwellers. She justifies it to herself like this. "I am a crisis, yes, I am a crisis at Christmas." It's a song, a 12 bar blues. She sings it to herself as she walks out into the street to catch the January sales which always start in December.

Jocelyn went to see the lights in Regent Street, the decorations in Hamleys when she was small. They said she could choose a toy. She wanted a Sasha doll all dressed up in a '60s mini-skirt, Twiggy-shaped body, long, black, sleek, malleable hair, hazel eyes and Latin skin – but Sasha, they said, was too expensive and *foreign*. She had cried, sitting on the floor of the doll department, clutching a Sasha doll which she had snatched off the shelf.

They bought her a toy spaniel. She swapped it for a bag of marbles with another kid in the street a few days later, after cutting the label off. It was the label that mattered. She'd figured that one out.

Today, in Hamleys, the shop assistants call her "Sir", looking at her quizzically and smirking behind their hands. She is not deterred.

"I want a musical box, a merry-go-round."

She counts out the payment three times. There is a long queue behind her at the counter. The shop assistants exchange glances. The song in the box is *The Entertainer*. Horses gallop round on their carousel.

"I want it gift-wrapped," she says.

"Of course, Sir. All our toys can be gift-wrapped at no extra charge."

She hugs the box in silvery paper with a golden bow and goes in search of a phone box. Most public phone boxes, she knows, no longer contain phone directories and, if they do, half the pages are torn out or burnt. There is a phone box in the basement of Hamleys. It has an array of directories. She thumbs through it, finding Dean's new address easily. She slumps down, takes the leftover change from her pocket and counts it. Still ten pounds left. Enough for a return ticket to Essex suburbia with its pointed roofed houses, double garages and garden gnomes, the stuff her nightmare cities are made of.

When she gets outside it's beginning to rain. She tucks the box inside her jacket and goes in Virgin Records to ask for a carrier bag. The nothing time between Christmas and New Year. No snow. Does that mean Father Christmas doesn't exist? No snowflakes, no sledge. Jocelyn rattles the carrier bag. There is a present, weighing heavily.

She takes the tube to Liverpool Street. It's busy with Christmas travellers but the commuter train she boards is deserted. She picks up an abandoned newspaper and hides behind it. She hasn't been out of London for years. What an adventure! There are fields among the sprawl and even a horse or two. She wants to shout, "Look, look. A horse, mummy!" but she doesn't.

There is something she has to do.

Yes. As she has dreamt, so the tidy drabness of the place hems her in so that she has to run, a fox pursued by hounds in alien, exposed territory. She panics, losing her way for a while, until, miraculously, her sense of direction returns and she finds herself in the right street. Burning curiosity, naughtiness, wistful longing. She stops to catch her breath, leans against a clipped hedge.

She remembers playing Peeping Tom through summer evenings while other kids catapulted stones at greenhouses or played kiss-chase in the abandoned tennis club hut near the air-raid shelter at the sports field. In her sneakers, she sneaked around the posh houses, scrambling up high walls to stare.

The grass is always greener.

The grass in the gardens of the posh houses was vividly green. Children played in the gardens, real gardens with climbing frames, fish ponds, swaying trees; daisied, neatly defined lawns; daddy with a sprinkler and mummy carrying strawberries and cream, freshly baked cake and freshly squeezed lemonade down towards the garden table, softly calling, "Tea-time, darlings."

Jocelyn crouched on the wall, behind creeping ivy, watching, listening, smelling newly mown grass and cake. The family sat round the table, munching contentedly. It seemed so peaceful, so simple.

When she got bored she'd go round to the front of the house, peering through the thick velvet curtains into the pristine living room with fake chandeliers, chintz suite and highly polished coffee table, antique sideboards with cut-glass decanters glittering, Persian rugs and, oh Christ, a whole shelf of china dolls and Sasha dolls, boys and girls, all staring at her.

She'd start to shiver, a dull cold creeping, although the weather was hot. The daddy and mummy in the room arguing, not loudly. Masked expressions of anger, bitterness, of love, an unbroken politeness, an unbearable coldness which she wanted to break into, snap with one quick movement of her fist.

The other end of the street, her end of the street, was different. Mansion blocks, the first high-rise, broken bikes and bits of cars, discarded johnnies and glue tubes. It wasn't so exciting sneaking round there. Mums with ironing, tins of Heinz baby foods, a toddler getting in the way, dads tinkering with motorbike parts or sitting in front of the telly.

Jocelyn leans against the hedge, her stomach rumbling. She bites her fingernails.

Once in a while, the table at home had groaned with food, at Christmas, when guests came, but mostly she was shouted at if she ate more than one piece of fruit a day or asked for a second helping. When guests came she would be silent, silenced, gradually sinking right under the table and away.

"Eat up your dinner," her adoptive mother implored weakly sometimes, under her husband's hostile glare. "Children in India are starving." She would eat up everything on her plate, no matter how much she hated it, picturing big, pleading, fly-ridden eyes and swollen bellies, as the food regurgitated in her throat. She was afraid of being like those starving children, pitied, dehumanised, and then, she was sure, ignored. "We only adopted you out of charity," her adoptive sister used to goad her during an argument.

Sasha dolls were foreign, starving children in India were foreign, the black men hanging around on street corners were foreign. "Be careful of them. They're not the same as us," her adoptive parents used to warn when she went off by herself, skipping along in clashing violet, magenta, navy and sky blue shades of skimpy jumpers and hot pants.

The black men, leaning against railings, called out *Hey, purple girl, blue girl, cheer up. It might never happen!* or *Come on spider legs, let me warm your blues away* and she'd think about it and wonder what they'd do if she stopped and smiled at them or let them put their brown arms around her. Would they be the same or different? The same as what? She wasn't the same as anyone else. She was different.

"Not the same as us?" she'd asked when her parents warned her. "Who's us?" But her parents hadn't answered.

Jocelyn has bitten each nail in turn. There's something she has to do now.

She finds a huge oak tree opposite the right house. She hugs it, hidden from view. She digs her sore nails into the mossy bark, begins to rip pieces off.

The door of Dean's house is opened and he comes out, wearing a tight suit with a sheen. Jocelyn giggles. He opens the boot of his shiny Ford Escort. It has a baby seat and a toy soporific rabbit in a hammock at the back. A few seconds later his woman joins him, blonde, petite, neat. Their heads meet as they search the boot for something. He strokes her hair. She pecks him on the cheek. She is wearing pink and white fluffy rabbit slippers. He passes something to his woman and she turns back to the house. He gets in the car, revs the engine and drives off.

Jocelyn's legs ache, nearly give way. Wait, she thinks, wait. She prays for the door to open again, for Amy to come rushing out and find her, embrace her behind the tree, play "Beep-bo." But when the door opens again and a child appears, cautiously peering out, Jocelyn takes a moment to recognise her. She remains in her hiding-place, hands sweating as she pushes them deep inside her pockets, letting the present fall to the ground, spill out of it's bag into the muddy mass of earth and roots.

Amy is much taller, much thinner now, her face long and peaky. A dog passes the gate and pees against it. They both watch it, Amy with more concentration than Jocelyn. The door moves slightly and Jocelyn, thinking that Amy is going back inside, comes out of her hiding-place. Amy opens the door wider, comes out onto the step and stares straight at her mother. She shouts back into the house. Jocelyn retreats behind the tree. A squirrel runs past her. She manages to pick up the present, wipe it on her trousers. She used to think she could make herself invisible if she thought it hard enough. Today she wishes it but knows it won't happen.

Dean's woman shouts back at Amy and they both come to the door, Amy gesticulating wildly. The woman shrugs and returns inside. Jocelyn can hear the faint wail of a baby in the background. She'd guessed they'd have another child by now. He'd pressurised Jocelyn to have one for him until she'd got sterilised after Amy. He hadn't been pleased about that, not pleased at all.

"Will she come across the road?" Jocelyn asks herself, her breath shallow, beads of liquid running down her armpits, her legs, her forehead. Please don't run across the road. Please do run across the road and let me take you...but there is nowhere to take you. There's nowhere to take me!

Amy is at the gate, surveying the tree, talking to herself. She hesitates, turns back to look through the doorway, begins to walk, but then a buggy is pushed out of the house, the woman's hands firm as she holds the buggy still on the left and grabs

Amy roughly with the right.

"Where do yer think you're going, young lady?"

Amy doesn't reply. She takes hold of the buggy and they walk down the road. Jocelyn's eyes follow their movements and Amy turns back once to stare.

Jocelyn rubs her fingers on her head, forgetting she has no hair to pull, to restrain herself from running after them.

"Keep a picture in your head," she murmurs as they turn the corner. "Now..." She darts over the road, lays the present down next to three empty milk bottles on the step. She looks at it. There is no name on it. Hastily she picks up a sharp stone and scratches the word "Amy" over the beautiful silver wrapping, tearing it, ruining its sophistication. She feels like a ghost with no hair who can't smile.

She walks away from Dean's house in the opposite direction from her daughter. She is satisfied that she has done something. "Something" is important, significant, whatever the "something" is.

Jocelyn gets back on the train, considering where she will sleep tonight.

On the Steps of Lalita Ghat

Jim Gleeson

Jim Gleeson was born in Manchester in 1972 and studied English at Jesus College, Cambridge. Awarded the Harper-Wood studentship for creative writing, he travelled for a year before coming to UEA. He has completed both a collection of stories and short screenplays in a Magic Realist mode.

Jim Gleeson

On the Steps of Lalita Ghat

Under the vertical sun, splashing down through whitewashed arches, Will stares at the profiled face of the woman he is conscious of having once been familiar with. To be more exact, he is on the staircase of the Hotel de Paris, Varanasi, and the woman in question is hanging from his arm. Not literally hanging, of course, since she is perfectly capable of walking on her own two feet and is, if the truth be known, undoubtedly the steadier. But hanging is the word Will finally settles upon as he hovers between this step and the next, one foot suspended in space, hanging for dear life over the edge of a precipice.

Justifiably uneasy, he glances up at the remaining nine steps, which the woman, having broken free of his arm, has just covered in a flurry of anklets and nail varnish. If it comes down to the issue of perspective, and it invariably does, then the himalayan dimensions of the billowing staircase must be a fallacy of his perception, spectacles notwithstanding; so that, bearing this focal adjustment always in mind, Will bounds up the final five steps almost in one go.

At the top he is embraced by the woman he half-remembers from somewhere, either in the recent or distant past, and regarded by a cleaner through an open doorway, bent over a mattress blotched red with mosquitoes. Their eyes meet for a second, then the cleaner's dart up the length of the door hinge, chasing the tail of a gecko.

Leaving the woman to fumble with the key in its lock, Will watches their reflection in a full length mirror to reassure himself of his, of their normality. His appearance – leather Jesus sandals, white cotton trousers, fake Raybans – is typical. The woman beside him in pink pyjamas and silk shirt could easily be mistaken for his lover or wife. She is tall (taller than Will) with bobbed brown hair and a long neck. He can see her mouth moving; she is telling him something. Now the mouth stops and she frowns at him, waiting for his reply.

"I'm sorry. What was that?"

It shocks him to hear his own voice answering, unmistakably his, but as if emerging through several metres of water, which leaves the words in their clear shape only momentarily, before bubbles envelop them.

He is pulled by his collar into a room fractionally larger than a single bed. The loose sheets and stray underwear, specifically Will's boxer shorts (whose appearance he is tempted to treat as the offspring of an elaborate fantasy), record the presence of lovers. Now that he has stepped into her territory he starts to recognise things about her. They are pressed together by the doorway, and his eyes roam over her dolphin-shaped ear-rings (he remembers the emerald dangling from its tail and the pearls that were its eyes), around the ridge of the whorl of her right ear and down toward the shadow at the root of it. She is still talking, but he has stopped straining to catch the words.

Will sits down on the armchair by the window. Down on Chaitgani Marg the traffic has come to a standstill. A cow in a cloud of dust has settled in the middle, forcing trucks, taxis and rickshaws into two bottlenecks either side of it. He can hear sirens in the distance, and sees a jeep passing the train station with a monkey swinging from its roll bar. A massive police operation is under way, in which he remembers himself to be implicated, through a bland conspiracy of chance.

When he looks back to the woman, she is huddled over the desk, heating resin by candle flame and crumbling it into a mound of tobacco. The action familiarises her. They shared a boat trip across the Ganges at dawn. She'd told him her name, which he instantly forgot. They were both travelling alone. One afternoon, on the deserted cricket fields at Benares Hindu

University, they smoked themselves into oblivion. Maybe he is sleeping with her? That would account for the bedding. He remembers a meal with Kingfisher beer brought to their table in tea pots and lizard-shaped bread rolls; then stumbling back to her room.

"Where've you been all morning? I went to the Hotel Buddha to look for you."

Once again he is conscious of having to respond in an alien voice.

"I found a dead body. A woman's."

"What!" She has leapt up and is poking him in the ribs. He wants to fasten his mouth on her lips as she blows smoke through the window. She is as distinct to him as if he had run his hands over her body.

"Very funny."

Part of him wants to argue with her, to insist, describe the position of the boat and her feet protruding (as if someone had dropped it on her from a large height), all those rupees in her purse. But an immense lassitude creeps over him. He has been walking several miles at high altitude with a heavy backpack. His mind is racing with all the events of the early morning. It is all he can do to reach out and clasp the joint. Soon the voices from the Marg below become part of the fan's movement – and gradually Will feels himself being carried, then pulled back, into sleep.

From the centre of the stopped fan above his head an eye fixes him for an instant, then flicks shut. He leans up to finger the cap, but as he approaches the fan it begins to rotate. Daylight threatens through the latticed air vent, awakening him to a different bed on the dawn of the same day. He has little to look forward to – only a bureaucratic vortex of embassies and giro transferrals. The borrowed seconds of his wristwatch tick into six fifteen.

Through the key hole of the door he watches three men peer over the banister onto the floor below. The sound of a shower suggests they are spying on a woman. Beyond them, the sky's dark grey is rapidly lightening.

The room is too small. Most of his clothes have tumbled onto the floor during the night. Those that haven't need laundering, but he can't afford a dhobi wallah, even at five rupees a garment. On the bedside table the first two pages of an unfinished letter quiver in a draft from the air vent. As he scrunches them up and throws them across the room, the paper transmutes into a white dove that wheels upward through the window above the door. He rushes after it, but the bird has already flown far away, past the lime outwalls of the Hotel Buddha, over the street sleepers of Godaulia and out across the Ganges and the plains of Uttar Pradesh. Will has never felt more lonely.

He lights the last third of a roll-up and thumbs through his passport – a global patchwork of stamps, Caracas, Harare, Denpasar, Nairobi, and the smudged green ink of his Indian tourist Visa, its date of expiry (now two months old) unhelpfully legible. He remembers their arrival at Dum Dum eight months ago. The first thing they noticed, the smell, like being in a cavern, the walls stale and dripping. A whole continent spread before them: sandstone palaces of Rajasthan, house boats on Dal Lake, palm-fringed backwaters between Quilon and Allepey. They had all the time, and most of the money, in the world.

When Will steps onto the hotel roof he imagines he can smell rain, and it springs to his mind that he would like nothing better than to get soaked to the bone, walking on and on through the tumbling bazaars of the city's old quarter, his skin clasped by wet fabric, as the streams run down Dasaswamedh Road and the waters swamp up to the temples. In the reception, the young waiter is stretched out on a Persian rug, wrapped in a sheet which squirms and pulsates over the sleeping body. Will is tempted to lift it a little. He has an horripilating vision of cockroaches swarming over the belly, but as soon as his fingers touch it, the twitching stops. The boy moans in his sleep and turns his back on Will, who sneaks out under the arch of the reception.

For the first time in eight months he has no money for a

rickshaw. Umej badgers him as soon as he steps onto Chaitgani Marg but he waves him on.

"Special rate Mr. William, sir." Umej spreads out an open palm. "Only five today."

Will shrugs, points at his pockets, pulls their lining inside out and continues walking. Birds come squawking out of the south east from the old city, dragging their black bellies across the horizon. The street is unnaturally quiet. It is the sort of street that should never be this quiet. It is intended for bustle, for the sweaty cries and elbows of the many, and in its present emptiness what remains bulks more threateningly: the carcass of a donkey, or the scarlet spattering of pan (as if the streets themselves were tubercular) or the sump and surge of the sewers bubbling up through cracks in the concrete. Will has seen this street at this time on several occasions, but what is it in the air – a smell, a colour – that makes him step uneasily?

Shop façades are opening in a tumult of silk brocades and Benares saris. From a simmering vat, an old woman pulls out honey rings and lays them to harden on cardboard egg boxes. The street is coming to life even at this grey hour: trilling bells of the furious peddlers racing to be first to bear their Japanese cargo to the Ganges; the sough of tabla and sitar emerging from cassette stalls. Across the corrugated roofs of the STD, monkeys gambol as if the sun will never rise, and as Will gazes up at them he is appalled and delighted to discover that the face of the monkey looking down on the street, the eyes that rivet him with their dark green density, are his own eyes, his own face, and that, contrary to walking down alleyways in threadbare trousers he should be up there on the rooftops, leaping higher and higher, a stone's throw higher than the furthest reach of the children.

Smells from the riverside, the sweet decay of crushed sabzi, the perfumes of incense, pepper his nostrils. He follows an old woman down a side street, her wide undulating hips swathed in a sari. She is bearing a letter but her trembling hands cannot open the letter box. He steps forward and yanks on the handle, his eyes scanning the name on the envelope as it skims down the shoot. Was it, by some uncomfortable stretch of the imagination,

William T. Dobson, his own name, the name he had been christened with? He'll never know for, as suddenly as the envelope, the sender has vanished, sucked into thickening hoards of pilgrims and shoe-blacks; and when, a week from now, the letter arrives at the Hotel Buddha, its recipient will have already checked out under mysterious circumstances.

From the east, high over the towering minarets of the Great Mosque of Aurangzbeb, daylight advances. The sky, bleached white by the plains of the cow belt, creeps over buses and bull carts, mercilessly wrenching dhotis from sleepers. Will pauses at an alley between a butcher's and chemist's. From the shadows he can hear a dog growling, a low whine in the throat deep as violence. Since he arrived in Varanasi, several dogs have chased him. But what is it about this particular dog, what strange new modulation in its slow gnarling, that roots him to the spot, his legs transfixed, framed in light at the end of the alley? He doesn't have time to consider. In its rabid fury the dog hurls itself toward him in one bound. At the same time a window opens and wash water cascades onto the flying dog, who collapses at his feet. Will looks up to thank his unwitting saviour, but the window has slammed shut and behind it several voices are shouting.

At last he has reached the Ganges. At the mouth of an impossibly thin bazaar, two crooks goad him to follow them.

"You see Ganga this way please sir."

They have tested this trick on him from the day he arrived and anyway, he is penniless. When he shakes his head, they are no longer looking at him, feasting their eyes on an American couple.

He follows a bend in the street, past the Sadhus and the crippled, beyond the children with their baskets of flowerbands and the songs of the blind. (Remember that song of the blind man on the train from Calcutta, the way the tongue let the tune loose, a patter of notes rising, then a pause whose length was constantly changing?) Dasaswamedh Ghat explodes in his eyes. Down by the riverside tourists are being pressed into boats with fantastically colourful sofa chairs and names like Gulshan

Delux. An armada of rowers have taken to the water to watch day blush the walls of the temples. In front of him, old men sit on stools, their faces lathered, while teenage barbers bend over them, razors flashing, each an artist daubing a canvas. And beyond the ticking hive of cameras and mantras, under the pink glimmer of a dawn he has never missed nor can ever imagine himself forgetting, the baked plains stretching south to Chunar Fort. From the centre of the river the contrast between city and plains is so great it is as though the Ganges were a mirror through which Varanasi saw itself reflected, a vast flatland of reluctant soil from which even the circling crows instinctively flinched.

He picks his way down past the shrine of Sitala, following his usual path upstream, towards the Mir Ghat. Some lone boat-wallahs stiffen at his approach, but he indicates his feet and passes them by, smiling. "Namaste" one calls out after him. To the left through the arches of the Nepalese temple, a monkey surveys east and west, its screech resonant down the length of the buttresses. Will's mind wanders back to the scene in Calcutta, in the Blue Star café, when Eve, delirious from the fever, had leapt from her chair and spat square in his eyes. Even then, with their relationship lurching dipsomaniacally from one crisis to the next, he was so stoned he thought she'd blown kisses on his eyelids. Not even the sudden silence, the wide-eyed stare of the proprietor or the way she locked the door on him for six hours afterwards had been enough to convince him and he met her declaration that she was sick of this she was leaving with the benign complicity one extends to a child who insists that the pitched duvet is a mansion. All the way from Shakespeare Sarani, up Chowringee Road past the ethereal Hooghly he had sat in a trance in the back of the taxi, no longer conscious of what she was saying (though he must have heard those sentences, for he could recall them weeks later with a terrifying lucidity). "I don't want to see you in this state. It's not good for us. Whatever problems you think you have you can tackle them alone, I've had enough. Phone me when your head's straighter."

Ahead of him at the Manikarnika Ghat, in the backwash of ragas from a guest house window, the cremation has begun. The sun heaves itself over the desiccated plains in a movement so palpable, like a speeded-up camera, he can feel the planet spinning on its axis and must fix his eyes on a point, like the middle of the rail bridge, to steady his vision. He stops thirty yards from the burning ghat. Each day he has woken up and lived through another dawn, another departure, watching the hot ash veer into the water as the sun rears out of it, the one formed of the other, in an ancient revolution of death and regeneration.

The fire is blazing now, its flames a thicket through which sparks like tongues crawl and fly, and the body, held up by slats that have withered into ash, is scarcely visible in the centre. Below the ceremony, by the cold ashes of earlier cremations, a dog snatches an arm and backs away, his eyes on the men above. Two men throw more logs on the fire and suddenly the legs, expanding in the heat, jerk upward, head and torso also, an unnatural snap, sprung, like a mouse trap. No one stirs. The faces are impassive in the golden spray of flames. Down by the water a child, barefooted, has shooed away the dog and is reaching out over the Ganges, launching paper boats of petals and incense.

Will steps up from the riverside, intending to walk round the top of the ceremonial group. As he approaches high on the left, however, he sees that the fire, collapsed in upon itself, a burning tent, has started to lick up the steps where the men are standing. Those nearest the fire are now knee-deep in flames, their heads bowed, unmoving, in honour of the dead, and no matter how often Will shouts or flags his arms they do not notice him or else choose to ignore him, standing there, sculpted, while flames leap the length of their dhotis. Will covers his eyes, but he can see, even in that pink darkness, that his mind has tricked him and that if he pulls down his hands the men will still be there, tending the fire. Nevertheless, it is still some time, a few minutes, maybe ten, before he opens his eyes and walks down past the mourners.

Already, the sun burns across his forehead. His throat is

parched and he needs something ice cool, a Limca, veri veri lime'n'lemoni, for which he has no money. Somehow he forgot to bring the bottle of purified water. The situation is serious. He could speak to Eve but the digital booths of the STD are cramped and unsoundproofed and he hasn't even enough money for a local call. He could pawn his watch, his Walkman and the box of Marlboro his brother had sent, registered, to Calcutta. As a last resort there were his parents, who could maybe arrange a giro transferral. At any rate, he still has a hundred rupees – or a little over two pounds. Three days spending if he put his mind to it.

The screech of crows circling above breaks his chain of thought. One swoops down onto a floating corpse and starts pecking at the muslin. When he turns away, nauseated, he glimpses something protruding from under an upturned boat. He is now a long way upstream, just past Lalita Ghat with its two turrets emerging from the water. Apart from the bathers down at the river's edge, no one is about. From under the boat, a pair of feet wearing gold sandals jut out, like the wicked witch of the East, the toes varnished red and gleaming in the sunlight.

Will crawls over the bellying ghats and leans on the rutted bow. As he moves towards her, light refracts off her gem-encrusted anklets, endowing her feet with the illusion of movement. He scrabbles aftward, as if to save the beautiful lady from the brink of suffocation. He calls out "Hello", knocking on the base to establish communication. Silence. He knocks again. "Can you hear me?" No time to think, he reaches under to grip the metal rim and heaves up. Light flooding in reveals the woman's legs. He looks over his shoulder to left and right, leaning the boat against his knees, but there is no one, not even a Brahmin dispensing his blessings. Down by the Ganges the pilgrims cleanse themselves under the seductive cover of their saris.

One final push and the boat rolls over onto a ridge below. He looks down at the body of a young woman, sari rucked up to her thighs, her green choli empurpled by a gash spreading down from the neck. His mouth opens to scream but a monkey perched high on the turrets fills the silence before him. He checks the pulse; then pulls down the hem of her sari. What is he going to do? He is sweating. In the back of his head he can hear the seconds tick, like rain, like miraculous rain drops in this season of Grishma. He must tell the police. He looks round for someone to help him, but this part of the ghats is deserted and the bathers, most of them almost fully immersed, are twenty, thirty feet below. When he pulls down her right arm to lay it flat on the stone a purse spills onto the floor. It contains a stapled wad of one hundred rupee notes.

Will leaps up and scans the river; calls twice, three times. No answer. Only the sound of ashen water, lapping bodies. He hovers on the next step, petrified, wanting to fling himself into the Ganges, but unable to move forward. Filtered by his Raybans, the shadows and contours of Lalita Ghat have assumed the dimensions of a Giant's Causeway. Will crouches to steady his balance, his eyes level with the woman's face, and notices that her mouth has remained fractionally open, braced on the verge of a scream, its syllables congealed on the walls of her throat.

The sun, no longer a well-defined sphere but a wide, expanding ellipse that fans out across the eastern horizon, pummels his temples until he can no longer think. For a moment he feels the onset of delirium. Voices approach from the left, fifty yards below. He has to do something, quick. So, quite casually, as if he has given the action very little consideration (which, in a way, he has) he bends over the body, eyes flitting from right to left and picks up the purse; then, facing downstream, descends the ghats. It is only when he reaches the riverside that he realises the body has been left uncovered.

From a parapet overhanging the Trilochan Ghat a gang of dogs bark wildly as he passes. Hundreds of metres downstream, other dogs pick up their call. The howling, amplified by the walls of the sliding temples, spins round and round in his head until he almost breaks into a sprint. There is a rending heave behind him, and, turning, he sees the stone figure of a cow subside into the Ganges. The dogs are yelping now, their paws scrambling and slipping on the newly diagonal slab, and the bathers splash out into the water. He doesn't even stop to pull up the Brahmin priest he has just knocked over as from everywhere, from speakers set inside lingams or perched on window sills, from the mouths of Sudrahs opening like gold fish, the dull throb of tabla and sitar emerges.

Stopping at the nearest stall he grabs the first drink to hand – two bottles of Gold Spot – and pays the wallah an incredible, a conspicuous, fifty rupees. The sign leaps out at him in red and black: Fun means Goldspotting. A traveller bumps past him, dressed in a purple sari just like the one Eve bought in Gujarat, and he stares after her, her black hair curling down over her shoulders, a faint limp in her left leg, like Eve every detail, down to the gold-crusted sandals. But he is too tired and terrified to run back and look at her face, and besides, he needs to get away from here.

At Dasaswamedh, he takes the nearest rickshaw, pedalled by a septuagenarian who can barely set the wheels moving. He has a vision of a young girl, back at Lalita Ghat, stumbling over the body, her cry so piercing (for it is her own mother she has stumbled over, for whom she has been searching through the night) even the dogs stop barking and the bathers tense at the sound, toothbrushes rigid. The wallah is so old and feeble Will must get down and push from behind. Bharat-bhagya-vidhata he warbles as he pedals, spitting out pan between the words.

When they have reached the Cantonment area the crowds, now slightly dispersed, have gathered round a dispute between a butcher and a Sikh chemist. Will interprets from their gestures that it is about some form of adultery, and that the empurpled butcher is accusing the chemist. The crowds sway on both sides, pinning back the arms of the protagonists and exchanging their own fusillade of insults. Will pays the wallah and backs away from the crowd. He needs to find somewhere quiet, somewhere he can arrange his thoughts in their proper order. The shouts pulse in his head: Jaliya, Ja-li-ya, JA-LI-YA, the syllables now punctuated by the tinkle of ox bells and the stamping of feet. It dawns on him that this scene and the murder are somehow connected, the woman slashed in a paroxysm of envy, and in his shock Will falls backwards through the revolving doors of the

El Parador restaurant and has to be dragged to a table.

Reviving with a swig of Gold Spot, he surveys the restaurant. The other diners, mostly Europeans, are staring at him and shaking their heads. He looks up at the ceiling, at the fan languidly rotating and the eye in its centre which fixes him again. He is about to spit up at it before he remembers that people are watching him. Sunita, the Nepalese proprietor suddenly appears by his side.

"You are OK, William? We have not seen you for many days." He counts with his fingers, "Seven perhaps."

"I've been unwell."

"Ah...the English stomach."

"Dysentery."

"Not nice, not very nice at all. But today you eat again." He nods his head encouragingly as he says this, then vanishes.

Fifteen minutes later, a brunch of waffles, pancakes and hash browns is set before him. Will has been dreaming of this breakfast for days. Yet now that the food is spread out, the honeyed waffles oozing with butter, the slice of lemon next to the pancake, he feels sick. He can't get the woman's face out of his mind, her pale lips, the hair unfurled from its bunch under the veil, and the glacial vacancy of those staring eyes. He tries to blot out the memory of those beached pupils, set in eyes already yellowed by sunlight. All about him in the El Parador, eyes seem to be avoiding him, skating round his table or over the camber of his flaking forehead. Even that eye in the fan which had followed him everywhere since the first days of his addiction, appearing in pendants, in matchboxes, in the middle of samosas, has now flicked shut, never to re-open.

The speakers above the counter howl with the latest track from a Bombay epic, making Will think of the billboards for it above the East India Arms Co. In the foreground an ape beating his chest to the lion's roar and Jane with her Tarzan, erect by the waterfall, their skin obediently pale as Hollywood teaches. Outside, a wallah sells dud batteries to people whose radios broke yesterday, a banana cart is pushed up a side street as the words of the song spin in Will's head: "I love you – I love you –

I love you", male bass to her soprano. He can feel his head giving way to the sump of sounds merging – laughter in the kitchen, Sunita humming, voices comparing hotel prices and stomach disorders, cut across by car horns and police whistles dispersing the crowd by the Sikh chemist. Sunita has brought him a bang lassi without even asking, as if following instructions in a script, and Will raises the tumbler full of green coagulant, staring down along the straw from which a pair of eyes peer up (he is almost relieved, things are normal again), and he winks at the eye winking back at him. This is dreary work, the day not done yet (it has barely started) and the green glue in passing down the walls of the throat will make him forget all, even the green choli and the flies creeping over it. He had been so struck by her chill beauty he'd blocked out the flies; the smell, sweet rose-hip and damask to his senses; the slash too straight and the blush vermilion against her celluloid paleness, some cheap scene in a movie thriller, that and no more.

He glances down at the book in his hand, a second-hand copy of Kipling's *Letters of Travel*, bought yesterday for two hundred paise at Ganesha bookstore. On the cover stands a gold-embossed elephant with a swastika crooked to the left of its eye, representing goodness, from svasti, meaning good in Hindu. Signs wrenched from their context, like the Arayavata, or the words that spool out from the paper, *"After the gloom of grey Atlantic weather..."*. He is uneasily conscious that there is someone smiling at the further end of the restaurant. His instinct is to fix the person with a withering stare, but he doesn't know how much that grin is conscious of. Each time the kitchen door swings open the grin widens.

To protect his face he holds up the menu. Names for fantastic dishes leap out at him: Spegthi Napoleon, Fried Squit or (Colonel Saunders' favourite) Fried Children. In Covalum, they had spent a whole evening at the Full Moon, laughing at its menu. Eve had even taken a photo.

Will signs a cheque on the air to Sunita, his fingers thrumming the pocket, as if the familiar pat could make those bank notes his and suddenly he feels like laughing, giggles bounce along his veins and up the stem of his throat. He watches his fingers (though they cannot possibly be 'his') extract a note from his pocket. They have thickened since he last used them, expanding like sausages on a barbecue. Before his very eyes, the note rises through the gaps between his knuckles, on up to the fan, an ash-flake ascending on hot air. He flails desperately after it but Sunita has already trapped it between palm and tray and bears it back to the kitchen, now an exquisite delicacy, a pheasant, for the cook to prepare. When he sits down again, aware that eyes have been focused on him all this time and are waiting for him to say something, an apology, an explanation, he confronts a woman he has never seen before opposite him on the same table, her lips curled into a grin.

"You're late, Will."

"Am I?"

"And stoned. I've been watching you from over there," she gestures to the table by the kitchen. "What the hell's the matter with you?"

"I'm hot. Listen – why don't we ask Sunita to speed up the fans?"

"I went to the State Bank this morning. They accepted my Visa card so," she pats her money belt, "we don't need to worry for the time being."

"Is this some kind of joke?"

"What are you talking about?"

"How do you know my name? Who told you?" A long pause. "Don't bullshit me!"

"Christ Will, you really are pathetic."

"Who are you? Just tell me that, will you."

"I'm getting out of here." She stands up, casually giving out over her shoulder, "I think you should come with me." She reaches down to pick up the change but Will beats her to it. "Christ your hands! Look at them!" He looks down at his hands, now the hands of an old man, withered and palsied with the strain of many years' use.

They take a rickshaw to the Hotel de Paris. It's only a few blocks away but 'she' tells him he's too weak to walk. On a doorway next to the Yelchico restaurant, two men crouch over a game of chess, the edges of the cloth board flitting up in the breeze. They pass market stalls with pyramids of mangoes, bananas, coconuts and as Will looks across the body of the woman (he still cannot bring himself to look her in the face) he can see the outline of her breasts under her blouse embroidered with elephants and wild palms. Up above, the sun, now perpendicular, throbs over the plains of the cow belt just visible beyond the tin roofs of the Cantonment. Will feels suddenly boxed in, as if an entire continent waits to be traversed, but he has yet to reach the city suburbs.

In the intense heat he has a dream of a frog he had seen once in the British Museum. They'd locked a North American wood frog – one of those cold-blooded animals able to survive freezing during winter – inside a human skull sculpted from ice inside a freezer. He imagines himself as that frog, Rana sylvatica, in the transparent cranium on a steel platform, his fingers compacted, iced for a millennium.

They are back in the hotel. Everything – the manager's smile, the cleaner chasing the gecko, travellers nodding – is the same. Will follows the woman up the stairs and into the room. The same questions: where had he been, his reply, her laughter. They smoke. He passes out. Police sirens still howl in the distance.

The revving of the generator and the heat from the stopped fan wake him. Another power cut. For a moment, he cannot remember where he is. On the bed, a woman lies in foetal curve with her back to him. She has removed her pyjamas, and along the length of her golden legs tiny follicles of blonde hair stiffen and quiver. Will is overcome by a desire to run his hands over her legs, but he is separated from them by the netting. Holding his breath, he untucks the gauze and rolls it up until there is a gap wide enough for his head; then slips under the net and lays himself down, inch by inch, his hands spread wide to distribute the weight of his body. As she hugs her chest with her knees Will slides his own into their moist hollowed backs. With his head propped up he looks past the pink flesh of her tiny lobe, down the silver chain across her neck and into the cleft of her compressed breasts. The swoop of his eyes pulls his whole body after it until he almost falls into her. Somehow, as he lies there, fingers suspended over the black elastic of her knickers, his mind abandoned to the moment (as if nothing – walking along the ghats, the bank notes, her body – had ever happened) he remembers her name. Rachel.

"Rachel," he whispers into her ear. "Rachel, Rachel."

An absurd notion seizes him: he sings the words of the Tarzan lovesong from the El Parador. Nothing. No movement. Will hovers over the little tendrils on her temple, holding his breath again. From the Marg below, a policeman is questioning an old woman. In the pauses he strains his ears. She has stopped breathing. He waves his hands against her lips.

"Rachel. Wake up."

Will shakes her shoulders. The body slumps onto its back on the hard mattress. He reaches to take her pulse. He is shaking all of a sudden; cannot control the rhythm of his breathing. What has he done? What is happening?

Then the hand he has been gripping wriggles free and wraps round his neck, pulling him down towards a face full of laughter. He is laughing himself now, as she whispers in his ear, a hot thunder of words impossible to decipher. His hands struggle to repress her ambulant legs. He asks her to repeat what she just said. "Fuck me," she whispers again; he is almost embarrassed to look her full in the eye as they fall into each other, and she plays dead again though this time he knows and the fan rotates, the power from the generator finally making the three stories, and sirens wail across the corrugations of centuries...but as his shoulders tense, and he half-turns, his teeth plunging deep into the pillow, he sees the body under the boat by the river and feels sick again, the last throb subsiding, a dying fall.

Soon she is sleeping. The wad, damp with sweat, throbs like a trapped rodent. He has to set it free. It fills the room with the stench of sewers. That tune again, Tarzan; he catches himself whistling it as he buckles his sandals. In the next room, a traveller claps his hands at irregular intervals, chasing mosquitoes.

Will moves forward to open the door. Something gives in his right leg, until he can't sense it any longer and has to drag it after him, a sack of wet sand. On the staircase he pauses for several minutes, gripping the banister. He can hear the sound of running water and is about to lean forward to peer at the bather. Then he remembers he's in another hotel. The manager waves him on as he walks past reception, and schoolchildren smile at him through the dark glass, so he waves back and joins them laughing. He takes a rickshaw (the same wallah, he notices, same pinks and greens in the lunghi, same tune through cracked gums). He has to lighten the load and push again, the whole morning played backwards along streets of fish guts and pan stains. He spies the first ghats at Dasaswamedh, and the open palms of the beggars by the shrine of Sitala. With the sirens in his head he doesn't stop to think. He has to be there before they reach her, past the Mir Ghat, past the cremation (the flames have now spread down from the steps and across the ganges, there's floating pyres of package tours and camcorders), past the temples and bhaktis.

Far ahead of him, on the steps of Lalita Ghat, a colony of travellers pirouette on tip-toe about the boat, in a dance that could belong to an ancient, pagan ritual. Above their heads, flashing Kodaks capture the spectacle of a body whose odour he is becoming conscious of with every second, every step. He stops outside the Nepalese Temple. Nobody notices him: neither camera crews jostling for close-ups on the face, nor journalists spitting into defective Dictaphones. Helicopters form in the sky, hundreds of them, thousands, and the riverside thrums with the jabber of tracker dogs. No inch of space is spared. Will can barely turn to fight his way back to the crowds at Manikarnika, finding himself swallowed up in shouting voices, whistles, boots.

At last he has reached the stall on the other side of Dasaswamedh. He reaches for the money in his chest pocket but his hand falls through the stitching. Behind him, as he swivels round on his heels, a vast trail of bank notes stretches upstream towards the crowd on Lalita. Somehow they have survived the conflagration. Two policemen trudge through the cinders, picking up the notes as they pass, their eyes fixed before their feet, blind to what's ahead of them.

Oxford

John de B. Pheby

John de B. Pheby was born in Europe in 1970. He dreams of *amour courtois* in the Glens of Antrim. He also frequents the Cherwell. Presented here is an extract from the central section of his recently completed novel, *Oxford*. This one is for Claire and for David.

John de B. Pheby

Oxford

As you took your breath, I turned away, focused on my telephone, ordered room service to bring up an English breakfast. Pensive and somewhat afraid of you, I stayed, thus, turned away, focusing on anything ... A wall, a room filled with blackness and/or an unkempt fresco, the curtain of my own eyes, anything but you.

Your words spun their magic for the last time. I was consumed by your voice, mesmerised by your youth. As you spoke, and as my eyes remained closed, I was able to imagine your voice moisturising your face and dyeing your hair. Back, back into the Adeline I used to know. I wished, hoped, demanded to see that Adeline again.

You should never have grown old.

But then I turned round, forced to do so by the wheeze in your breath, concern over-riding misogyny and selfishness. I was dismayed to see egg in the wrinkles of your face and crumbs of toast in the grooves of your wrinkles. I really wanted to reach across and wipe your face clean. Instead I cried out my blatant frustration and wicked lust. You had no hesitation in wiping my tears. You're a fine old moll.

And you continued your archaeology. Forty years ago, the day that you abandoned our Elaine, the day that you murdered your muse, the last day that you were able to comprehend her sick perfection. I demanded that you tell me why you left her. But you did not hear my petulance. Are we that old, Adeline? So old that we do not know either the will or the way? So old that we have neither the eyes nor the ears? Are we that impotent?

Yes.

But, of course, you told me, you answered me, anyway, by-and-by.

Adeline It's time, I suppose, time to square up to the big sky.
Elaine Everything there.
Adeline May I have the pleasure? Mademoiselle? Save this one for me.
Elaine Bien sûr. But I'm a pumpkin at midnight. You got the whole package, darlin'. You got the rough with the smooth. You got the cancer with the chancer.
Adeline With the dancer.
Elaine So take me. Here. If I fall here, catch me. Keep me.
Adeline Now.
Elaine Dance away with me. Until we fall, drunk, loving, dizzy, loving.
Adeline Fall down.
Elaine Take me away.
Adeline Anything wrong?
Elaine Oh, all the celebrations hurt my head.
Adeline Away from the punctured excess.
Elaine You drive me away from home, and it feels divine. So fine, so hip, so right.
Adeline The sun sets on the clean sheen of metal.
Elaine Sheer love highway.
Adeline Waltz the wheel.
Elaine Take my hand.
Adeline Uh-huh.
Elaine Hold me safe.
Adeline Yeah. All the way. Into the big land.
Elaine Across the orgy shack of border where wrens wank with weapons and liquor flows in mufti unto the horizon.
Adeline We race past Grianan Ailech.
Elaine Blessed be.
Adeline PleasedearGod, please cease these fucking waterworks.
Elaine Love you too, darlin'. Love you always. Too.
Adeline Listen.
Elaine Oh yeah. Cool.
Adeline Happy drum beats lace the night with electric orange amalgam.
Elaine The skies of Donegal are so huge.
Adeline Reach out.

Elaine And eat them. Live them.
Adeline Lick them.
Elaine Love them. Drum.
Adeline Vaulting into the quilts of luxury.
Elaine Everything is young and softlyrecently plucked.
Adeline And feels so fine.
Elaine And it feels so fine.
Adeline Always. Always. Always. Fine.
Elaine Cool.
Adeline In the wilds. Cruising the nouveau riche hick strip of Letterkenny. Gobbing at the cute ethnic whores.
Elaine What happened to the sweet colleen? The delicacy, the homemade jam and the rosary, the intacta hymen and all the nice boys?
Adeline Oh shucks, where have we all gone wrong?
Elaine The good old days.
Adeline There was never enough drumming then.
Elaine Now I love this land.
Adeline Now we cry and dance. No anomaly.
Elaine You're the white keys. I luxuriate in black. Happy infant black. Black sky now. Don't watch the stars. Want the claustrophobia of a forever slumber night.
Adeline Do you want me?
Elaine To hold me tight? Lost in your huge eyes, like the huge sky.
Adeline We plough through scorched bracken and broken borders.
Elaine Oblivious and wonderfully lost.
Adeline A tunnel of neon.
Elaine And. Or.
Adeline Driven on by your tears.
Elaine Hold me tight.
Adeline Then I'd be above the limit.
Elaine Then stop. Stop the car. Please. Just. Please stop. Stop and love me.
Adeline Here at the energy of the elegy.
Elaine The Rock of Doon...
Adeline If we spoke here...But...if...'twould be roccoco in the extreme
Elaine Hell, you mean we've been on the level up till now?

Adeline Woh...
Elaine I'm on the level. Oh yes. Really fucking together. Sharp and aware and poundin' yer night. Through.
Adeline Alright.
Elaine All. There.
Adeline Neat.
Elaine Y'see this? This exciting skirt? This sex. This micro turn-on.
Adeline Yeah. Yes. Love it.
Elaine Well look how it goes. See.
Adeline How it unravels.
Elaine See? I'm together. Do you like what's underneath?
Adeline What you've -
Elaine - Uncovered. Pretty clear.
Adeline You must be cold.
Elaine Clean and cold as ice.
Adeline What do you want? Now?
Elaine Up to the rock.
Adeline The Rock of Doon
Elaine Crown me.
Adeline The world is huge. All around. Ready for a dusting of dusk.
Elaine To clean me and modest me.
Adeline In night.
Elaine Svelte yeah.
Adeline Of course. I supervise you.
Elaine Timeless old me.
Adeline Lovely you.
Elaine Thankyou.
Adeline Oh, you know, you.
Elaine Should I?
Adeline In all this?
Elaine I'm not cold.
Adeline But proud ...
Elaine Fine.
Adeline Beautiful.
Elaine That's lavender isn't it? Lavender from the causses?
Adeline No. No, Elaine. That's you.

Elaine Do you love me, then? Now?
Adeline What, you, a slip, a wee Derry scut?
Elaine The very one.
Adeline Sure.
Elaine Your hand here, desperate, flailing for me, an extension of your clumsiness, your clothing.
Adeline Yeah ...
Elaine And then a graceful part of the red horizon.
Adeline Prize ribbon.
Elaine Arms of flame. Hatred.
Adeline Huge. So vast. Boundless flame and love.
Elaine And I'm reaching for you. But I'm drowning.
Adeline And I'm not there.
Elaine The ribbon of Donegal is so huge. The land is ugly.
Adeline And boundless flames.
Elaine I adore its ugliness! I love my cancer!
Adeline Reach out ...
Elaine And eat it. Live it.
Adeline Love it. Drum it.
Elaine Louder and louder. Until I collapse, mash head into Doon and scars into blood again.
Adeline What are you?
Elaine Alchemist? Completely fucked?
Adeline Beautiful again.
Elaine Kiss it better. Kiss it all better?
Adeline With what?
Elaine Adrenalin.
Adeline I love you.
Elaine You adrenalise me. Shivery with your excitement my nakedness slips into Doon.
Adeline And so you own the big land. And so you rule the corrugated mountains.
Elaine Both of us.
Adeline Both of you.
Elaine Me and my consort. Me and my cancer.
Adeline Nice ...
Elaine A small kitten by the spring of Doon.
Adeline I watch you, feeling callous.

Elaine Kittykittylovey ...
Adeline You don't touch me any more.
Elaine Ah ...
Adeline You touch cat. Ignore me. Cat.
Elaine Oh!
Adeline Cat runs away into the night, fucking perspective, growing with every step.
Elaine See it! In the sky. My cat is the sky ...
Adeline The midnight purrs over Kilmacrennan and the Rock of Doon.
Elaine Butt naked, I lick it.
Adeline Screaming fucker ...
Elaine Love it. Jesus. Good, good boy.
Adeline What? Where?
Elaine See! See ... My cat, my cancer, living in the grand manner, up in the grand sky.
Adeline You hop, Wiccan stylee. Why you hop?
Elaine Hop? You see me?
Adeline You lady ...
Elaine Heh! Well, this lady's got hops in her garden.
Adeline Do you come from a hopping community?
Elaine Do I come from Kent?
Adeline Nah.
Elaine Eden's beer ...
Adeline I send you up the walnut tree to get the hops down, because they've gone up the walnut tree, because nobody trims them.
Elaine Really, you hear, if you get your hops up -
Adeline I know, you don't have to pick so many to make a bushel.
Elaine Oh!
Adeline Yo?
Elaine Let's go.
Adeline So how's it hanging dude?
Elaine Just drive away from Oxford.
Adeline We're well away.
Elaine Drive far away from Oxford. Away from spires and scrolls. Away from the Union. Away from the privileged oranges. Away from Louis Macniece.

Adeline No better man!
Elaine Aye. Whatever. Just away, though. Just. Truly. Just.
Adeline Odd thing, driving through a dream.
Elaine Is that what this is?
Adeline Phallic verges inspiring paranoia.
Elaine Vastness instilling a sense of futility.
Adeline Night clad beauty.
Elaine Unseen. Kinetic.
Adeline Hope.
Elaine I'm so tired. All the pills ...
Adeline Then sleep.
Elaine Nothing I want, nothing I need, more.
Adeline Oh?
Elaine Other than a helping hand.
Adeline Then?
Elaine Then I'd smile a smile as wide as the meadow, obvious for the world, oblivious of the darkness.
Adeline Now?
Elaine I'm tired. But the last thing in the world I could do is sleep.
Adeline Why?
Elaine Too many doctors using too many needles.
Adeline Ah. Oh. Them.
Elaine Too many rapists in white coats fucking me.
Adeline Sure.
Elaine Their wild abandon ...
Adeline What then?
Elaine Continue West. Stop at the Atlantic. Give me a room with a big window and a portal onto the ocean. Please ... give me waves and too much time.
Adeline Close your eyes, then. Picture this room.
Elaine Picture the present.
Adeline Picture my gift.
Elaine And though we arrive -
Adeline At a boarding house where the waves inspire mould and coughing.
Elaine No matter. Eyes are closed. I feel Heaven.
Adeline Sodium splinters into the peeling ...

Elaine I watch the sea ...
Adeline In the abstract afterglow, I watch you.
Elaine The waves spray the window.
Adeline Through the beautiful cacophony, you turn me on.
Elaine I love this, Adeline.
Adeline Ah well ...
Elaine This is my dream ...
Adeline Bummer!
Elaine Adeline, go wash, go powder, go eat.
Adeline Why? What?
Elaine Want the sea for myself.
Adeline Go fuck yourself ...
Elaine Yeah ...
Something like that.
Me, myself and sea.
Over and over. For ever. All that sound.
Where is all that sound? How is all that sound?
Drowning in that sound.
Hiding this beautiful forswearing.
I love you because who can know?
Who can know I love you?
I supervise the sea.
Nothing else restricts me.
Smell disinfectant. Smell death. Floundering in all the majesty, all the sound.
Of the sea.
Of the sick bay.
A hypodermic slices my nakedness.
A nurse reflects into my consciousness, smeared in a rain drop, real in a sea drop.
And buggers me, wound fucks me, drops me into this ocean.
Breath comes quickly. Too much oxygen spirals me into panic.
Naked ambition flails me along a cultured corridor.
Into a bathroom.
With a fine, sturdy lock.
And a wonderfully fashionable handbag. Full of drugs.
Hitchcock observes inbetween the shortness and sharpness of my respiratory problems.

This is too nasty ...
Droplets pound, form ugliness across the nicotine tinted window.
The ugliness attracts me. The wounds around my face ...
Suddenly ...
It's me! The whole big universe is me.
Everything I see.
Me.
And it's all way too ugly. Big much.
It's all too nasty ...
I created this monster.
Jesus.

Adeline Elaine ... darling ... my Elaine ... where are you?

Elaine Barricades. Barricades ...
Thought they'd all gone huh? All the barriers. All the words.
Enough dialogues.
There's still violence. There are still doctors.

Adeline Are you in here?

Elaine Who are you?

Adeline You know me.

Elaine Only your lies. You always lie.

Adeline When? When, my darling? When do I lie?

Elaine You keep telling me how beautiful I am.

Adeline You are -

Elaine - No! No. I know where the scars are. Here. Here they are.
They're in the mirror.

Adeline Let me in!

Elaine Ask nicely, stranger.

Adeline Please ... Please ...

Elaine No.

Adeline Fuck you! Fuck you! But please, fucking open this door.
Let me in!

Elaine Can't a woman enjoy some privacy in the bathroom?

Adeline What are you doing?

Elaine Pissing. In a moment, I'll crap. Scream **then** if you want.
It'll hide the noise and save my blushes.

Adeline Christ. Oh Christ! I'll do anything. I love you. Fucking
Christ. Oh please, my littlelittle, please, please. Fuck. My God.

Elaine Listen to yourself! Let me be.
Adeline Let me see.
Elaine Perverse. That.
Adeline Give me strength. Merciful God, strength.
Elaine Sixty pills in pairs and a beaker of cloudy water.
Toothpastey.
The animals go down two by two. And very calmly.
Very pretty indeed.
I want to know nothing, Adeline ...
Don't want the guilt.
Don't want the illness.
Don't want you. Don't want me.
Don't want to have to slash my face to be pretty.
Simply. Don't. Want.
Another two.
Two more.
I sing popular songs.
You help with your screams.
Together, separated by the last barricade in Ireland, we subvert the joy.
Popular music.
Another two. Two more. Water's foul.
I'd like to rot in the sea, methinks. The sea would clean me.
But would my cancer be like oil for all the lovely fishies ..?
Can't have that. You pound the door. I pound my face.
I nick my cheeks, smear the blood onto my pale lips.
Lovely.
And so I swallow pills down with blood and toothpaste and water.
Cool.
Patheticfine. It's a justrightdose.
Adeline
Elaine The door gives way. The world comes in.
You look me in the eye.
Bravado races.
I wilt.
See these tears?
They defeat me.

Adeline
Elaine You piss on my pile of pills.
You ruin my hope.
You could have used the loo.
Adeline
Elaine
Adeline
Elaine
Adeline
Elaine
Adeline
Elaine
Adeline Worship me.
Elaine
Adeline
Elaine No.
Adeline
Elaine
Adeline
Elaine

Adeline Last drive.
Elaine Can't think straight.
Adeline No. No. Hush.
Elaine Dull land. Faces everywhere. That noise?
Adeline Your head.
Elaine Oh.
Adeline This is the last drive.
Elaine Will you abandon me?
Adeline Yes.
Elaine Why are you crying?
Adeline You are a mystery. I love you.
Elaine Then?
Adeline But you won't love me.
Elaine I'm dying, Adeline. And I don't love myself. I don't want to die thus, broken hearted.
Adeline I don't like you dying. There is nothing I can do.
Elaine So?
Adeline I'm going to leave you in the mystery.
Elaine Everything is so dark.
Adeline Darker for you.
Elaine There's random malice in the rain.
Adeline So claustrophobic.
Elaine And such infinity!
Adeline How are you?
Elaine Oh. You know. Dying.
Adeline Ah.
Elaine Tripping.
Adeline Here. This is the Poison glen.
Elaine Nothing to see.
Adeline Right. It's night. But if you last until the dawning, you'll find a lake, a mountain, tranquillity, ease of thought.
Elaine Where are we?
Adeline In the transept of an open Church. It's burnt and dead.
Elaine It's beautiful, yeah?
Adeline You might find out.
Elaine It's dark. I can't see you.
Adeline No.
Elaine But I can hear your tears. There ... I can see your tears.

No, only stars.

Adeline Pray for your salvation. Please.

Elaine

Adeline

Elaine Adeline?

Elaine

Elaine

Elaine Can hear the car starting. And now, so far away it might be part of the storm, it might be natural.
Can't see anything.
I close my eyes and imagine that I'm beautiful.
Ever. So. Alone.

Elaine Adeline?

Elaine No. Storm. Just.

Elaine

Elaine So this is freedom.
Freedom is blindness, loveless, coldness, useless.
Nekkid, gal.
Hypothermia. Cool. Reeling from a deferred OD.
Fantastic.
Kiddies ... Check out. Happy shapes in the darkest night.
A smiley face.
I'm excited and excitable. My skinny frame pronounces muscles.
I clap and hop gagfree.
There's nothing inevitable about the end of this night.
Even when Sheela-Na-Gig deigns to begin the dawning, she seems to devour rather more of the land and the soul and the girl than she illuminates.
I can't get no.
Satisfaction.
Stop and think, wistful and calm, about the rape.
About the 'cure'.
And Sheela tells me this. And that. A vast lake swallows the dawn, remains wholly dark and bottomless.
I'm no virgin. My grail's drained of innocence. I'm no lover. My grail's drained of affection.
No. So check this out. A paralysed reflection in a dark lake.
I am a Mother to cancers now.
There's wisdom now. In my chalice.
But I still hurt.
Oh how I hurt.
There's nobody to laugh at me. And so I cry.
The feeble day asserts itself, dimly, an endless nonentity.
A hollow church surrounds me on the shore of the poison.
The mountains smell.
Here. Still. Four walls.
Four fucking walls. No voice. Nothing.
No empathy at all?
I just want to talk.
Really. I'm dying. I'm shouting, yeah. Just want someone to hear.
The response is my own echo.
And so I scream and rip out roothair.

This is freedom.
Unimpressed, I imagine a hospital ...
A man's brogue crushes a left breast.
Another pins my windpipe.
This is the cure.
Spittle from a great height.
Seems so real. Poison fills my mouth and blood pours from a lumber puncture.
And nobody hears my screams.
So I must be spoofing!
Fuck that honey(?)! I hurt.
A mirage on a cold day. Banishing such self-referential tosh, I retch into the meadow and count my blessings ...
In this auto da fe. Burning in this mist. I paddle the shore.
Each step splinters stillness and conscience.
Could have been a teenager on a joyride in a joyless world.
Cancer Kid. Circles and thistles. I'm not in Chechnya.
Nettles and napalm. Not in Bosnia. Or Greater Serbia
Or Laos. Not Iraqi/Kuwaiti. Not from China. Or
North Korea. Or the US of A.
Have a fucking nice day.
I'm neither Iranian nor Colombian. Aushwitz does not threaten me.
I'm not being fucked with AIDS in Thailand or fucked with money and snow in Panama or bulletfucked-in-labour in dear Kampuchea.
Wicked, man! I'm fine.
Absolutely fine.
Except that I want the joy ride to be terminated.
I want to die and I deserve exhilaration.
Luckyluckylucky me. But I can't stop crying.
Call me selfish. But do call me.
Hold my hand.

Elaine

Elaine Back in the Church's shell, I hide and watch the sky through the empty windows.
I stain the sky.
A montage of a dying family.

We're all fighting.
Daddy kicks my head.
My head, welded to his foot, smashes into the ornament cabinet.
Someone conducts the ornaments into my thigh.
I am a windmill. Violence whirls on and on.
We all scream hate sounds.
We all shout damnation words.
Someone 'sections' me.
Strange word.
I ask the pigs if this is the ward for mad girls or crying girls?
From the lake to the church is 22 paces.
It must always be
1,2,3,4,5,6.
1,2,3,4.
1,2,3,4,1,2,3,4,1,2,3,4.
Over and over in my loneliness.
It's my birthday.
34. Forever 22.
We love each other even as we kill each other.
Across the stained glass mosaic of the sky.
Don't know what they look like.
Guilt is a bottomless lake.
Just think 22. Concentrate on your feet. Keep your feet on the ground.
Night comes early.
Oh! And I was having so much fun.
I lie in the water and the day's fire is doused.
Cease fire.
Close my eyes as the darkness trickles up my legs and sexes me.
I picture the beautiful boy.
The water whips into me and I kiss the lash.
Moon violates clouds and shatters the love and lake into storming watermarks.
Kiss my imagination. Imagine my halo.
Tender as this light braille, the beauty holds me in strong, shy hands.
Into his room. Into his womb.
His white flesh slips through fingers ripe as delicate chastity.

His white flesh slips in and around the moon rays.
This hideandseek love. He flits from moonpillar to mistpillar. I reach out to
touch man ...
But fall into edible moon, drinkable poison.
Kiss the webbed surface of my imagination. So still, despite the disturbing
embrace.
I reach for his illusion, loving this photosynthesis, crying at the diabolical counterpane of sad lust and futile romance that the sky has become, the
tapestry
that the sky proclaims.
He's in my eye, though. He's in my mind's eye.
The celerity of the stillness. And still ... blowing kisses into ridges and ripples.
The viscid nature of this glorious fuck.
I masturbate with shadows. The surface reflection shows me a beautiful
woman,
but no beautiful boy. That figment flees.
In the black and white silence of this nature, this film, I am mainlining distortion.
Therefore, I am very pretty, a crying melody.
The lake sub-edits, takes away my cancer, my fresian tones, my ugly bones. My blood is splendid and stunning.
I am seductive. I am the bait. Fishing in this
lake.
Fishing for my cancer. For I am a Mother to cancers.
Alone in the Poison Glen, I go down on my fantasy.
I suck it off, feeling no shame or sleaze, just love and contact.
With the empty air.
Cancer's placenta surrounds me.
I am a Motherfucker of cancers.
Heh.
I orgasm in the chandelirious lake, staring upwards into the chinks of eternity.
I am allowed. My screams bounce off ancient vistas as

soothing, indelible, edible joy.
There are two beautiful boys.
The salvation in my mind's eye, who shall save me and marry me and make a 'good woman' of me.
And my friend, my son, my cancer.
We lie with each other.
We hold each other away from harm. We brighten the night with acceptance, patience, breath.
I am sincere. I know that I am a Good Woman.
I am a lover, floating, lost in this last dance, bewildered by this peace time.
Giving birth was a smile! I have known real pain ... I have wanted death.
Pain has pinned me to the centre of the world.
Linked forever with my friend. Bosom buddies with my fantasy and my cancer.
Rain falls, impacts loud as cymbals.
In the silences, the sound of my emptiness is the dub **and** the rub.
Having fucked to our hearts' content, me and my cancer share a cigarette.
The inhaleglow is all that illuminates the road, runwaying up the Glen.
Followtheyellowprickroad.
Never more alone or more wary of the silence.
Stamp my feet to keep the snakes away.
Bawl my bagged eyes and limp tongue truth to keep the snakes away.
The only snakes are corpses, boiling in this Maryland humidity.
So many. Hopscotch between them.
A 7-11. Classic Coke stops the fever.
I'm not black, else I'd be dead.
But my cancer is black, and he lives.
In the long grass of the baseball pitch, I am nothing.
Home run.
Yeah right.
On the tarmac, I boil. This bag boils.

This hag's boil. This maiden's cancer.
Real thing.
Don't want to nurture insanity or the ol' brokenheart thang.
Crawl back to water.
Drink the poison.
1,2,3,4,5,6. 1,2,3,4. 1,2,3,4,1,2,3,4,1,2,3,4.
Desperate drinking and numbers, drinking and numbers and nothing but.
Keep the pain away. Better to disintegrate than to hurt.
I'm humble enough.
I'd rather I was dead than you, you being everyone else.
Wade into the water, Avalonian, Sheela-Na-Gig. Saved from snake, slag slakes thirst.
Hands cupped, inevitably baptised.
No, just thirsty. Fidget and pretending to be happy.
Rilly. I mean, if someone's watching. It's important.
Of course, I am invited to the medicine ball.
Because Sister Horrible smashes it into my head while Sister Nasty treats my body as a pin-cushion with her tipped needles.
Everything swims. I'm ill and doped.
Can't see anything. Blind, on useless legs, so this
Unable to eat without an incendiary device erupting within my head, shattering every thought.
A drip trips me onto the floor.
Smell death in the next bed.
A Doctor gags me with a bandage, tells me to stop screaming.
Then he tickles, screws me, the usual.
So much laughter. So much fun.
I want oblivion, in order to exorcise these memories.
Want to drown in all this semen.
Sink. And swallow.
Swallow, but refuse to harm my figure. 22. Beautiful as the land itself.
Open my legs. Water in. Water out.
Shivers close my eyes.
Hopping and hoping. Jesus. Little girl. Little boy.

Jesus.
Swim, body open, senses horny.
Tendrils of memory sting, while eyes are white and unknowing.
Break the surface, hair and head a greedy, gasping river.
Hard to know if I'm crying.
A progressing beauty etched around my eyes. Fear swims in my eyes.
I am perfect.
The most beautiful part of the world.
My eyes are a fire now. My skin is perfect. My hands invite **you**.
To be held. By me.
I kiss the air. The air glows, static as the hawk that centres on the sun and moon.
My arms caress my body. My arms hold me safe.
I am my friend. I am beautiful. Gorgeous dead drop.
Calm now, in my auto da fe. Coy defence of palm pleasured face.
Imagine, from the top of the mountain, seeing such a Goddess!
Seeing Sheela-Na-Gig, genitals open, sexy as Hell, smiling through her self abuse.
And everything beyond.
Oh happy sunstruck land.
Imagine standing on the top of the mountain.
Just that.
Standing above a happy world, so tired.
The rain pains me. It bludgeons and blunts such illusions.
The rain, unnatural, makes no sound.
Or perhaps this scream even drowns the storm.
Sink to my knees. I pray.
For you. You being everyone else.
Head enters black combo poison of mind and lake, rams the surface, stays put.
Weight the straining, evil neck down with boulders.
There really is
Nothing.

Elaine
Elaine Now.
Elaine Nothing
Elaine whatso
Elaine ev
Elaine
Elaine

David It's the saddest thing I know.
With ...
The audacity of the last throes, I swim torrent, cut through lovelorn thrombosis, recallamnesia of birth and repair your churning fontanelle. Hold back the water. And I'm holding you up, up to the sky, feeling your beat, your body. Dieu. My hand disguises your dolorous stroke, my eyes clench against it, my hands swear water away. Worship your face. Not stealing, healing. I trace God-given and self- inflicted wounds in your map and experience, skinned. So there, alive in your lake, half crying my sweat, half pissing my fear, holding your life.

Elaine Don't hurt me.

David Dry you. Just.

Elaine One funky good samaritan.

David Your life, uh, guard.

Elaine Don't hurt me.

David Home. I'll take you home.

Elaine Thank –

David - Shhhhh. Close your eyes and dream it all away.

Elaine I know who you are.

David Really?

Elaine Yeah.

David And who might that be?

Elaine You're the beautiful boy.

David

David Come again?

You were foetal in a corner, having finished your wandering tale. My more staccato tones had crept into the room. But I stopped, feeling romantic and perverse, even here at the end, even unto oblivion.

I played Elaine's old Joy Division collection and we boogied, groovy and orthopaedic on my balcony.

You told me how the sky was a fire behind me. I knew already – your face was red, and usually it is so pale. Whatever, your news prompted me into thoughts of cremation. I thought about the River Alzou. I thought about the River Cherwell. I thought about the River Styx, Charon on the River Styx carrying a beautiful girl and carrying her cancer – all the way to the crematorium.

I wanted to save her, even then. But, of course, she died a long time ago.

Bugger.

Columbus Day

Janette Jenkins

Janette Jenkins was born in Bolton, Lancashire, in 1965. She trained in London as an actress before completing her first degree in Literature and Philosophy. *Columbus Day* is her second novel.

Janette Jenkins

Columbus Day

One

My mother's eyes worked so hard, that all the blue turned into milky egg-shell circles, even before her fiftieth birthday. She never stopped looking for him; her sharp eyes flitting from one face to the next. To be with her was exhausting, and I was grateful when the sun came out, and she'd hide the rolling blue lenses behind her dark, cat's-eye sunglasses, so it seemed that only her eyebrows were moving, in high honey-blonde arches.

We went to places she thought she might have been with him, in her long white socks and Princess Elizabeth coat; my grandfather in tweed, stiff enough to burn her cheek, and shoes you could see your face in. She couldn't remember exactly what they were doing, but she knew all about his shoes. "And they weren't suede," she said, throwing pebbles listlessly into the sea. "He'd never wear suede."

It was 1973, and we were in Blackpool because she thought she remembered the trams, hoop-la, and a circus with a bowler hatted clown. It was a cold July day, and the pavements were crammed with shivering crowds, straining their necks, turning their toes in their sandals, and waiting for the clouds to turn white. Outside arcades, boys in jeans and bomber jackets dropped aspirins, two at a time, into their cans of Coke.

"I know we came here," my mother said, pulling in her lips and narrowing her eyes at a sea-covered dog. "It was at least twenty years ago." She turned to face a row of deck chairs, their legs sprawled,their covers banging in the wind, "And I know he won't be back. I know it's ridiculous, but it's so awful here, that it feels kind of familiar."

We started to walk in long criss-crosses, from the beach to the prom and back again. Across the tramlines, the sea was thick and the colour of coffee. A man was tap dancing on a piece of board, and a woman with long grey hair grabbed hold of my mother's coat, and told her in urgent whispers that the manager of Louis Tussauds was a thief, and they were all on the fiddle, and that the air conditioning had jammed at least three seasons ago. "Well," my mother said, brushing down her sleeve, "they're hardly in danger of melting, are they?" I moved in, close to her safe side, swinging my bagful of greasy pennies, collected from pockets and the powder-smelling lining of her handbag.

"They're not real wax anyway," the woman shouted, backing into the crowd. "And Princess Anne's got the wrong wig on."

We ate shrimps from paper tubs with the rain dripping into the vinegar. My legs shivering in the shorts I insisted on wearing, even though I knew it would be colder than at home. I wanted to leave my mother's eyes and run off across the rippled wet sand and up towards the donkeys, who bowed their heads because of the bells they had to wear, the sticky hands and sharp heels, and the bright blue saddles that announced their names in daisy-chain letters. Molly, Dolly, and Peggy-Sue.

The wind blew up behind us, and our hair streamed out in long flat ribbons, tasting of salt and thin grits of sand. My mother turned into the wind, her eyes red-rimmed and streaming, looking as though we'd left someone important behind. The spread-out crowd dragged their things together, throwing sand-stained towels over their heads. "The North," she moaned, "I don't know how I stand it."

Our clothes flattened onto our shiny wet skins, and mother looked in scorn at the people shivering under huge umbrellas, dressed in bikinis and too-small swimming costumes. "Where do they think they are?" she smiled into her collar. "The Algarve? Now wrap yourself up, or you'll look like the rest of them."

"But I feel alright," I chattered.

"You'll catch your death." But then she squeezed my hand, and pulling me tight and close, whispered, "but are you having fun?"

"Oh yes!" I laughed, as my feet sank deeper into the mud. The sea looked a long way out now, a wide brown line on the horizon, my raw, red knees stinging in the wind, my pockets full of mussel shells and flat pink stones that I'd take home for my aquarium. "But can we do inside things now? Please?"

We walked towards the town, and into shops selling walking-stick rock and shiny plastic towers. You could have your name printed on T shirts and newspapers that said you'd been caught streaking down North Promenade. The shop smelled of toffee and its steamed up windows were piled high with chocolate-covered fudge and jars of sugar curls. I stood watching the woman behind the counter, the way her hair stuck down across her forehead as she wrapped fat sticks of rock. Biting her thick lips, she smiled as she took the money and dropped it into the drawer. She must live here. And just think, every day she can ride the trams, paddle, eat hot dogs and long candyfloss sticks. Across the shelves rock could be anything. Bacon and eggs. Kippers. False teeth or giant sugary dummies. I stretched upwards, pulling down a green paper box filled with fruit. It was all there, an apple, an orange, a bright green pear.

"Can I Mummy? Can I?" My mother was standing at the back, smoothing down her skirt, licking her finger and rubbing mud-freckles from her face. In the shop light, her hair stood out, like shiny gold spun cotton.

"All right." She pulled out her purse and began fishing for coins, but her athletic eyes moved up and down an old man in a long brown coat, fumbling with his wallet, his curled-up fingers struggling to get inside the narrow compartments. His sagging face trembled as he tried to pull out his money; his hands were all fist and knuckles, his skin the colour of nicotine. Mother shivered as he pushed his way past us, shuffling his thick, old-fashioned shoes on the worn-out linoleum. "Are you OK?" I asked, staring triumphantly into my stripy paper bag. The old man's hand slipped across the door handle. "But he couldn't be Grandad," I whispered, as he dragged himself over the step, "*could he?*" I imagined my grandfather then to be a stately old gentleman, with slicked white hair and waistcoats, a mahogany stick –

if he needed one, and the scent of cologne drifting across his stiff, button-down collars.

"Of course not," she swallowed, and then with hoarse whispers, she pushed me towards the door, "Now lets get out of here."

Through the large plate-glass windows, I could see that we looked different from everyone else, though I couldn't exactly say why. My mother's back walked in a straight line, her coat blew sideways as she moved, and her heels clicked softly along the tarmac. Other people gave her more than passing glances. Sometimes they smiled, and sometimes they gave her a wide, roundabout berth.

Behind my mother's eyes, a collection of silent pictures were held in storage . Occasionally, she flicked through these images as she moved along a pavement, her blank face giving nothing away, her shoulders weaving through people, waste-bins, lamp-posts. Crisp images that slowly blurred into lumps of coloured shapes. A hat. A pair of hands. Straight white teeth. And in all of them, her father's face. A man in his twenties, with oiled-back hair. He wore a trench coat and two-tone shoes. In the pictures, he would be doing simple things. Opening a refrigerator door, coughing, lighting a cigarette.

"Does he ever speak?" I asked her.

"No," she said, jutting out her chin, "but sometimes he whistles *Edelweiss*."

In the thick afternoon drizzle, my mother pulled her coat tight and began to walk up and down the side streets. "But there's nothing up here," I moaned. The flashing lights, the bingo-callers' drones, the breathed-over cases of push-penny were behind us, and my fingers itched inside my drawstring purse, rolling the pennies, sure I could win more. These streets were ordinary looking, with butchers and fruit-shops and dustbins. It didn't look like Blackpool anymore.

"What are we looking for now?"

My mother sighed, as we passed a warehouse selling cookers and giant fridge freezers, *For The Catering Trade*. "Ice cream," she said.

"But -"

"Not that stuff," she hissed. "Not Mr Whippy, all air and water. Real ice cream. Real Italian ice cream. There must be such a thing." She thrust her tiny white hands into her deep black pockets, "I mean, even Blackpool must have its immigrants."

We passed the back gates of boarding houses and fish and chip shops, gusts of steam pouring from wedged-open windows. My legs slipped against each other, my anorak barely covered my flapping red shorts. "Isn't it too cold for ice cream?"

"It's July, Jessica," she said. "And anyway, I'm sure that cloud's doing something up there. There's a definite hint of sun." She pulled out her sunglasses, tipping back her head in proud defiance.

A shop with green film on its windows had a rotating metal sign that promised Marco's Famous Gelati, but inside, the man was from Liverpool, with dirty hands and gaps in his teeth. The ice cream was solid and yellowing in giant plastic tubs. The man insisted it was Marco's, but my mother told him it was only Lyon's Maid. Eventually, we found a parlour selling milkshakes in tall glasses, and wafers with nougat in the middle, and even though the ice cream came from a spout called Robert's Best, my mother said it would have to do.

"Papa once let me eat three knickerbocker glories," she said, dipping the plastic paddle into the tip of the curl. "He took me to a parlour with swivelling stools and chrome plate, and men in long white aprons sprinkled hundreds and thousands all day long."

"Where was that?" I asked, striding towards the shoreline.

"I don't know," she smiled. "But it was lovely, and I wasn't even sick, though mother said I deserved to be."

"Come on!" I urged. "I want to do things."

"Don't you want any ice cream?" she asked. "It isn't bad."

"No..." I moaned, "*I just want to do things.*"

I left her in a pagoda-shaped shelter, sand-strewn, smelling of driftwood and dry, empty oysters. "I'm too tired to be doing things," she said, her knees hunched, her map-blue eyes following the backs of passers-by. "You go on." She scraped back her long, yellowy fringe, "I'm alright here. Watching. It's fascinating, I mean look at that woman with the legs," she sniffed, sitting on her hands. "Now that one really has let herself go."

"*But will it be alright?*" I asked, looking across at the wide expanse of promenade, the piers in the distance, the wobbling lines of linked-up people.

"Of course it will. You'll have fun. Just avoid strangers, cars and tramlines, and you'll be fine. And don't buy any plastic rubbish."

The Golden Mile was strewn with fortune-telling gypsies. Between red velvet, they sat with their heads on their folded arms, sipping cans of lager and cups of real coffee. A painted-on sign read: *Fortunes Told. The Original Princess Rosa's Granddaughter.* Pressed behind glass were yellow newspaper cuttings, and black and white photographs of stars from the 1950s. Girls with bouffants and puffed out skirts, and wide toothed men with slick, brillianteened hair held out their palms for the camera. I'd only heard of The Beverly Sisters. I longed to go inside, I'd never seen a real crystal ball before. A man in a long raincoat pushed a woman up the rickety steps, "Go on !" he urged, "or I'll never hear the last of it." The curtain swished and an olive-skinned woman growled through her lipstick, then smiled as he offered her a five pound note. "No change," she shrugged. Her hair was all tied up with shoelaces and Princess Rosa's granddaughter wore flip-flops.

"Have you lost your mum?" the man asked, as I hovered by the door, trying to hear the woman's whispered future.

"No," I told him, "she's in one of those huts."

"She thinks she's going to die." He jerked his head towards the curtain. "She thinks it's going to be in a plane crash. Let's hope she puts her straight, or we'll never get to Majorca, and it'll be Blackpool all over again."

The woman appeared, her head sticking out of the thick red material. It looked like she'd been crying. "Oh bloody hell..." the man breathed, "look at the state. And it cost me a fiver."

I wasn't sure I believed in gypsies, not these gypsies anyway. They didn't look real enough, with their glittery eyeshadows and glued-on nails. I wanted to believe that they could tell the future on their fold-away tables, see if a person was lucky, had money, or the love of their life. I wanted to ask the lolling chestnut heads if I'd ever meet my grandfather, and how; and if my mother's eyes would ever rest easy behind their soft baby-pink lids.

My grandfather was never real to me. He was a story. An old-fashioned looking man with soft bleached hair and a voice like my mother's. His skin had a thin, grey pallor, and his suits had red silk linings and stitching-by-hand. He was a gambler, half-American, he collected birds eggs in cotton filled drawers, he never smiled on photographs and danced with all the best looking women in London.

"He swept Nanny off her feet," my mother said, moving her arms, to imaginary music. "He wore emerald cufflinks and Italian leather shoes. And he knew all the right people."

"Important people?" I asked, trying to catch her wild flapping hands. "People like the Prince of Wales?"

"Oh," my mother said, falling exhausted onto the sofa, "I don't know about that, but he knew the man who invented glow-in-the-dark jewellery."

Leo James Forrester was really all-gone. He left home shortly after my mother's eighth birthday, and before that, he would be gone for weeks, months, and the occasional year. Even as a child, my mother would plan their reunion every night. There would be tears, promises, and a house with television and real garden swings. She would meet him accidentally in a cinema queue, in the park under the giant oak trees, on buses, in a Lyon's Cafeteria. Over twenty years on, and she still hadn't seen him, although she thought she might have seen the back of his head as he moved in and out of the crowd in Great Yarmouth. "I was eleven," she told me, "and the shape of his head, the way that he moved, I'm sure it was him. I wanted to run after him. I called out but he didn't hear me. We were near the bandstand and it was loud and mother told me not to be so silly, and what would he be doing in Yarmouth anyway?"

In a cigar box, under her cream silk lingerie, she kept the left-over scraps of her father. A hymnbook with a soft black cover, and across the fly leaf, a pasted-on bookplate: Leo J Forrester,

St Brendan's Sunday School, 1922. A silver cigarette lighter, blackened at the edges. A timetable with routes underlined in red ink. A diamond-shaped cufflink, a Premium Bond.

On Sunday nights, when my father was playing cards, she would get out her cigar box and empty it onto the bedspread. She would smell the inside of the hymnbook and read the bent-over timetable. She knew exactly where the number 19 bus stopped in 1946, that it went via Hawthorn Street and didn't stop in town on market days. In a spiral notebook, she copied down the addresses of all the L Forresters she could find from various telephone directories across the country. And sometimes, when my father was out, she would ring the number and wait for someone to answer, in the hope she might recognise his voice. Usually, she would put the receiver down, but if she was feeling brave, she would ask if Leo was there, and then invariably apologise for getting the wrong number, drawing a line through the roughly, scribbled-down address.

"You mustn't tell your father about all this nonsense," she said, covering the flat wooden box with camisoles and lace-edged knickers. "You know it's our little secret."

"But he might be able to help."

"He doesn't want to know," she whispered sadly, closing a drawer, trapping the strap of a white silk vest. "That's just the way he is."

"He said he'd pay for you to do it properly," I told her, remembering the day he pulled out his chequebook. "He said he knew people who -"

"But that's just it, Jessica," she said, stretching out along the bed, her flowery scent escaping from under her arms, her blouse riding up, revealing her soft, white stomach. "Don't you see?" she yawned. "That way, it would just be *too easy*."

•

My feet left muddy-brown stains across the carpet of the amusement arcade. Wet sand clung to plimsolls, stockings, un-wrapped hair. A man with a wide red face and gold rings sat at the door selling see-through raincoats, but mostly people shrugged, pulled down their sleeves, and huddled around one-armed bandits, under the warm, light-bulbed ceiling.

The close, humid air, clattered with rattling change, from machines and small glass booths, where girls in pink dresses swivelled on stools and counted out change. A bingo-caller in a frilly blue shirt said his name was Michael and the next game ladies was in two minutes time. I tried to get to the tables, where pyramids of pennies were waiting to be nudged into wide black holes, but gangs of boys with bruises and bony arms stood banging the tops and sticking chewed gum across the polished glass sides. Reluctantly, I changed my pennies into five pence pieces and went outside to the small tin caravan that sold hot dogs in sweet white buns.

The man looked at me strangely. He asked if I was on my own. I shook my head as he scooped up onions, throwing them into the sizzling fat. His arms were covered in purply scars, and a swirly blue tattoo said: TINA and LOVE.

"Looks like you need some fattening up," he said pulling the sausage from a pan of boiling brine. "There's not much meat on you."

"I'm average," I told him, "for my age and height."

"Skinny," he said, "and plenty of mouth."

I shivered as he leant on his elbows, watching me eat, and quickly I began to move through the crowd, past the mosaic walls of the circus and down towards the shelter. The wind pushed back my head, and out of breath, I waited for a tram to pass, watching its sparks fly into the air, then disappear under the sagging black wires.

I didn't have to remember which shelter my mother was in, I could see her already, her coat flying back, her arms outstretched to the side of her. She looked like she was walking a tightrope.

"You're back early," she said, leaning backwards over the railings. "Did you win or lose?"

"I didn't even get to have a go," I said. "It was too busy. And a gang of boys -"

"*Boys*," she grinned, her eyes moving up towards the banks of dismal looking clouds, "that's all they are. Why let some gawky adolescents stop your games? You should have stood your ground. Asked them to move aside."

"But Mummy," I said, watching her hug her arms around herself, her long coils of hair glistening with rain, "they were all so much bigger than me."

"You'll grow," she grinned. "Girls always do. Now look at my face," she said, turning it into the light. "Has the skin all cracked in the wind?"

"No," I shook my head at her. It still looked smooth and milk-white, her cheeks like two apple-pink circles.

"Well it feels like it," she said, digging inside her bag for face cream.

Side by side we sat hunched in the shelter, the wind whistling through the cracks in the boards. My mother's head crammed into her coat collar, my legs stiff and aching, and it wasn't even lunchtime.

"Did you see anyone interesting?" I asked, popping strings of hard, black seaweed.

"Not really," she sniffed. "But then I never did expect to see Papa, at least not today. I did see a very beautiful dog though."

"What did it look like?"

"It looked like your father," she said, in all seriousness. "Though of course," she pouted, "it wasn't nearly as fat."

Two

My father lived in a red room. He called it his study, but he never read any of the leather-bound books that lined the walls. Books that had foreign words printed across their spines in deep gold lettering, in between Tennyson and Donne and the collected works of Shakespeare. In a creased leather armchair, he would read the *Financial Times* from cover to cover, staining the ceiling with his fat cigars. The lid of the drinks cabinet was always wedged open, the smooth mottled walnut patterned with white circles, where wet glasses had rested before being refilled. Above the cases, butterflies with emerald-tipped wings were pressed behind glass. The room smelled strongly, of tobacco, hair-oil, *Famous Grouse*. At weekends, he spent most of his time in this room, reading the newspaper, drinking, sleeping, listening to music that came crackling out of an old fashioned wireless, whilst my mother sat in the kitchen with her Van Morrison cassettes and piles of thick magazines. Behind the study door, I would crouch, balancing on my hands. Through the panelling, I would listen to him smooth out his paper, open drawers and rest his glass on the arm of the chair. I smelled the cigars, the lemon oil, the warm whiskey breath, and I never dared go inside.

Roland Philip Rhys met my mother at a charity club ball. He was thirty years older than her, his face already patterned with the thin red lines of drink. She was wearing clothes that were too old for her at seventeen; a long velvet dress and black feather boa. She smelled of her mother's Number Five and wobbled in kid leather shoes.

"I practically tripped into your father," she giggled, sitting by his feet as he spread himself across the sofa. "Fell right into his lap."

"You were drunk Olivia," he growled back at her. "You were pissed out of your brains, darling."

"I was not!"

"Oh yes?"

"Well, I was merry."

"Merry as a fart."

"But wasn't I beau-ti-ful?" she lisped, resting her head against his wide, squashy knees.

"You were that alright," he softened, pushing his hand through her curtain of hair. "You were all blonde and honey, sweetness and light." And as he bent over to kiss her, my mother said she would pour them a scotch each, "Just to cheer us up..." And as usual, I slipped out, unnoticed, back to my silent room, overlooking the long flat lawn and the honeysuckle bowers, that were trimmed once a fortnight by Bill. In his flared jeans and purple vest, he would push the cranky lawn mower, whilst mother walked about, picking up the occasional twig, and dead-heading the roses in shiny stiletto shoes.

"Don't you wish Daddy was different?" I asked, as people drifted in front of the shelter, peering in to see if there was room, then walking swiftly away.

"Different? How?"

"Well..." I screwed up my face, I don't know. More energetic perhaps? Wouldn't you have liked him to have come with us today?"

"Not really," she said. "This isn't his thing – and anyway, I wouldn't change him for the world."

I wished he were different. I wished he would wear jeans and t-shirts instead of his three piece suits and floppy bow ties. I wished he would take me to the Wimpy and to the pictures on Saturday afternoons, but then as I sat there, watching my mother tie up her rain-drenched hair, I remembered how he used to take her out, every Friday night.

They would dress up, drinking vodka and laughing to music in the sitting room. The songs were old, and had words that my father could remember, and he would mime to them, as they held each other, colliding round the furniture. My mother wore tight silver dresses and long strings of pearls. They would go out laughing, and come back past midnight, in silence. I would watch out for them, leaning through the curtains until my elbows hurt. The taxi would rattle at the pavement, and the doors would slam, and they wouldn't be holding hands anymore. My father striding in front, my mother dragging her heels in the gravel. And later, my father would walk the babysitter home, and they would sit on a wall whilst he lit her a cigarette, and she would push his hands away, and then reluctantly it seemed, she would let him bury his face in her long red hair, and slide his arm around her half-hidden waist.

"It's time we went for lunch," my mother said, "though it looks like you've had something already. You've ketchup all over your face."

"I'm still hungry." I rubbed my hand across my mouth. "Starving."

"Well," she said, dabbing her hair with wads of crumpled tissues, "make yourself look presentable, we're going somewhere nice."

I tried to drag a brush through my knotted hair. My mother sat serenely, staring ahead at the railings, the flat expanse of sea.

"Was he different when you married him?" I asked, my eyes watering as I pulled at the tangled matted threads. "Was he handsome and everything?" I stared at the curve of her neck, the perfect symmetry of her face. She looked like the women in her magazines.

"Don't you think he's handsome?" She didn't move, then she dipped her head towards the dark circle of floor, "He was different." she said.

"How? Nicer?"

"He was different from the other men I'd met. *The boys*. He had style. He was lavish with attention. He sent me presents. Good presents. Real Swiss chocolate, fat bottles of perfume. He sent a boy round with bouquets of lilies and hundreds of roses. Not red," she said shyly, "He wasn't quite that gauche. He would send tiny headed tea-roses, the colour of apricots, and cards that just read *love*."

"But what did Nanny say? He was even older than she was."

"Well, what do you think?" she pursed her lips, and a grey-headed sea gull cried into the breeze. "She ranted on about father figures and how stupid I was being. But then who was she to say?" She stood up, stock still, her back to me, her hands pushing themselves together, "I've kept him longer than she ever kept Papa."

"Do you still love him?" I asked, wrapping my arms around her, smelling the scent that came pouring from her neck.

"Of course I do!" she shouted, ignoring the mothers pushing their prams across us, the scatter of faces that turned towards her strangled high-pitched voice. "He's everything. And doesn't he look after us good?"

My throat tightened as I pictured his dark old-fashioned clothes. His white-haired friends, the way he said 'luncheon' and a sneering 'Palais-de-danse'.

"But he isn't like other fathers." I thrust my face into her sleeve, screwing up my eyes, trying to stop the tears that came whenever I thought too much about it. "I don't know why, but he just isn't. Amanda's dad plays rounders with us. He does funny walks and tells bad jokes. He goes to football with her brother, and he calls Amanda 'Titch'."

My mother arched, "He's just different, that's all. What's wrong with that? I bet Amanda's father hasn't done half the things that Roland has."

"No," I said, thinking of his round baby face, his creaseless eyes, his thick, dark-brown hair, "but he's less than half his age."

My mother's hand flew up from out of her coat and slammed across the side of my face, a stinging whoosh of long fingers and a stiff, sea-filled wind. But then she began to cry.

"He's your Daddy, Jess," she stuttered. "Don't be mean to him. He might be older, but it doesn't matter. At least he's here with us. I wish I could look at my father. His eyes. His long, sweet face. He could be anywhere," she swallowed, "anywhere in the world. He might have gone back to America even. Montana. Southern Illinois. *Anywhere.*" A small boy clung onto the railing in front of us, his eyes wide and staring, but my mother ignoring him, went on, "Your father doesn't know anything about little girls, and I'm sorry, sorry, sorry, but we do have fun sometimes too, don't we, Jess? Don't we?"

And leaning in the sand-swept doorway, I cradled my mother, and told her that I remembered when he took us to the zoo, and we laughed at the penguins, and how he drove at a hundred miles an hour and let us scream all along the motorway, with our heads sticking out of the windows. I told her that I thought he was kind, and good, and much better than any of the other fathers I'd seen.

"He read me stories when I had the mumps," I told her, "*Mrs Pepperpot*, and *The Gingerbread Man*."

"Did he?" she said. "I don't remember that." And then somewhere at the back of my mind, between the warm red blankets, the lemon tea, the swollen face covered in cool, damp flannels, the voice that read me stories was somewhere in my head, a voice that could change into anything. The old woman, the gingerbread man.

"But your father was in Brussels when you were ill," she said, scowling at the boy, making him jump through the railings and onto the steps beyond. "Don't you remember?"

"No," I told her, biting my lips, "I'm sure he came back that time."

•